PRAISE FOR *HALF UPON A TIME*

"Snappy dialogue, fast-paced action,
unexpected twists."
—*School Library Journal*

"This fractured fairy tale features
a hip, contemporary voice."
—*Kirkus*

"'Quick-paced' is an understatement, as
our heroes move swiftly from one danger
to the next, with hardly a breath in between.
The only disappointment is that all of the
bad guys get away—but there's pleasure
in that, too, as it means we'll get to see
May, Jack, and Phillip track them down
to set things right in a much-anticipated
sequel. Highly recommended."
—**ChildrensLit.com**

"*Half Upon a Time* has it all—voice,
charming fairy tale characters with a twist,
hilarity, and an adventure-filled plot."
—**Bookinistas Blog**

HALF UPON A TIME

JAMES RILEY

Aladdin
New York London Toronto Sydney

This book is a work of fiction. Any references to historical events, real people,
or real locales are used fictitiously. Other names, characters, places, and incidents are
the product of the author's imagination, and any resemblance to actual events
or locales or persons, living or dead, is entirely coincidental.

ALADDIN

An imprint of Simon & Schuster Children's Publishing Division
1230 Avenue of the Americas, New York, NY 10020
First Aladdin paperback edition September 2011
Copyright © 2010 by James Riley
All rights reserved, including the right of reproduction in whole or in part in any form.
ALADDIN is a trademark of Simon & Schuster, Inc., and related logo
is a registered trademark of Simon & Schuster, Inc.
Also available in an Aladdin hardcover edition.
For information about special discounts for bulk purchases,
please contact Simon & Schuster Special Sales at 1-866-506-1949 or business@simonandschuster.com.
The Simon & Schuster Speakers Bureau can bring authors to your live event. For more information
or to book an event contact the Simon & Schuster Speakers Bureau at 1-866-248-3049
or visit our website at www.simonspeakers.com.
Designed by Mike Rosamilia
The text of this book was set in Goudy Old Style.
Manufactured in the United States of America 0714 OFF
10
The Library of Congress has cataloged the hardcover edition as follows:
Riley, James, 1977–
Half upon a time / by James Riley.—1st Aladdin ed.
p. cm.
Summary: In the village of Giant's Hand, Jack's grandfather has been pushing him to find
a princess and get married, so when a young lady falls out of the sky wearing a shirt that says
PUNK PRINCESS, and she tells Jack that her grandmother, who looks suspiciously
like the long-missing Snow White, has been kidnapped, Jack decides to help her.
p. cm.
ISBN 978-1-4169-9593-7 (hc)
[1. Fairy tales. 2. Adventure and adventurers—Fiction.] I. Title.
PZ8.R433Hal 2010
[Fic]—dc22
2010012714
ISBN 978-1-4169-9594-4 (pbk)
ISBN 978-1-4169-9595-1 (eBook)

Dedicated to anyone
whose story didn't go as planned.
Seriously, who writes these things?

HALF
UPON
A TIME

CHAPTER 1

Once upon a time, Jack wouldn't have been caught dead in a princess rescue. Yet here he was, in the middle of a cave—a dark and *stupid* cave—on his way to do just that. This was all such a waste of time, and after that last fight with what was apparently supposed to be a troll, his arm really hurt.

From deep within the cave came what was probably supposed to be a bloodcurdling roar. Jack sighed, rolled his eyes, and slowed down to wait. A roar like that could only mean bad things . . . and sure enough, a ball of fire came burning down the corridor, exploding just a few inches from his left arm. The heat caused him to jerk his body to the right, saving him from the second fireball, which blew through the spot he'd just been standing in.

"Hey!" Jack yelled indignantly. "You almost *hit* me!" Without waiting for a reply, he dropped to his knees, yanked out the blunt prop sword he'd been given, and whipped it end over end toward the source of the fireballs.

A second later Jack heard a dull thunk, followed by a groan and what sounded like a body hitting the cave floor. He smiled, then helped himself to his feet and continued on, the corridor now thankfully free of fireballs. As he walked, he looked himself over, realizing with annoyance that somewhere along the line his tan shirt and pants had both been ripped. Perfect. As if he had that many clothes to begin with.

A bit deeper in, a bright green dragon mask lay on the floor in two separate pieces, split by the otherwise completely useless sword. Just past the mask was an unconscious boy dressed all in green, a deep red bruise spreading over his face. Apparently, Jack's aim had been better than he thought.

He briefly felt bad about knocking the boy out, but then remembered how close the fireballs had come, and all guilt disappeared. Picking up his prop sword, Jack started to leave when a thought stopped him in his tracks: *Why play by the rules?*

There it was, on the boy's right hand: a sparkling red ring. Jack quickly worked the ring off the boy's finger, then slid it onto his own. Satisfied, he started back down the hall, trying to ignore the growing ache in his shoulder. Stupid fake troll. At least the fake dragon had missed.

A bit farther in, torches flickered on the cave walls, creating what would have been an eerie effect if it hadn't been so transparently designed to be. Again, Jack slowed down, moving as silently as he could despite the sword banging against his leg at every step. As the torchlight grew brighter and the cave started to widen, Jack stopped completely.

This was it . . . the final challenge. The first challenge required a strong arm, he'd been told, though if the pain in his shoulder was any indication, his arm hadn't exactly been up to it. The second challenge took a brave heart, facing the fireballs. And the final challenge, the most difficult of all, could only be won by a wise head.

Wise, huh? This might not end well.

Still, it couldn't hurt to get a little information before rushing in. Jack drew his sword and angled it around the corner. In the sword's reflection, he saw two torches hanging from the ceiling over an old, blackened stone altar. Strapped to the altar was what looked to be a teenage boy in a white dress, a golden tiara decorating his blond hair.

A boy playing the princess? Classy.

Over the boy in the dress stood a man wearing all brown, holding a knife to the boy's chest. On the other side of the room, a hunched old woman leaned against a large staff. The woman's black robe covered everything but her wart-infested nose, which looked more like a carrot than anything.

"My knight will rescue me," Jack heard the boy princess on the altar say in an unnaturally high-pitched voice. "He *will*! Just you wait!"

Jack sighed. A knight? Yikes. He fiddled with the ring a bit to ready it, then prepared himself to move quickly, knowing he was going to need the element of surprise if he had any hope of saving the boy . . . princess . . . whatever.

"The knight is *here*," the woman in black hissed.

Okay, apparently surprise was out. Still, even if they knew he was there, maybe Jack could still throw them a bit.

"I *am* here," Jack said, stepping out from around the corner. "But . . . I surrender." With that, he held his sword up, then slowly placed it on the ground.

"You what?!" the wart-covered woman said.

"You what?!" the boy princess said.

"I surrender," Jack repeated, stepping away from the sword. "You win."

The man in brown held the knife closer to the fake princess. "It's some kind of trick," he said.

The woman nodded. "I agree. Cut out the princess's heart!"

"*No!*" the boy princess screamed, his voice breaking in panic.

"Quiet, princess!" the man in brown said, lifting his knife high into the air. "The witch orders, and I obey!"

"And as for you, little hero," the witch said, "you will join your princess in death!" With that, she aimed a gnarled wand in Jack's direction, shouted a magic word, and shot a bolt of lightning straight at him.

Jack dropped, then quickly dodged a second blast by rolling to the right.

"Princess, your heart is mine!" the man in brown screamed, driving the knife down toward the boy on the altar.

"I have you now!" the old woman shouted, aiming her wand right at Jack.

Jack glanced quickly between the woman and the man in brown. He could either save himself or the princess, there was no time to do both. He instantly made his decision, aimed the ring, and fired it . . .

Right at the witch.

A fireball three times the size of the previous ones erupted from the ring and exploded into the witch's chest, lighting her black robe on fire. The witch screamed in terror as she frantically tore at her flaming clothing. The man in brown gasped, then rushed to the witch's side, dropping his knife to the ground as he ran.

Jack used the distraction to retrieve his sword, then duck under the altar to quickly cut through the captive boy's bonds. "Get up, Princess!" he hissed, standing back up. "We have to—"

And then he stopped, realizing he was too late. The boy princess's white gown was now stained with some kind of red liquid, and he lay on the altar with his tongue sticking out, not moving.

Dropping his sword to the ground, Jack put his head in his hands. He had failed. The princess was dead.

The furious witch grabbed Jack by his shirt and pushed him against the wall, her eyes narrowed dangerously and her fake nose singed. "*Jack!*" she roared. "You could have *killed* me!"

"I know, I'm sorry!" he said, his face turning red. "I didn't know it would do that! When Stephen used the ring, the fireballs were a lot smaller. . . ." He quickly removed the magic ring and held it out to the woman. She glared at him for a second before grabbing it from his hand. Then she smacked him in the head.

"I don't *care* what Stephen did," Julia, his teacher, told him as she tore off the rest of her makeup. "*He* knew enough to miss you! You, on the other hand, aimed right at me!"

"Okay, *ow*, first of all!" Jack said, rubbing his head. "Second of all, you said to treat this test like it was real. And you were shooting lightning at me! What was I supposed to do?!"

"Um," said the princess from the altar, "can someone rescue me already?" The princess's voice had gotten remarkably deeper since she "died." Jack took a closer look and recognized Bertrand, one of the other boys from the village. Apparently Jack had missed some of the ropes, and Bertrand's arms were still tied down.

Jack rolled his eyes. "Rescue yourself," he said, tossing his fake sword to the "princess." It hit the boy in his stomach, knocking the wind out of him.

"Well, congratulations, Jack," Julia said as she finished removing her costume. "You *failed*. Not only did you handle every single situation wrong—*every single one!*—but you went after me when the real threat was the witch's servant. He *killed* the princess, Jack!"

"But you were attacking *me*!" Jack protested. "If I had saved her, I would have died. And then what good would I have been to either of us?"

"And what good were you now?" Julia asked as the man in brown, Jack's teacher Stewart, quietly walked over to untie the still complaining princess.

"It's all useless anyway," Jack said, his face burning from his failure. "We all know there are no unmarried princesses left. Even if there were, I don't want to marry *anyone*, let alone some stuck-up royal. I'm just fine where I am!"

Jack turned to leave, but Julia grabbed his arm. "This is important, Jack. You're the son of a . . . well, a . . ."

"A criminal?" Jack said, his eyes narrowing.

"And I don't want you to follow his lead," Julia said. "This is for your own good! Being a hero, rescuing a princess, killing a dragon . . . these could really turn your life around! At least, if you survive long enough." She glared at him. "You're the only one in your entire class to fail the princess rescue test. Just go home, Jack. We'll talk about this later."

Jack sighed, and turned to leave. "I don't care how the world works," he said over his shoulder. "All this? It isn't me."

"And it never will be at this rate," Julia said, helping Stewart to yank the ropes off the fake princess.

"Thanks for nothing, Jack!" the "princess" yelled at him, his wig and tiara falling off as he sat up.

"That's a pretty dress, Bertrand," Jack said as he left. "Your mother must be so proud."

The walk back through the cave was a bit more peaceful this time, though that wouldn't last long. His grandfather would be waiting, and Jack's test results weren't going to go over too well.

Outside, the brightly setting sun blinded him for a moment. He raised a hand up to block it, as the green trees of summer weren't helping too much in that regard. He realized that it wouldn't be much longer before the trees picked themselves up and migrated to the warmer south, leaving their dead, leafless brothers behind.

Lucky trees.

Between those trees, an old man tapped his foot impatiently. Jack's grandfather was covered in three or four layers of different-colored clothing, while his long white beard poked out from his shirt in several places. None of that was out of the ordinary, though. The tiny, golden girl sitting on his grandfather's shoulder, however, was a bit unusual. The girl's wings shimmered in the sunlight as she flapped them absently.

"Hi, Grandpa," Jack said, hoping a smile would help hide his failure. "New friend?"

His grandfather snorted, then gently offered his palm to the fairy on his shoulder. The creature daintily stepped into it, smiling shyly up at Jack as his grandfather walked over. "Just caught that bully Robert hunting some of these things," the old man said. "The other three flew off when I rescued them, but this one seems to have a thing for me."

Before he could even finish speaking, though, the fairy jumped out of his hand and flew over to Jack. She landed on his head, settled herself into his hair, and let out a contented sigh.

"Or not," his grandfather said with a grunt. "How did the test go?"

Jack took in a deep breath, then blew it out without a word.

"Right," said his grandfather, nodding. "Can't say I'm surprised. What was the problem this time?"

Jack turned red. "I kinda let the princess die."

His grandfather groaned. "You *do* realize that's not a good thing, right?" the old man asked.

"So I'm told," Jack said.

His grandfather patted him on the shoulder. "You'll save her next time. Until then, you'll practice every minute that you're not working in the fields."

And there it was, pretty much the worst punishment his grandfather could have laid down. The last thing Jack wanted to do was practice more princess rescuing. The whole thing was just so *useless*!

"It's not useless," his grandfather said, apparently reading his mind. "You think I'm going to let my only grandson stay a farmer for the rest of his life? That's a job for kids too young or adults too old to go out on a proper adventure. Now, let's get back to the cottage. There's a chill in the air."

"You realize it's the middle of summer, right?" Jack asked as they started home. "I'm pretty sure any chill is just in your head."

That earned Jack a whack on the head from his grandfather's cane. "I fought an ice giant, you little idiot!" the old man snapped. "The monster froze my bones to their very core, and they've never properly healed! Usually it's worse when I'm around the truly stupid." He gave Jack a dark look. "You see where I'm going with this."

"I'll start a fire when we get home," Jack said with a sigh. On top of his head, the fairy made herself a little nest, tugging some of his hair in the process. Unlike this one, most fairies were shy, scared of humans for a good reason: Their wings sold pretty well to wizards and witches for their magic. The practice was horribly cruel, but that didn't stop some of the village boys from hunting the little fairies.

"A fire's a start," the old man said. "And then tomorrow we'll go over my adventuring lessons again."

Jack gritted his teeth. "Grandpa, I'm *not* going to waste my time anymore!" he shouted. "I'm not you . . . and I'm *definitely* not my father. What's the point, anyway? There aren't any unmarried princesses left!"

"And how would *you* know?!" his grandfather shouted back. "You're not even looking! If you go looking for adventure, *it* will find *you*! At least, it would if you had the brains nature gave your little fairy friend—the one who's scratching her head with her foot, I might add."

"If adventure's going to find me," Jack growled angrily, "it can find me right *here*. If you're right, it shouldn't matter where I am. I should be able to just stick out my arms and have a princess fall right into them!"

He stuck out his arms to highlight how stupid his grandfather's argument was.

Above him, a circle of blue fire exploded open in the middle of the air. Out of the middle of the flaming circle, a person fell to the ground less than a foot from Jack's outstretched arms.

For a second, both Jack and his grandfather were too shocked to say anything.

As usual, though, his grandfather recovered first.

"You really have to work on your aim, boy," the old man said.

Jack quickly ran forward to see if the person—a girl—was hurt. She was lying on her stomach, so Jack quickly turned her over, sighing in relief when he saw she was still breathing. He looked her over, trying to figure out if she'd broken anything, but she seemed okay . . . that was, other than her odd appearance.

The strangest thing had to be the streak of startling blue playing through the girl's dirty blond hair. That couldn't have been natural; some sort of magic had to have been involved. Not that her clothing was normal, either. Her pants were dark blue, worn through in some places but almost new in others. Her black shirt was a much thinner material than her pants and barely had any sleeves. And then Jack saw something that made him gasp in surprise.

"What?" his grandfather asked, creeping up behind Jack to look. "Is it dead?"

The old man noticed what Jack had seen, and he leapt into the air, almost giddy with excitement. "Jack, my boy!" he shouted. "You've done it, you've found one!"

Jack shook his head, still staring at the girl. She couldn't be . . . could she? He read the words on her shirt again, out loud this time. "Punk . . . Princess."

This girl was a princess? And where exactly was Punk?

CHAPTER 2

Think she's all right?" Jack's grandfather asked, tapping her leg with his foot.

"Don't *kick* her!" Jack whispered. "She's a princess!"

The old man kicked her again. "That doesn't mean she's all right."

"Just let me handle this, okay?" Jack said as he bent over the girl protectively. His grandfather grunted and wandered off in the direction of their cottage, hopefully to get a blanket or something. Meanwhile, the girl hadn't woken up, which wasn't a good sign. The short fall from the fire circle in the sky shouldn't have been enough to knock her out, so it must have been something else.

A spell, maybe? Jack frowned. If it was a magical sleep, there was a very specific way to wake up a princess. Jack crinkled his forehead, struggling to remember his lessons from school. She had to be kissed, yes . . . but did the kisser have to be a prince? Why were there so many rules to these stupid spells, anyway?!

This had been the sort of thing he ignored on general principle. How often did someone just trip over a sleeping princess, after all? Jack had been much more interested in learning why bees stung or what part of the month were-rabbits transformed into humans, rather than how to deal with spoiled royals who couldn't get out of bed.

"Do you have to be a prince to wake a sleeping princess?" Jack whispered to his returning grandfather, who instead of bringing back something useful had dragged out a chair to sit on.

"Who knows?" the old man said. "Smooch her, see what happens."

Jack glared at him. "I'm not just going to kiss her."

"If you don't, I will," the old man said. "You think she wants to wake up to this?" He pointed to his bearded, wrinkled face.

Jack nodded. "Good point." He bent over the girl, then paused, suddenly nervous. Whoever this girl was, she was all kinds of cute and about his age. Plus, she was royalty, whereas he was just some idiot covered in cave dirt.

"*Do it already!*" his grandfather shouted. "In my day, she'd be awake and married to you by now!"

"*Shhhh!*" Jack hissed, his face just inches from the princess's. "I don't want to do this wrong!"

"You've never kissed a girl, have you," his grandfather said, then snorted. "We really *do* have to get you out of this village."

Jack just growled in response, and turned back to the girl. "Good luck, Princess," Jack whispered to her, then smushed his mouth against hers.

The princess's eyes immediately flew open, and she sat up so fast her head smacked right into Jack's. A hollow *bonk* echoed through the clearing.

"*Ow!*" the princess yelled, grabbing her head.

"*Ow!*" Jack shouted, falling backward and holding his forehead as well.

His grandfather almost fell backward out of his chair too, though only because he was laughing so hard.

Now extremely awake, the princess glared all around, looking confused, scared, and pained all at once. "Grandma?" she yelled. She started to get to her feet, but quickly fell back down, apparently still woozy from whatever had knocked her out. "Grandma?!" she yelled more urgently, then turned to

Jack, her eyes wide with fear. "Who are you?! Where am I? Where's my grandmother?" Abruptly, her look went from scared to annoyed. "And what made you think that *kissing me* was okay?!"

Jack turned fiery red. "Yeah, uh, sorry about that," he said quietly.

The princess grunted, still glaring. "Where's the guy in green?" she asked. "And where's my grandmother?!"

Jack shook his head, a little done with all her questions. "No idea," he said, trying to stay patient. "You're the only one who fell out of the sky."

The girl looked up at the now empty sky, the sun setting in the distance. "Wait, the fire tunnel," she said, almost to herself. "And it was after midnight a second ago . . . why's it so light here? Where *am* I?!"

"Giant's Hand, Princess," Jack's grandfather said, pushing past Jack. "A small village in the kingdom of Blunderbush." The old man waited for a sign of recognition, but when he got none, he just shrugged. "It's a pretty small kingdom," he admitted.

The princess stared at Jack's grandfather for a second, then turned back to Jack, where she seemed to notice something for the first time. The princess's eyes popped, and her mouth dropped open, a small squeak echoing in her throat.

The fairy in Jack's hair just stared right back at her.

"What?" Jack said finally, the silence making him a little uncomfortable.

The princess pointed at the fairy, still not saying anything, her mouth still wide open.

The fairy pointed back with a smile, enjoying the game.

"It's a fairy," Jack said, his annoyance starting to creep into his voice. "What's *wrong*?"

"There's a little . . . *person* in your hair!" the princess said, her voice cracking. "You're asking *me* what's wrong?!"

Jack reached up and gently picked the fairy out of his hair, then held her out for the princess to get a closer look. "See?" he said. "Just a fairy."

"Just a *fairy*?!" the princess said, shoving herself away from the fairy in a panic. "That's not right! It can't be *real*! It's a special effect or something, right? I mean, I can deal with little monsters with axes and blue fire tunnels and everything, but *that's not right!*"

The fairy's smile turned into a frown, and she stuck out her tongue at the girl. Jack held his other hand protectively in front of the fairy, shielding her from the princess's outburst. "There's no reason to be *rude*," he said.

"Rude?!" the girl said, her voice cracking again. "*Oh*, I get it! I'm asleep! This is all a dream, right?" She reached out and pinched Jack.

"Ow!" he said, and pinched her right back.

"*Ow!*" she yelled, pinching him again.

"All right," Jack's grandfather said, inserting himself between the two of them, stopping Jack's return pinch in a very unsatisfying way. "I think we've all established that no one's asleep. Why don't we introduce ourselves? I'm Jack, and this is my grandson here, also named Jack. He's Jack the thirteenth . . . the lucky one, I call him." The old man laughed, but no one else did. "And you are . . . ?"

The girl paused, then said, "May."

"Well, Princess, you're obviously in distress," Jack's grandfather said, reaching a hand out to help the girl to her feet. "Did you say your grandmother is missing? Maybe we can help."

Jack glared at her, not really over the whole pinching fiasco. "Who said we *want* to help?" he muttered.

"Was that what you call kissing me?" the princess asked, throwing him a dirty look. "Helping?"

Jack blushed, angry and embarrassed at the same time.

"The boy was trying to wake you up," the old man said before Jack could say something rude in response. "He wasn't sure it would work, since he's no prince, obviously, but apparently they're relaxing the standards."

"He's not a *prince*, huh?" said the princess, one eyebrow raising as the old man helped her to her feet. Then her eyes shifted to the fairy in Jack's hair again. "Oh, c'mon," she said with a weak smile. "Princes? You can't be *serious*."

"No princes around here, obviously," Jack's grandfather said. "The nearest one's a good day or two away. But why waste the time when my boy is ready to help? He's not much, but he'll get the job done, Princess."

Her eyes narrowed. "Okay, let's back up. When you say that word . . ."

"Princess?" the old man asked.

"Yeah, *that* one," she said. "You're not just doing that whole old-person thing where you call girls cutesy names 'cause you think it's charming or whatever, are you."

"Certainly not," Jack's grandfather huffed. "I don't *think* I'm charming, I *know*—"

"Missing the point!" the princess said, her voice edging on panic. "*Why* are you calling me a princess?"

Jack pointed at her shirt. "It's not like you're hiding it too well."

She followed his gaze down to her chest, then gave him a disbelieving look. "It's a *T-shirt*," she said.

"So you're not a princess?" Jack said.

"*No!*" May yelled. "I'm not a princess!"

"Whatever you say, *Princess*," Jack said, his eyes narrowing as he glared at her.

"Uh, Your Highness," Jack's grandfather said, inserting himself between them again, "why don't you and Jack go over to our cottage, so you can explain how you ended up here? I'll go grab something for us to eat from the inn." When the princess started to object, Jack's grandfather interrupted her. "Don't you think we'll be able to better help you once we know the full story?"

The princess looked like she wanted to disagree but couldn't think of a good enough reason to do so. "*Fine,*" she said. "Let's go. But I'm keeping my eye on you both. *Especially* you," she said, pointing at Jack. "You come at me with those lips again, there's gonna be pain."

"Can't be worse than the last time," Jack said to her as his grandfather wandered off toward the village's inn. Jack nodded in the direction of their house, and he and the princess walked down the path toward it, an awkward silence filling the air as they went.

Not ten seconds after Jack closed the cottage door behind them, the blue circle of fire reopened in midair, and a giant of a man dressed entirely in green dropped out of the center, landing silently in a crouch. The man carefully touched the spot where May had landed just minutes earlier, then glanced in the direction of Jack's cottage.

The man in green smiled, stood up, and slipped silently into the forest to wait for his prey to emerge.

CHAPTER 3

Jack sat down at the rickety table his grandfather had built. The princess glanced at the table's other chair, then pointedly took a seat farther away, on one of the tiny beds. Apparently she wanted some distance, something she wasn't going to get much of in the cramped cottage. With a table, two beds, a chest of drawers, and a fireplace for cooking, there just wasn't room for distance.

"Okay, let's get on with this," Jack said, opening the large book on the table to the marked page . . . only it wasn't the page he'd been expecting. Text filled the left page, while on the right—

"What's that?" May asked, coming over to stand behind him.

She pointed at the elaborate illustration of a man holding a golden harp, facing down a rampaging giant.

"Nothing," Jack said, quickly flipping to the first blank page. "Apparently my grandfather's been reliving the past."

"Did he draw that?" May asked.

"Nope," Jack said. "It's a Story Book. It's actually pretty rare; there were only four made. My grandfather got this one when he rescued an old woman who used to ride a giant goose." He flipped to the very front of the book and pointed to the picture of his teenage grandfather creeping through a dungeon to free an imprisoned woman and a very annoyed-looking goose. "Anyway, the book writes down any stories you tell it, painting whatever you're thinking as pictures. It's not only a good way to keep track of them but it fills in some blanks that most people leave out."

"So what, it'll record it?" May asked, raising an eyebrow. "So not only do you have fairies and stuff, you also have magic voice-recognition books? Weird."

At the mention of her, the fairy in Jack's hair perked up, spread her wings, and gently flew over to May's hand. The princess's eyes went wide, but she held up her palm for the fairy to land on, staring at the creature with wonder. The fairy, though, just smiled, then climbed up May's arm and into her hair, burying into it and sighing contentedly.

"That might have been the cutest thing I've ever seen," May said. The fairy waved a bit in response, then settled back to fall asleep. "I guess you don't need technology when you've got fairies, huh," May said, then seemed to realize something. "Speaking of technology . . ." She reached into a front pocket and pulled out a small, fat card with numbers on it, some of which she pushed a few times. When nothing happened, she frowned and slipped the card back into her pocket. "I figured there wouldn't be a signal, but it would have made things a lot easier."

"Well, *yeah*," Jack said. "We . . . we don't get a lot of signals out here. Not anymore. We used to. But they all died. Eaten. By monsters. It wasn't a good situation."

May nodded slowly at him. "Sounds . . . pretty bad," she said, turning back to the book. "So what, I just have to start talking, and it'll write down what I say?"

"Try it," Jack said, flipping back to the blank page.

"Well, I was up later than I was supposed to be, so I had all my lights off," May said. "I was—" And then she stopped as text began to appear in the Story Book.

"Once upon a time," it read, "a beautiful young girl disobeyed her grandmother." On the opposite page, an illustration appeared, showing May in a dark room, her face lit blue by some kind of glowing square.

"That's so creepy!" she said. "I didn't even say I was on my computer!"

"It takes both what you say and what you think, Princess," Jack said, ignoring the fact that he had no idea what a computer was. "And don't think I didn't see the part about calling yourself beautiful."

"It's a smart book," May said, the corners of her mouth rising a bit. "All right, then. I was up late when I heard Grandma coming upstairs, so I quickly turned off my computer and jumped into bed." Text rose to the surface of the Story Book's page as May talked, but Jack soon forgot it, as he always did when someone was telling a story. The illustrations were so realistic—it was hard not to stare at them.

"Grandma knocked, and came into my room," she said, and a new illustration appeared: a woman silhouetted in a doorway, light spilling in behind her.

"That's my Grandma," May said, her voice catching a bit.

If she was, the woman certainly didn't look the right age: Her face was perfect and beautiful, unmarred by any worry or smile lines. Her long black hair was tied up in a bun, though Jack could make out a white streak or two playing in and out of the hair.

Despite May's protests about not being a princess, this woman clearly had a royal bearing. In fact, she reminded Jack of nothing less than a queen, even in what looked to be a simple dressing gown.

"Wow," Jack blurted out.

"Yeah," May said. "Kinda intimidating, but you get used to it. She told me I had to get up, but she sounded . . . worried. She said that someone had broken into the house, that they had stolen something: a box she'd always had, a box with a heart on it."

An illustration appeared of a wooden box with a heart on its front. Jack couldn't tell much else about it, since most of the box was obscured beneath piles of books, clothes, and other items he didn't recognize.

"She never let me near that box," May said. "It was always hidden away somewhere. The only time I ever saw it was when we'd move, which we did a lot."

"So this box . . . it was stolen?" Jack asked.

"That's all she said was taken," May said. "Not sure why

someone would just steal that, and not take any of our valuables. She told me it wasn't safe, though. At the time I thought she just meant because someone had been in our house, and they could come back at any time, you know? It made sense. So she told me to get up, that we were leaving. Oh, and she handed me a note with emergency numbers on it and told me to call them if anything happened."

"Numbers?" Jack asked.

She frowned. "Yeah, kinda useless, though, considering my phone doesn't work."

Jack nodded, pretending he understood any part of what she'd just said.

"She wanted to leave right then, so I quickly got dressed and followed her out," May said, glancing at the illustration forming on the page. "Or, at least, I started to."

A picture slowly formed of a room more richly furnished than any Jack had ever seen. An enormous bed covered in linens filled most of the room, right next to the large wooden desk that May's glowing square sat on. The walls were some kind of smooth, uninterrupted stone, white as clouds.

All but one small part, that was. Though the May in the picture seemed oblivious to it, a small, familiar blue flame burned on the wall right behind her. And inside the blue flame . . . Jack leaned closer to look.

Inside the flame was a small hand, like that of a child. The hand was reaching for May.

"See?" May said sadly. "This is where they come for me."

CHAPTER 4

"Downstairs I heard this huge explosion," May said quietly, staring at the picture of the hand in the flame. "Voices yelling, too. One of them was Grandma, but I didn't know who the other one was. So I ran to the stairs to look."

A new illustration began to paint itself onto the page, this one showing May glancing down the stairs to find her grandmother and one of the largest men Jack had ever seen, dressed entirely in green.

"They were talking about something . . . I can barely remember," May said softly. Jack nodded, then absently glanced over at the text, where words that May could barely remember drifted up from the ether. *Snow White . . . betrayal . . . cursed . . . Mirror.*

And then three words that made his blood run cold: *The Wicked Queen.*

Jack gasped, suddenly understanding who the man in green was, and what might be happening.

"I know, right?" May said, not exactly on the same page as he was, at least not figuratively. "And things are about to get worse, 'cause while my back was turned, the things from my wall attacked."

The picture showed what May remembered: A vicious monster about half her size leapt at her, a horrifying axe in one of its hands. Behind it, more monsters were swarming in from the burning blue hole in the wall, eager looks in their eyes.

"They all jumped on me," May said with a shiver. "I kicked as hard as I could, and I know I hit a few, but there were too many of them. They picked me up and carried me into the hallway."

The new picture showed May held in the hands of the monsters, being presented to the man in green like some kind of gift. Her grandmother's hands, feet, and neck had all been chained together with huge iron bands, and the older woman looked both furious and worried.

"He asked me who I was," May said, pointing at the man in green.

"Who might you be, girlie?" said the man in green, according to the book.

"And I called him some names," May said.

The book printed something garbled.

"They weren't the nicest names," May admitted. "Anyway, he told those monsters to take me back to the palace, then to look for something."

"Find that crown; we need it to use the Mirror!" the man in green yelled in the book.

"My grandmother struggled," May said, her eyes locked on the illustration, "but he just picked her up and carried her over his shoulder like she weighed nothing. And then he said something I didn't understand, and another blue fire showed up."

The next picture showed a circle of blue flame burning on the wall in front of the man in green, who was carrying May's grandmother into the circle. Inside the circle, Jack could make out some kind of tunnel of the same fire, ending in a second circle. And in that second circle of blue flame stood a figure he couldn't make out, a figure that looked almost like a woman. Jack shuddered, the room feeling colder all of a sudden.

"Grandma yelled something about how he should leave me behind, that I wasn't important," May said, "but he just laughed and said if she cared that much, I'd definitely be coming along. So they carried me in right behind her. Only . . ." She trailed off briefly, then shrugged. "Only I struggled while we were in that tunnel. I guess the fire wasn't that stable, 'cause it didn't take much for me to knock one of the monsters off balance, and they dropped me. Not knowing what else to do, I jumped."

She pointed at the picture now painting itself onto the page, of May diving headfirst into the tunnel's wall, childlike hands reaching out to grab her fleeing form.

"And that's all I remember," she said.

In the book, three dots appeared, as if the story wasn't quite finished.

"That's when we found you," Jack said, and a final illustration appeared, showing Jack bent over the unconscious princess, the circle of blue fire still burning in midair, his grandfather looking on with a big smile on his face.

"Right," May said. "So if you start talking from here, I should find out why you started making out with me?"

Jack blushed. "We can probably skip that part."

May glared at him for a second, then reached into her pocket and pulled out a folded piece of paper. "Emergency numbers," she reminded him. "Probably pointless, but who knows."

May unfolded the paper, then gasped as a silver necklace slipped out. She caught it as it fell and held it up to get a closer look.

At the end of the chain was a golden crown. "This is my grandmother's," she said quietly. "She never takes it off."

Jack frowned. "What does the paper say?"

May slipped the chain over her head and unfolded the rest of the note. "'May,'" she read. "'Keep this hidden. It's the key to everything.'" She paused, holding up the necklace to examine it.

"I think I understand," Jack said. "Keep reading."

"'If I am taken,'" May continued, "'you'll find help in the Black Forest. Remember I—'" May stopped reading suddenly, swallowing hard before continuing. "'Remember I love you always, my beautiful month of May.'" She put the note down and turned to Jack, her eyes wet. "I guess I shouldn't have shown you the necklace, huh?"

Jack sighed. "Thanks for the trust. But it all makes sense, Princess. I just can't believe you didn't mention the most important part of your story before!"

"Which part?" May asked, wiping her eyes. "The guy in green?"

"Not the Huntsman, no," Jack said. "Though he was my first clue."

"The Huntsman?" May repeated. "You know who that guy is?!"

"Only from stories," Jack said. "But that's what I'm talking about. That's how I know who your grandmother is!"

May stared back at him. "Who she *is*?" May asked. "But how would you know that? You've never met her. She's not from . . . wherever here is."

"Oh, yes she is," Jack said. "But she's been gone for years. This is huge, May!"

"What are you *talking* about?" May shouted at him.

Before Jack could answer her, someone banged on the front door. Jack jumped up to open it, wondering why his grandfather didn't just come in.

Except it wasn't his grandfather. Instead, it looked to be about twenty, maybe thirty, of the village boys. And standing at the front of the boys was Robert, the oldest, meanest, and strongest of all the boys in their village—not as much a bully as some kind of horrible tornado of evil.

"Hey there, Jack," Robert said with a smile. "Your grandfather's been telling the whole town that you found yourself a princess." He looked over Jack's shoulder to where May stood with a confused look on her face. "Congratulations, Princess. Me and the boys here have come to rescue you!"

May glanced from Robert to Jack and back again. She started to say something, then looked down at her shirt.

"Okay, that's the last time I wear this stupid thing," she said. "Seriously."

CHAPTER 5

Don't you worry, Jack," Robert said, stepping forward. "We'll take things from here."

"Give us the princess!" shouted a high-pitched voice from the back of the mob.

Jack stood on his toes to see who'd spoken. "Wait, was that Justin?" he asked. "Justin? You're like eight years old!"

"Ten!" Justin shouted back.

"Shut up!" said Robert, glaring at the other boys, who all quickly quieted down. "The princess needs a husband, right? Well, I'm just the man for the job."

A few of the boys raised objections to that, but a second look from Robert shut them up again.

"She's not looking for someone to marry," Jack said, moving to stand between Robert and the princess. A thought occurred to him. "You're not engaged already, are you?" he asked May.

"I'm fourteen!" she said.

"And?" Jack said.

"So *no*, I'm not!" May shouted.

"Get her!" someone yelled, building up the mob's courage.

"She's mine!" someone else yelled.

"I love you, Princess!" yelled Justin.

"Give us a minute, okay?" Jack said, then pushed Robert backward and slammed the door shut.

"What is going *on*?!" May asked, her voice getting higher pitched by the minute.

"We've got a problem," Jack said, shoving his back against the door. A second later, his whole body shook as Robert pounded on the door.

"Let us *in*, Jack!" Robert yelled from outside. "There's nowhere for you to go!"

Jack considered that for a moment. Robert had a point—the boys would see them if they tried to sneak out one of the cottage's small windows.

"*Open the door!*" Robert yelled, and the other boys began to join in.

Jack sighed, then turned around and yanked the door open. "*Listen!*" he yelled. "I said, give me a *minute*! I'll bring her back out then, and you can all fight over her!" With that, he slammed the door shut again, then whirled around, only to yell out in surprise when he found the princess standing an inch away from him, staring at him angrily.

"What is their *deal*!" May yelled at him.

"They want to marry you," Jack said, pushing past her. "If one of them marries you, then he becomes a prince and gets his own kingdom."

"*Marry* me?!" May said, following closely behind Jack as he made his way through the cottage to the fireplace. "I'm fourteen!"

"You said that already," Jack said as he moved the wood in the fireplace aside. He levered up the grate beneath it with one hand, then reached in with the other and pulled out a bag covered with soot. "Hold this for a second," he said to the princess, handing her the sack. He lowered the grate and stood up.

May just glared at him, now completely covered with ash. "Thanks for that," she said.

He smiled, grabbing the bag back. "They're just cinders, Your

Highness. You can pretty yourself up later. For now, let's deal with the boys, okay?"

Jack walked to the door, but May didn't move. He glanced back with a questioning look.

"You're not helping me just so *you* can marry me, right?" she said suspiciously.

Jack laughed. "Nah," he said, and she relaxed a bit. "I'm keeping my options open in case something better comes along." As he turned away from her, he could almost feel the heat of her hateful gaze burrowing into the back of his head.

Before Robert could pound on the door again, Jack pulled it open. "Everyone, back up!" he shouted, pushing Robert and a few other boys away from the doorway so he and May could get out. The village boys grudgingly backed up, silently waiting to hear him speak.

Jack leapt onto the pile of firewood next to the door and addressed his audience.

"Gentlemen!" he shouted. "You all know that the last thing in the world *I* should be doing is helping this princess. We can all agree that I have no idea what I'm doing. But you . . . you're *all* obviously much smarter and stronger than me." After a few boys voiced their agreement, Jack continued. "Still, only *one* of us can help the princess on her quest—"

"Why?" asked Justin.

"Because only one of us can marry her and become a prince," replied Jack. "Will someone shut him up?"

A resounding thump answered his question, and the top of Justin's head disappeared from within the group of boys. "Thank you," Jack said.

"No problem," said a deep voice from the back.

"But still, we need a way to figure out who will get the honor," Jack said, looking up thoughtfully. "The question is, how to choose which of us is the most worthy?"

At this, various suggestions came flying from the crowd.

"We fight for it!"

"No, we should race!"

"We all know about your stupid magic shoes, Wallace. We're not racing!"

"Gentlemen! Gentlemen!" Jack interrupted loudly. "There's only one way to decide this!" He held up the bag so they could all see it. "It just so happens that my grandfather brought back the incredibly powerful Eye of Courage from one of his adventures. In fact, he plucked it right out of the head of the Cyclops of Cater Pual!"

Jack paused for some impressed murmuring, then continued.

"Exactly. Now, you may not have heard of it, but the Eye of Courage is perfect for our little problem. Basically, if you look at the Eye and aren't completely fearless within your heart of hearts, it kills you dead."

The impressed murmurs immediately turned to stunned silence.

"Nice, huh?" Jack said with a smile. "I think we'd all agree that only the bravest, most courageous of us should be the one to help the princess. So all we need to do is take turns looking at the Eye, and whoever's still standing can take the princess."

"Are you kidding me with this?" May whispered to Jack.

He ignored her. "Who's first, then?" Jack asked the crowd.

At first, no one moved. Then a few of the boys realized they had some urgent chore or errand they had to do right away, while others just silently slipped away. Within a minute, the mob was half the size.

"Is no one brave enough to face the Eye?" Jack asked, faking surprise. "She's a *princess*, guys! Isn't she worth the chance that you'll fall over dead right here?!"

"I'll take that chance," Robert said, grinning arrogantly. He stepped forward, towering over Jack by at least a foot. Out of the corner of his eye, Jack noticed the fairy in May's hair dig herself in deeper, hiding from the boy who'd been hunting her earlier that day.

"Just between you and me," Robert whispered in Jack's ear, "I know you're lying. Still, I'll play along and back up your story. That way I get the princess, and no one argues."

"You've got a deal," Jack whispered back, and opened the bag for Robert to take a look. Robert flashed the mob a smile, then turned and stuck his head into the bag. . . .

At which point Jack drove his knee right up into Robert's face.

The older boy went stiff, shook for a second, then collapsed to the ground, the bag still covering his head. A collective gasp went through the crowd as Jack carefully removed the bag from Robert's head. None of the mob had seen what actually happened, as Robert's body had blocked their view.

"Guess he wasn't brave enough," Jack said sadly, then turned to the crowd. "Who's next?"

CHAPTER 6

Most of the boys didn't bother with excuses after that—they just ran. A few of the older boys seemed to suspect something was up, but they still left, murmuring their doubts. They could be a problem later, but at least there was some room to breathe now.

"That . . . was the biggest display of stupidity I've ever seen," May said.

Before he could respond, the sound of hoofbeats made them both look up to find Jack's grandfather walking down the path toward them, a tray full of food in one hand and the reins of a horse in the other.

And then Jack took a good look at the animal and realized it wasn't a horse at all: It was easily the most evil, horrible monster he'd ever faced.

"Watch out, Grandpa, that thing's a killer!" Jack shouted, his voice cracking in terror.

"Oh, calm down," his grandfather said. "Samson here probably won't bite . . . assuming you don't get him all riled up like you did the last time. George said we could borrow him if we needed him to help the princess."

"It didn't just want to bite me," Jack said quietly, stepping back. "It's been waiting to kill me for years now, biding its time until we were alone."

If there was a meaner, nastier animal within one hundred miles, George's horse would have run it down out of spite, eaten it, then maybe stuffed it as some kind of trophy. All that stood between Jack, May, and a death by trampling were the thin leather reins held in his grandfather's naive hands.

"Did I miss something here?" the old man asked, nodding at Robert's unconscious body.

"Not much," May said. "Just a mob of boys fighting over who could marry me."

"In other words, nothing special," Jack agreed, still eyeing the horse. The horse stared right back, following Jack's every move with his dark, dead eyes. "By the way, I wanted to thank you for telling the entire town about the princess."

The old man coughed to cover his blush. "Yes, well, sometimes words slip out," he said. "Sorry about that."

Jack rolled his eyes. "Slip out? Sounds like you've been shouting about her from the rooftops. Anyway, we should get out of here before Robert wakes up. If the other boys see he's still alive, things are going to get ugly."

"Things already look ugly," Jack's grandfather said, tapping Robert with his foot. The boy moaned slightly at the touch. "Whoops," the old man said quietly. "Get on the horse. Hurry, now."

"I'm *not* getting on the horse!" Jack whispered, his anger rising with his fear.

"Quit being a baby," May said to Jack, and walked up to the horse. "You're not mean, are you, buddy?" she said to Samson.

Samson turned his gaze on the princess, and May immediately took a step back, shivering in the cool evening air. "I think it wants to eat my *face* off," she said quietly.

"It's nothing personal," Jack told her, pulling her away from the monster. "It wants to do that to everyone."

At that, Jack's grandfather grabbed his bag from Jack's hands. "You two are both pathetic. Still, I've got just the thing." He reached deep within the bag, all the way to his shoulder, despite the fact that the bag was only large enough to fit his arm up to the elbow. May's eyes widened at the magic while Jack just tapped his foot impatiently.

Finally, his grandfather smiled in triumph and pulled out what looked to be a horse's bridle. Only this bridle was made out of flowers—daisies, to be specific.

"Years ago," the old man said, handing Jack the flower bridle, "I was kidnapped by shoemaking elves. That was back when I was working as a cobbler—and making a good living at it too, I might add. In fact, my shoes were the reason the elves took me prisoner: They were jealous! Eventually I got to be friendly with one of my captors, a little elf woman named Mariella. She helped me escape by giving me one of the elves' magic bridles, capable of taming even the wildest beast." He smiled widely. "Had to use it on a frog the first time, actually. Did I mention they shrunk me to the size of an apple? Amazingly, the bridle grew with me when I turned back to normal, but that's another story—"

"I've heard it," Jack said, eyeing the horse, then the bridle. At this point, he wasn't sure which was worse. Magic was all well and good when it worked, but it had a tendency to go wrong just when you needed it the most. Say, for example, when you were trapped on the back of a devil horse.

On the ground, Robert moaned again, and Jack realized they didn't exactly have a choice. He sighed, took the bridle, and planted his feet, facing Samson. He took a deep breath and held the bridle out between his hands, then thrust it at the horse's mouth.

Samson immediately opened his jaws to bite one of Jack's hands, but Jack quickly jerked them to the side, so Samson bit down on the flower bridle instead. Immediately the beast froze completely, although his cold, dead eyes still glared at Jack.

"Huh," Jack said, honestly impressed that the bridle actually worked. "I've seen that story a million times in the Story Book, but I still thought you were making it up."

"Show's what you know," his grandfather told him, helping May up onto the unmoving horse. After she was up, the old man handed Jack the bag. "Take this too."

"What is that, anyway?" May asked.

"Ah!" Jack's grandfather said, lighting up. "It's a magic sack, Princess! No matter what you put in it, it'll never weigh you down or fill up. It's also where I keep my most treasured magical items, may they come in handy on your trip." He threw Jack a look.

"That includes one of your father's beans, by the way. Try not to eat that. Come the morning, you'd have more than indigestion."

"Thanks," Jack said he leapt onto the horse behind May. "Are you going to be okay here alone?"

"I'll be fine. Get out of here!" his grandfather said, eyeing the growing crowd of boys standing on the path back to town. "And try not to mess this up, huh?"

"Thanks for the optimism," Jack said, then shook the reins. Samson immediately began to walk, then trot. All the boys in town knew enough to stay out of the horse's way, but several of the boys threw Jack dirty looks as the horse approached.

And then, just as Jack and May passed by the largest group of boys, an angry voice yelled out from behind them. "Hey, what's going on here?!" Robert yelled. "You tricked me, Jack! Get him, guys!"

A loud *conk* shut Robert up, as Jack's grandfather smacked him with the food tray, but it was already too late. Jack kicked Samson into a gallop, and off they went down the path, a screaming mob of boys right behind them.

CHAPTER 7

The village of Giant's Hand barely qualified as a village. The story went that some hero had killed a giant nearby, and as the monster fell to the ground, one of its hands crushed a few acres of trees, clearing room for the town. The tree line did follow a handlike pattern, if you squinted . . . and ignored the fact that there were only three fingers. Still, people loved their stories.

Every building in Giant's Hand looked alike, each with a slate roof and wooden walls. The inn was the busiest building in the village, mostly due to the pub on its first floor. Besides the schoolhouse and open-air market, there just wasn't much else to do in the village—another none-too-subtle reminder for children to leave to find adventure when they were old enough.

As Jack and May galloped through the town just ahead of the enraged mob of teenage boys, Jack wondered if he'd ever see any of it again. Glancing back at his old schoolmates, he hoped not.

Although Samson was galloping, more than a few of the boys had kept up because the path's twisting slowed the horse's pace, and now rocks whizzed past Jack's and May's heads every few seconds. Fortunately, most of the boys couldn't hit the broad side of a barn—the closest rock sailed more than a foot over Jack's head, almost taking out a large blackbird in one of the nearby trees.

Still, it was only a matter of time before one of them got lucky. Turning back around to push Samson to go faster, Jack almost bumped his head into May's, she was so close. Out of nowhere, Jack realized that her hair smelled like vanilla.

"Do you know where we're going?!" May yelled at him, turning her head slightly in his direction.

Jack quickly leaned away, in no way sniffing her hair still. "The Black Forest," he shouted back. "Your grandmother said we'd find help there, so that's where we go. It's only a couple of days' ride from here."

"A couple of *days*?!" May said, her voice rising as she ducked beneath a rock.

A little ways back, a horse neighed loudly. Jack kicked Samson lightly to speed up, and the horse obliged, fairly bursting out of the village and up the path leading out of town as the last bit of sunlight faded away completely. The last of the boys gave up, but the horse behind them neighed a second time, much closer now.

"That can't be good," Jack said, glancing back . . . and there was the horse, one of George's farm animals. Only, it wasn't one of the village boys riding it.

Instead, a giant man dressed entirely in green barreled down on them, swinging an enormous axe over his head.

"It's him!" May screamed, trying to kick Samson to go faster, but only managing to hit Jack instead.

"Stop kicking me!" Jack yelled. Tree branches ripped at their clothes as Samson galloped down the completely dark path out of town, as not even the light of the moon could penetrate the trees. Normally, no other horse in the village could outrun Samson, but the Huntsman's horse wasn't carrying two riders. That, combined with the fact that the Huntsman seemed to know how to ride, a skill Jack hadn't exactly mastered yet, meant that he was gaining on them.

"Run all you want!" the Huntsman shouted from behind them. "I'll track you down no matter how far you go, no matter where you hide!"

"I've hidden from bigger guys than *you* before!" Jack yelled back.

"Way to stand up to him," May said over her shoulder.

Jack glanced back, ducking his head to avoid branches as he did. Another minute and they would be within reach of the Huntsman's ugly looking axe. That was it. They weren't going to outrun him. They needed a new plan.

"Hold on," Jack said in May's ear. "Hold on *tight*."

"What?" she said. "Wait, why?!"

Instead of answering, Jack jerked back on the magic bridle, commanding Samson to stop. Magically controlled as he was, Samson planted all four feet in the dirt and leaned back, instantly skidding to a stop.

The force of the halt threw Jack into May and May into Samson's neck. Jack managed to lock his legs around the horse and grab May just before she flew off the horse, while the fairy just dug in, almost yanking out a patch of May's hair as she tumbled forward too.

The Huntsman, meanwhile, galloped right past them, screaming at his own horse to stop. Though his horse did slow down, it wasn't dumb enough to try what Samson had been magically compelled to do. All in all, Jack figured they had about five seconds to figure out what to do before the Huntsman could make it back to them.

"We need to get off the horse," he told May, jumping off himself.

The princess quickly dismounted as well, then started to run for the trees, but Jack grabbed her hand and yanked her back behind Samson. "What are you *doing*!" she said, pulling her hand from his. "He's going to kill us!"

"Not you, girlie," the Huntsman said, stepping off his exhausted horse. "Your boyfriend, on the other hand, is fair game." With that, the Huntsman swung his axe around and aimed it right at Jack's face.

"Oh, I'm not her boyfriend," Jack said, taking a quick step to the left. Unfortunately, the axe followed him. "I just met her, in fact. If you want to take her, she's yours."

"What?!" May said, turning to stare at Jack. "You're letting him take me?!"

"Brave lad, aren't you," the Huntsman said, shaking his head with a smile.

May growled. "You know what, Green Man?" she said to the Huntsman. "If you want to take *him*, then *he's* yours! I don't even care!"

"With that attitude," Jack said, throwing a dark look at the princess, "maybe I *will* let him take you!"

"Oh, *really!*" May said, her eyes flashing with anger. "You don't seem to be doing a whole lot to stop it!"

"You have no *idea* what I'm doing!" Jack said, turning to face the fuming princess. "Maybe you could try *trusting* me?"

"Trust you?!" May yelled. "You just told him to take me!"

"I was tricking him!" Jack shouted back. "I'm outwitting him!"

The Huntsman burst into laughter at that, dropping his axe's tip slightly as he did.

Instantly, Jack yanked the magic bridle out of Samson's mouth.

The cold, dead eyes came to life, their pure, unadulterated hatred focused straight ahead. Jack quickly grabbed May and pulled her behind Samson, out of the horse's sight.

"What's this, then?" the Huntsman said, quickly aiming his axe at Jack again.

Jack looked from Samson to the exhausted farm horse and back. George owned the only two horses in town, which meant the Huntsman had just ridden Samson's mate into the ground. And Samson didn't look too happy about that.

The monstrous horse let loose an unnatural growl and slowly advanced on the Huntsman, his eyes burning red with hatred. The Huntsman froze, then quickly turned the axe toward the horse, the enormous man's expression turning from curious to worried all in the span of a few seconds.

"I think he wants to eat your face off," Jack suggested helpfully.

"It's just a horse," the Huntsman said dismissively, though his eyes never left the animal.

"A demon horse," Jack replied, smiling now. "And you just rode his mate almost to death."

At that, Samson reared up, neighing horribly, his evil hooves clawing at the air in front of the Huntsman. Desperately, the Huntsman brought his axe up, but Samson drove his hooves down right into the Huntsman's chest, crashing the enormous man backward into a tree. The force of the impact actually cracked the tree trunk, but didn't seem to do more than knock the breath out of the man.

Samson wasn't finished, though. Before the Huntsman could move, the horse blocked him in, rearing up on his hind legs again. The Huntsman slipped between the trees for protection, but Samson reared again, then drove his hooves into the tree trunks on either side of the man, sending wood chips flying.

The Huntsman threw one last furious glace at Jack, then disappeared into the forest. Samson, robbed of his prey, squealed in fury and followed the Huntsman into the trees with a neigh that sounded almost hungry.

Jack took a deep breath, then looked at May. The princess's eyes were as huge as dinner plates, while the fairy in her hair looked just as shocked, if not more.

"You okay?" Jack asked her.

"I'm going to see that thing in my nightmares," she whispered. "Well, maybe both those things. They deserve each other."

"Samson may be evil," Jack said, "but he's still just a horse. The Huntsman will outsmart him . . . or kill him. Either way it's not going to take too long. We've got to get out of here."

Jack grabbed the magic bridle and stuck it into his bag, while May glanced over at the horse the Huntsman had stolen. "Should we ride her?" the princess asked.

Jack shook his head. "She's so tired, I doubt she could carry us both. But even if she could, do you really want Samson coming after *us* next?"

"Good point," May said.

Jack grabbed her hand and led the way into the forest, on the opposite side from where the Huntsman and Samson had gone. As dark as it was, they both stumbled with almost every step, but fear kept them moving.

They ran for what felt like hours, trying to put enough distance between themselves and the Huntsman so they could hide. From the stories, Jack knew the man would eventually track them down, but finding their trail in the dark would take a while, and hopefully they'd find some kind of safety first.

The problem was, the farther they ran, the more lost Jack got. They'd taken a few unfamiliar twists and turns when riding Samson, and now Jack had no idea where they were. There weren't any landmarks that Jack could see, either—just forest in every direction. For all he knew, they were heading back toward Giant's Hand.

Or worse, toward the Huntsman.

"We have to stop," Jack said, his breath coming out in gasps.

May didn't bother replying, she was so out of breath. Instead, she just nodded, then fell limply to the forest floor and leaned against a nearby tree.

Jack settled himself next to her, and for a few minutes, they sat in silence, catching their breath.

"We're going to kill ourselves, running through the woods like this," Jack said finally. "What do you think about waiting until the sun comes up to keep going?"

May nodded, still not saying anything. The fairy in her hair, despite having done nothing more than hang on all night, looked just as exhausted.

"Are you all right?" Jack asked the princess.

She paused, then turned to look at him. Even in the dark, Jack could tell her eyes were red from crying. "Am I all right?" she asked, her voice quiet. "This hasn't exactly been the greatest day of my life, has it?" A tear rolled down her cheek, and Jack immediately felt guilty for no particular reason.

"Oh, hey," he said, awkwardly patting her shoulder. "Don't do that."

She sniffed loudly. "Oh, *okay*, then," she said, a bit of a smile showing. "I won't. Thanks."

"Sorry," he said. "I know this hasn't been easy on you."

She looked at him and sighed. "No, it hasn't. But since we're not going anywhere for a while, why don't you tell me how you know my grandmother?"

"Oh, right," Jack said. "I mean, *everyone* knows her. I just wish you'd mentioned that your grandmother was Snow White. That would have explained a lot."

May blinked. "I'm sorry, what?"

CHAPTER 8

I said, I wish you'd mentioned that your grandmother was Snow White," Jack repeated. "Would have been easier than figuring it out on my own."

"Snow *White*?" May said, her eyes narrowing as she glared at him. "Just because I'm in some kind of fantasy world doesn't make me stupid."

"Nah," Jack said. "If anything, you would have been born that way."

She punched him for that. "*Explain* what you're talking about," she growled. "You're talking about *the* Snow White? Like, with the Wicked Queen and all?"

"Yes! Did she ever talk about the Wicked Queen?" Jack said, his eyes going wide.

"No, because my grandmother isn't a character in a fairy tale."

"Fairies don't have tails," Jack said, pointing at the fairy in May's hair, whose behind was sticking straight up into the air as she snored. "Not too observant, are you," he said.

May snorted. "I'm gonna observe me punching you again in a second. Not tails . . . *tales*. Stories. Anyway, Snow White isn't real. She's made-up."

"That's what the Wicked Queen used to say," Jack told her. "The Queen started rumors that Snow White wasn't real. Other people thought Snow White had died. But I guess she was just . . . well, in Punk." Jack smiled. "You have no idea how great that news is, that Snow White is still alive."

"Okay, fine," May said. "Snow White's real here. You've got fairies, you've got magic books. You probably have cats walking around in boots too."

"Not anymore," Jack said. "If there ever were cats like that, they were hunted down years ago with the rest of the talking animals."

That shut the princess up for a moment. "What, seriously?" she said finally. "Are you kidding?"

Jack shook his head. "It's a long story. Anyway, Snow White disappeared back at the end of the Great War, and no one's heard from either her or the Wicked Queen since."

"But why would you think *my* grandmother is Snow White?" May asked. "I mean, her name's Eudora Winterbourne. And don't make some kind of stupid connection between 'winter' and 'snow.'"

"Look at the facts," Jack said. "First, your grandmother is the spitting image of Snow White: pale skin, black hair, beautiful . . ."

"Right," May said. "The fairest one of all. I get it. But you just described like half a bajillion women."

"Second," Jack continued, ignoring her, "did you hear what she and the Huntsman were talking about? They mentioned the Wicked Queen and betrayal and Snow White . . . and the Mirror!" Jack shuddered. "If the Wicked Queen has her Mirror again, we're all dead."

"Mirror?" May asked.

"It's the Wicked Queen's most powerful magic," Jack said. "From what people say, her Magic Mirror knows everything, and answers any question you ask it, even if what you're asking about hasn't happened yet."

"That doesn't make sense," May said. "How could it know the future?"

Jack looked at her oddly. "I just said, it's magic."

"Oh, *okay*, thanks for the explanation," she said. "So my grandmother mentioned something about a mirror and the Wicked Queen. That doesn't make her Snow White."

"Think about the stories you've heard," Jack said. "The Wicked Queen sent her Huntsman out to kill Snow White, but Snow White escaped. The Huntsman must have been tracking her down this whole time. And when he finally found her . . . and you . . . he brought her back to the Wicked Queen."

"That's not exactly how I remember it," May said, her forehead crinkling. "But who knows, my grandmother never let me listen to any of those stories for some reason. Anyway, what was that Great War thing you mentioned?"

Jack paused, forcing himself not to remember certain bad memories. "Basically, the queen of a tiny kingdom invaded all the lands around her, destroying everything she came across. She'd taken over the entire eastern half of the continent before the Western Kingdoms decided to unite against her. Most people say it was Snow White who actually brought us all together to fight the Wicked Queen, as people started calling her. But it didn't go well. The kingdoms couldn't stand up to the Wicked Queen's armies of goblins, trolls, dragons—pretty much any kind of monster you can imagine. It also didn't help that the Wicked Queen had her Magic Mirror. It's hard to win a battle when your enemy knows exactly what you're planning."

"Well, yes," May said.

"But something happened that the Queen somehow didn't see coming. I guess that's the limit of the Mirror: If you don't ask the right question, you're out of luck. One of the Wicked Queen's inner circle of knights—people call them her Eyes—one of them betrayed her. This knight supposedly fell in love with Snow White and helped her and a small group of rebels break into the Wicked Queen's castle. You've probably heard of most of them: Rapunzel; Rose Red, who people say was Snow's sister; the piper and his magical flute; Edward, the cursed prince; and the Wolf King."

"I thought you said all the animals were gone?" May asked.

"The Wolf King might be gone now too," Jack said quietly. "The only one of Snow White's group that anyone's seen since then is Rapunzel, who is now queen of the Western Kingdoms. We know they succeeded in defeating the Wicked Queen somehow, because all the Queen's armies dispersed and the Great

War ended. But Snow White, the Wicked Queen, and the rest were never seen or heard from again. That was like twelve years ago now."

"So," May said, "if no one's seen Snow White since, how did she end up in the real world?"

"The real what?" Jack said.

"The real world," May said. "Where I'm from." She rolled her eyes. "Okay, fine, how did she end up in *Punk*?"

"She must have hidden herself there," Jack said. "Some stories say that Snow White broke the Queen's Mirror during their final battle. And when your grandmother was taken, the Huntsman told the little monster things to look for a missing piece of the Mirror." Jack paused, then slowly turned to look at the necklace hanging around May's neck.

She noticed his gaze and pulled the golden crown out from under her shirt. "This?" she said. "You don't really think . . . *this* is a piece of the Queen's Magic Mirror?"

"She told you to keep it hidden," Jack said. "And if it is, that might be all that's been stopping the Wicked Queen from coming back. If she had a working Mirror, she'd be all-powerful again." Jack swallowed hard. "Which means the only thing keeping the Wicked Queen from taking over the entire world is that necklace."

May shot him a dark look. "Well, at least you're not being overly dramatic." Despite her sarcasm, she shuddered and slipped the necklace back under her shirt. "I'm not willing to say you're right, but I guess you could be close to somehow being *almost* right. Either way, sounds like we're going to need that help my grandmother mentioned in her note, huh?"

"Sounds like," Jack agreed. "Only, let's find it in the morning." He laid down a little more, with his head against the tree, exhaustion suddenly smacking him in the face.

May did the same, and pretty soon their eyelids were drooping.

"I have to warn you," Jack said quietly. "I'm not very good at this sort of thing."

"Good at what sort of thing?" May asked, opening one eye slightly.

"Well," Jack said, "if your grandmother *is* Snow White, then you really are a princess."

"Ha," May said drowsily. "That a problem for you?"

"A bit," Jack admitted. "I can't stand royalty."

May laughed softly. Jack smiled too, taking one last look at May as the princess fell asleep. She really was cute, all things considered. And she didn't act like princesses in stories did—all useless and vulnerable and needing rescuing. Maybe some royals weren't actually that different from the rest of the world.

He stopped himself there—his sleepiness must have been messing with his head. May was the granddaughter of Snow White, a member of one of the oldest royal families in existence. And she'd grown up in the lap of luxury, with more wealth than he could even imagine. She was as royal as they came, and therefore was nothing like him.

Wouldn't it be funny if she were, though?

The last thing he heard before he fell asleep was tiny, high-pitched laughing from all around him.

Apparently, someone else thought it was funny too.

CHAPTER 9

Jack woke up from nightmares of a man in green to find that the forest he'd fallen asleep in was gone. Instead of leaves above him, now there were pink and white tiles, and whatever he was lying on was smooth, unlike the rough forest floor.

He started to sit up, but something held him firmly in place. Hard ropes of some kind covered his chest and legs.

Well, *that* probably wasn't good news.

"Hello?" Jack said, looking around as much as he could while being held in place. A massive headache pounded the sides of his skull, and for some reason, his feet were really warm. "Huntsman?" he asked more quietly, a little afraid of the answer.

"You're awake, darling," said a woman in a raspy voice. The speaker leaned over his head so that Jack could see her face . . . except there was no face to see. Instead, a black hooded robe covered what looked to be a smooth white orb, almost like an egg.

And then the egg cracked across the center, splitting jaggedly in half in what seemed to be a horrifying mouth. "My children found you in the forest and were growing ever so hungry!" the faceless woman said. "I almost let them eat you whole, there on the ground, I did. But that wouldn't do, darling, no. My children deserve a home-cooked meal, they do indeed."

And just like that, the situation plummeted past bad and headed for can't-get-much-worse. Despite his pounding heart and the sudden sweat all over his body, Jack took a deep breath, knowing nothing would be helped by panic—at least not until he could run screaming. "Who are you?" he asked, slowly flexing every part of his body to see how strong his bindings were. He felt a little give in the ropes around his legs, but not much.

"I'm No-One-in-Particular," the woman said with a small giggle, the crack in the eggshell giving the impression of sharp teeth.

"You're a witch," Jack said, recognizing her nonanswer. "So you're not going to tell me your real name?"

"Names have power, darling," the witch said, stepping out of Jack's vision. For a second, he wasn't sure where she was, but then he heard her down near his feet. "Yes, they do, don't they, Jack?"

Uh-oh. "My name's not Jack," he said. "Who told you that?"

The witch cackled, still out of his sight. "The girl, of course, darling. The one who said your name while she slumbered! Quite a tasty treat there, darling."

At that, Jack abruptly stopped sweating as his insides froze up. "What did you do to her?" he said quietly, barely able to hear his own voice over his heartbeat.

The witch put a hand on his leg, and where she touched him, his skin went numb. "Don't you worry about her, darling, yes. She's quite safe, she is. Recognized her necklace, I did, and that one's worth more alive than in my stomach, yes. But you, darling, you're another tale altogether, yes. You're to go in the oven, for dinner. Then we'll see if we can't trade your friend to the Wicked Queen for some dessert."

And then something sharp pressed into his skin next to the witch's hand. Jack bit his lip to keep from yelling out in pain, only there wasn't any. Whatever it was didn't seem to be cutting him, only his pants. "Don't fret, darling," the witch said. "I'm just removing your clothing skin . . . gives such a burnt flavor if you leave it on, darling."

The witch brought the sharp object down again and sliced.

The feeling of sharp metal on his skin sent Jack into a terrified frenzy, and he frantically kicked out with both legs. He missed at first, but a second kick managed to knock the witch's hand away slightly, sending the sharp metal in her hand right into the rope tying Jack down.

Suddenly, he was free, as cutting the rope on his legs had loosened the rest of his bindings. Jack quickly pushed himself up enough to see the witch, then launched his foot right at the witch's eggshell face.

The kick connected, knocking the witch backward off her feet. Jack quickly pulled the rest of the strangely sticky ropes off himself, then threw his legs over the side of the table, noticing for the first time why his feet had been so warm. Only a few inches from his toes was the most enormous black metal oven he'd ever seen.

And then a gnarled claw sunk into the table next to him.

"Oh no, darling," said the witch, her white head rising up over the side of the table. His kick had knocked the witch's hood off, because beneath it . . .

Beneath it was nothing at all. The white orb that made up her head didn't go past the halfway point, like someone had broken the eggshell in two. The back was completely hollow.

And not only was her head empty, she now had an indentation in the shell where he'd kicked her. As Jack watched with horror, the dent slowly pushed back out with a nauseating pop.

"You mustn't struggle, darling," the witch said, shuddering to her feet as she pulled her hood back on. "That won't do at all, not at all. You'll make your meat all tough, yes you will, and—"

Jack kicked her again, but this time, her gnarled old hand came out of nowhere to catch his foot. She held it in place for a second, then cruelly twisted it, sending a lightning bolt of pain all the way up to his waist.

"It's rude to interrupt, darling," the empty face said. The witch yanked upward on his leg, pulling Jack up and off the table, dangling him in midair. "I intend to crack these little bones," the witch said in a delighted tone. "Yes I do. There are such tasty flavors in your little bones, darling, and they're just going to waste."

Jack kicked out desperately, trying to free himself from her grip, but the witch just held on tighter, her claws cutting into his skin. Giving up on his legs, Jack groped around on the strangely sticky floor for something to hit her with, but there was nothing within reach.

The witch yanked the oven door open, and the heat from inside exploded over both of them. The witch bent to look Jack right in the face as he swung helplessly over the floor. "Thank you, darling," she said, drool dripping out of the crack that was her mouth. "Thank you for letting me eat you."

As Jack stared in horror, her mouth began to close in on his leg, as if she was going to take a bite out of him right then and there. He punched her with both hands, but his blows just sank into her robes as if there was no body to hit. As the witch's face-less head got closer, a flickering tongue pushed past the cracked mouth, licking the edges in anticipation as she closed in.

And then something startlingly red and blue slammed into the witch's head, knocking her over.

Jack crashed to the floor, landing right on top of the witch. He frantically pushed himself off the witch's squirming body and tried to crawl away from her on the sticky floor but didn't get very far.

And then hands pulled the witch's body away from him. May, a disgusted look on her face, had hooked her hands underneath the witch's arms and was dragging her body toward the black ropes that had tied Jack up. On the floor next to May lay a large blue and red circle with a white stick.

It was a lollipop, easily as big around as Jack's head.

"Uh . . . what?" he said, having trouble following.

May quickly circled the ropes around the witch's body, then pulled them tight, eliciting a groan from the groggy witch.

Jack grabbed the table and slowly pulled himself to his feet, his legs still wobbling under him. "How . . . ? Where did *you* come from?"

May nodded over his shoulder. "She tied me up and threw me in the closet." The princess smiled. "She might want to empty it out next time instead of leaving all kinds of sharp gardening tools around for someone to cut themselves free with."

Jack grunted. "I'm actually kind of glad she didn't think that far. And . . . the lollipop?"

May picked her weapon up off the floor. "What, this?" she said. "Have you taken a look around?"

Jack raised an eyebrow, then took a closer look around the room. "Oh, wow," he said, his breath catching in his throat.

The walls, the ceiling, the furniture: Everything was made of candy.

Peppermint chairs had gumdrops for cushions. Walls made

of graham crackers were held in place by white frosting. The table Jack had woken up on was made of chocolate bars; the end nearest the oven had even melted a bit. And the ropes now tied around the witch looked to be black licorice strings braided together.

The oven was metal, probably for practical reasons, but the chimney above it seemed to be made of hard toffee. The colors on the ceiling that he'd noticed when he woke up were actually . . . well, he couldn't tell what kind of candy they were, but they looked good. Even the windows looked like thin panes of lollipop candy.

Jack's stomach rumbled in spite of everything. "It's . . . it's a candy house!" he said, taking a step toward the graham cracker walls. As he walked, the sticky floor caught his attention: peanut brittle. "Don't you want to *try* it?!" he asked the princess, fighting off a wild desire to taste everything at once.

May gave him an exasperated look. "Are you kidding?" she said. "Don't tell me you're actually thinking of . . . Jack, you're *not* going to eat any! After what the witch was going to do to you? Do you know how disgusting that is?!"

"Very?" Jack said, not really listening as he considered the chocolate table.

May gagged. "She's been *walking* on this stuff! Sitting on it! Not to mention the fact that I haven't seen a bathroom. And you're going to put it in your *mouth*?"

"It's *candy*," Jack said, running his fingers over the chocolate table. "Who cares where it's been?"

May sighed. "I can't tell you how disgusted I am right now. At least don't eat the floor. Or the chairs or tables. The walls might be the cleanest, up high."

Jack nodded and climbed up onto the chocolate table to get close enough to the wall for a taste. He picked a frosting seam to try first, put a hand on either side of it, then stuck out his tongue and licked the wall.

A sugary explosion burst in his mouth, and he almost fainted in pleasure. It was as if every candy or dessert he'd ever eaten had been in preparation for this one moment! The sweetness, the texture . . . it was making him light-headed!

Actually, it really *was* making him light-headed. And when had the room started spinning?

And then everything went dark, and Jack was falling. He heard May scream something right before he tumbled off the table and slammed into the floor.

A few seconds later, Jack opened his eyes to find May

standing over him, shaking her head in amazement. "I hope that was worth it," she said, pulling him up to a seated position, then leaning him against the same wall he'd just tasted.

"It almost was," he said, still a little faint. "Too bad . . . she must have poisoned all the candy."

"Poisoned it?" May asked. "Is that what happened?"

"I should have realized," Jack said, shaking off the lingering effects of the frosting. "Of *course* she'd poison it. That's probably how she caught most of her prey. Bait the trap with a house made of candy, then add a little something to knock out anyone who eats it. Wham, she's got dinner."

"That's pleasant," May said, helping Jack up. "But that's not how she got us. How exactly did we get here, anyway?"

"She mentioned something about her children," Jack said, his head clearing as he slowly followed May to the candy house's front door.

"Her children? Wonder what she meant by that?" May asked as she yanked the door open. One look outside, and the princess immediately slammed it shut and spun around with a look of terror in her eyes.

"What?" Jack asked, his stomach going queasy, and not from the frosting. "What was out there?"

In a very small voice, she said, "I think they're her children . . . ?"

Jack frowned. "Okay, so there are a few kids. We should be able to get past them." He picked up a nearby lollipop. "Especially if we have weapons," he said with a smile, a smile that May didn't return. "What?" he asked her again.

"A lollipop's not gonna cut it, Jack," May said quietly.

From outside, Jack heard a giggle, the same one he'd heard before falling asleep. A second giggle quickly joined it, then a third, and soon what sounded like hundreds of the creatures began laughing right outside the door.

A second later, the witch began laughing too. "Come in, my children!" she shouted. "I know I said the girl was to be left alone, but mother's changed her mind. Come untie us, and we shall feast on both of these delicious morsels!"

CHAPTER 10

Jack sighed, grabbed May's lollipop from the floor, and knocked the cackling witch on the head. May, meanwhile, grabbed one of the peppermint chairs and slammed it down into the peanut brittle floor to hold the door shut, just in time: The chair crunched into place just as one of the little giggling monsters outside pushed the door open, its little hand reaching in. As the chair slammed the door shut again, the creature's cry of pain harmonized eerily with the witch's.

"There's no escape, my darlings!" the witch screamed. "My children will not let you leave until they've eaten their fill!"

"Can you shut her up?!" May yelled. Jack swung the lollipop again, but this time the witch was ready. Her cracked eggshell mouth grabbed the lollipop and crunched down, biting it in half.

"Gah!" Jack shouted, dropping his half of the lollipop.

"I took her down on my first try, you know," May pointed out.

"She's not the main concern," Jack said. "We need to find something to use against her children!" As he spoke, they could hear loud scraping sounds on the door, followed by little plaintive cries, as if the witch's children were babies crying for milk.

"What about that?" May said, pointing at the curved knife the witch had been using to cut open Jack's clothing when he first woke up.

"We might want to think bigger," he said. "One knife's not going to protect us very long against all those creatures."

"Fine," May said. She paused, then grabbed Jack and pulled him toward a small door in the corner of the house. "We still have all the noncandy tools in the closet, though!" she said, yanking the door open. "Maybe there's something in here we can use as a weapon."

Jack made his way over to her, dodging random gardening equipment she threw out of the closet. A hoe, a saw, a rake . . . none of these were big enough. There was some wood for the fire, still not enough . . . oh, his grandfather's bag! Jack grabbed it as it flew by and threw it over one shoulder. May hadn't stopped, though. A hammer whizzed by his leg, followed by a broom, then a metal pot . . .

A broom?

"Hold on!" Jack yelled, spinning around to pick up the broom. He hated to use magic, but it didn't look like they had much of a choice.

May tossed a few other assorted instruments out of the closet, then turned around. "What?" she said. "That hammer's no better than the knife."

"Not the hammer," Jack said. "The broom. That's our way out."

Outside, the clawing grew louder, and not just at the door. It sounded as if the creatures were trying to claw—or eat—their way right through the walls of the house. Apparently the poison didn't affect them.

"Are you still drugged on candy?" May asked, narrowing her eyes. "You do realize that's for sweeping, right?"

"Don't you know anything?" Jack said. "How do you think witches get around?"

"Don't touch that!" the witch cried out, struggling harder against the licorice bindings.

"One more word, and you're going in the oven!" May said, then turned back to Jack. "You're saying witches actually ride around on brooms?" she asked, one eyebrow up. "Wow, how old-school."

Jack shrugged. "It's tradition."

"So how does it work?" May said, taking the broom from him. She straddled the handle and began hopping around the room with it under her. "Giddyup!" she shouted. "Let's go! Bibbity-Bobbity—"

"Don't just *yell* out magic words!" Jack shouted at her. Did she even know what she was saying?! Who knew what spell she might cast!

"I think we're safe," May said as she came to a stop. "And apparently I just ran around on a regular broom. Great idea, genius."

Jack grabbed the broom and looked it over, thinking. Finally he shrugged, held it horizontally at shoulder level in both hands, then brought the broom down as hard as he could toward his knee, as if he was going to break it in half.

Just before it hit his knee, the broom leapt out of Jack's hands and into the air with a squeal. It bucked wildly, then tore off around the cottage, madly flying in every direction like a trapped insect looking for a window.

May threw herself out of its way, but as the broom tore past Jack, he jumped up and grabbed it with both hands, holding on tight. The broom didn't even slow down, continuing its frantic dash around the cottage, only now dragging Jack along behind it.

"Little help?" he asked as he flew by May. The princess grabbed Jack on the next go-around, and between the two, they managed to pull the broom back down to the floor.

"I think I figured out how to make it go," Jack said, grunting as he held the still struggling broom with both arms.

"How'd you know it would do that?" May asked, tentatively approaching the broom, which seemed to be calming down a bit.

"It was just a guess," he said. "I figured I'd try scaring it, see if that got any reaction out of it."

"Just a small one," May said, reaching out to pet the broom. As she touched it the broom jerked a bit, then quieted down, as if it were a frightened cat. "Where'd you learn this stuff, anyway?"

"School, mostly," he said with a shrug. "The rest is just common sense."

"Glad you caught the witch lesson," May said, still petting the broom, which now seemed to be purring.

Suddenly, the lollipop chair holding the door closed bumped backward. Fortunately, the chair stuck briefly in the peanut brittle, falling back into place after the initial jolt. A second hit from outside, though, knocked the chair completely out of the way just as Jack leapt forward and smashed the chair back into place. The chair's legs cracked a bit, but held firm in the sticky floor.

May turned from the front door back to the broom. "Right," she said. "Time to go."

As she straddled the broom again, Jack quickly grabbed the knife from the table and threw it into his bag. It wasn't much, but it couldn't hurt. "Ready to try this?" he asked May as he threw a leg over the broom behind her.

"Not even a little bit," she said, turning around to look at Jack. "Let's go."

Before Jack could respond, another hit sent the chair skidding across the floor as the door banged open.

Seeing the creatures for the first time, Jack gasped. The witch had called them children, but these creatures looked nothing like any child he'd ever seen. Yes, they were small, no more than two feet tall, but not many kids in his village had sharpened fangs and claws. Also, most children he knew didn't have empty sockets where their eyes should have been.

Even without eyes, though, every one of the witch's children managed to look at them hungrily.

CHAPTER 11

Grab them, my children!" the witch shouted.

"Get us out of here!" Jack screamed, kicking up from the floor. "Go, go, go!"

"Fly!" May yelled, pulling up on the broom. "*Fly*, broom!"

At the princess's command, the broom leapt into the air just above the first few children that lunged at them, then shot forward like an arrow, straight at the monsters blocking the doorway. Jack ducked his head and May screamed in terror as they plowed right into the creatures.

Claws and teeth ripped at Jack's clothes and skin as the witch's children grabbed and bit, but the broom never stopped. A second later, they were through the mob of creatures and out into the night sky. A few of the witch's children held on to May, Jack, and the broom, but Jack managed to kick and poke the little monsters off as May angled the broom up into the sky.

As the monsters tumbled off the broom, Jack watched them fall. Despite the fact that it was now dark again (how long had he been knocked out?!), the lights inside the cottage lit up the area around it, giving Jack just enough light to see by. And what he saw made him sick.

The entire forest floor, as far as Jack could see, was covered in the witch's children. There must have been hundreds of the tiny, swarming monsters, including the ones climbing all over the cottage . . . the same cottage that just minutes ago Jack had tasted.

He swallowed hard, pushing down the bile. That'd teach him to eat candy from strange houses.

"If we hadn't found the broom . . ." May said, then stopped in midsentence, thankfully. Jack glanced down again, but as they rose, the children quickly blended into the forest floor. Soon, even that was blocked by the trees, the tops of which they quickly rose past.

"We're a bit high, aren't we?" Jack asked, feeling his toes go cold with nothing beneath them.

"This?" May said, looking down, which tipped the broom.

Jack tapped her on the shoulder more and more urgently until she leaned back. "I've been on roller coasters higher than this."

"Good to hear," Jack said, fixing his eyes on the horizon, not really caring about her rolling coasts or whatever.

The moon lit up the cloudless night despite its only being half-full, and the whole land unfolded before them. If the moon didn't eat soon, it'd risk fading away completely, but from what Jack had seen, it never learned, disappearing from view at least once a month.

Now that he could see where they were, Jack glanced around for any landmarks he might recognize. The forest extended in all directions, and there was no sign of a road or path. Giving up on landmarks, Jack started looking for the nearest farm or town, anything with people who could give them directions. He couldn't find one of those, but he did see the turrets of a castle peeking out above the trees up ahead. A castle meant royalty, but at least the royals wouldn't try to eat them.

A low standard, yes, but an important one.

"See?" May said, pointing down as she twisted back to look at him. "*Now* we're getting high."

Jack looked to where she pointed and almost toppled off the broom. They hadn't stopped rising, and now they were so high

Jack could barely make out individual trees below them. "Broom!" Jack yelled, his voice cracking. "Stop going up! Go forward!"

The broom ignored him.

"Broom!" May shouted. "Stop rising, and fly straight ahead!"

Instantly, the broom stopped rising and began to inch forward.

May turned around and smiled. "It likes me better," she said, and the broom purred beneath them.

Jack sighed, happy not to be flying any higher. "It's probably used to listening to the witch. Maybe you remind it of her."

She glared at him. "You want me to tell it to drop you?"

"I take it all back," he said quickly, not willing to test if May was joking or not. "You're wonderful and beautiful and amazing."

"That's what I thought," May said and turned back around.

"Point it toward that castle over there," Jack said, and she pulled on the handle until they were pointed at the large stone fortress.

And just like that, they were off . . . if by off, one meant moving along at about a slug's pace. And not the pace of one of those magic slugs that were larger than a horse, with super-slick oil that they skated on top of, either. Granted, their oil was valuable, since it kept metal hinges from sticking, but still.

"I'm going to give it some gas!" May yelled, interrupting Jack's slug-oil musings. Before he could wonder what she meant by gas, the princess leaned back to brace herself, an act that almost made Jack lose his balance again.

"Stay still!" he hissed at her, his heart in his throat. "I almost fell off!"

"Oh, calm down," she said, reaching an arm behind her to hold on to him. "Ready now? Broom! Fly forward as *fast* as you can. Ready? Go!"

Jack doubled his grip on May, locking his hands around her stomach and his knees around the bottom of the broom.

It wasn't enough.

The broom bolted forward like lightning, faster than a galloping horse . . . faster than a winged horse, even. At that speed, they were going fast enough to pass the castle that'd been several days' walk away in less than a second.

At that speed, they were also going fast enough to send Jack tumbling right off the back of the broom.

CHAPTER 12

"*Jack!*" May shouted as he flew off the broom. She threw herself backward, both arms desperately reaching for him, hanging from the broom with just her knees.

While her left hand missed completely, her right hand grazed his shirt, a fraction of an inch from grabbing it.

Jack's flailing arms fortunately made up the difference. He grabbed on to May's right arm with both hands, almost yanking her off the broom as well.

Jack locked his fingers around May's arm with a death-grip as he hung suspended over miles of empty air. He tried to yell at her to stop the broom, but for some reason his lungs wouldn't work, and he couldn't get out more than a wheeze.

"Hold on!" May yelled to him. "And don't look down!"

Trusting that she knew exactly what she was talking about, Jack fixed his eyes forward again, expecting to see the horizon. Instead, he saw something large, gray, and rocky.

They were headed straight for a mountain.

Jack frantically sucked in some air, intending to make his voice work whether it wanted to or not. *"Pull up!"* he screamed.

"What?" May yelled, the wind making it hard to hear much of anything. Unfortunately, hanging backward as she was, the princess couldn't see the large amount of stone they were about to slam into.

"Mountain!" Jack screamed back.

Not knowing what else to do, he flexed his arms, pulling himself up a bit, then dropped suddenly, jerking May and the back of the broom down as hard as he could. The front of the broom shot up, rising just enough for them to miss the mountain.

At least, May and the broom would. Jack, unfortunately, lost his grip on May's arms when the broom began to climb and down he fell.

"Jaaaaaaaaaaaaaaaaaaa . . ." Jack heard May yell until the wind in his ears and the growing distance from the princess wiped out the last of her scream. As he tumbled through the

open air, his heart beat so hard it felt like it was going to break open his chest.

Jack quickly reached over his shoulder and pulled off his grandfather's bag with all the old man's most powerful magic items. As the trees rushed up at him with an alarming speed, Jack knew he had time for just one try. He thrust his hand into the bag, grabbed the first thing he found, and pulled out . . . a feather.

A *feather!* Jack's eyes lit up and he smiled, the wind pulling at his cheeks. A feather might be perfect! If it was the feather from some kind of magical bird, maybe its magic would let him fly!

Desperately, he wiped the feather all over himself, hoping to make the magic work that way. When nothing happened, Jack frantically blew on the feather, then crushed it in his hands, closing his eyes, and willing himself with all his might to stop falling. . . .

And as if by magic, he stopped! The sudden jolt sent his stomach into his shoes, and Jack glanced down to find himself maybe a dozen feet above the trees, swaying slightly in the wind. The feather had done it! He wasn't dead! He was flying!

Jack's laughter grew almost hysterical, he was so happy. "I'm flying!" he shouted to no one, flapping his arms like a bird. "I'm *flying*! Up, feather! Let's go up!"

And just like that, he rose higher in the air.

He flapped his arms a bit more, but it didn't seem to be necessary, so he stopped. Not that it mattered: He was going to be just fine. "Princess!" he shouted, looking up. "Princess! I'm flying! I'm fly—"

And then he noticed two log-size fingers pinching his shirt.

He wasn't flying. He was being lifted into the air.

The excitement he'd felt a second ago up and took flight, unlike the rest of him. The huge fingers ended in an enormous hand, and that hand connected to a massive arm, which ended at . . . the mountain.

Except it wasn't a mountain. It was a giant.

The mountain was a giant.

The mountain was a giant.

"Oh, *great*!" Jack screamed. The feather—the stupid, useless feather—fell from his hands and floated gently to the ground below, but that didn't really matter. He'd probably managed to destroy whatever spell it had by crushing it anyway. *Fantastic*.

As the giant lifted him higher, Jack could start to make out the creature's proportions. What he'd thought were stones was actually a rumpled gray shirt, its buttons larger than Jack's head. Hair jutted out from holes in the shirt, looking exactly like leafless trees. Surprisingly, the shirt had a pocket, and for a second, Jack considered what a giant would possibly need to keep there.

And then he remembered something fairly important. "*Princessssss!*" Jack shouted into the night air. "Can you hear me?!" He imagined her ramming the broom right into the giant, or flying straight up into the sky until she hit a city in the clouds or something. When he got no response, he grimaced. Out of all the options, her landing safely on the ground didn't seem too likely.

The giant apparently didn't like Jack's yelling, though, as it began to wiggle its fingers back and forth. That small act threw Jack around violently, knocking his grandfather's bag right out of his hands. As soon as Jack's eyeballs stopped shaking in their sockets, he lunged to grab it, but he was much too late . . . the bag was already far out of reach. As he watched it fall to the ground, Jack said good-bye to his best shot at saving himself.

Satisfied that his captive was done screaming, the giant began lifting Jack again. He passed the creature's squat, creased neck and what seemed to be a chin or two before finally stopping at the giant's face.

A few feet below him, the giant exhaled, sending a brief, tornado-like wind that almost blew Jack right out of his shirt. The smell of the giant's breath was even worse than the strength of the wind, though: If a herd of animals had died in the giant's mouth, it couldn't have stunk more.

Jack gagged his way past the breath, only to find himself staring up into a virtual jungle of hair jutting out from twin cavernous nostrils beneath the giant's enormous hooked nose. Trying to look away, Jack found himself eye to eye with a pupil the size of his fist in the middle of an eye as blue as a robin's egg. The monster stared back almost curiously.

"So," Jack said, twisting around at the end of the giant's fingers. "*You're* a big boy, huh?"

The giant opened its mouth to respond, then paused, its enormous eyes spinning skyward, its attention suddenly elsewhere. Something was distracting the giant from above.

This was it. This was his chance to fight! Jack took a deep breath, prepared himself, then kicked at the giant's eye as hard as he could.

Unfortunately, he didn't come close to reaching, and only succeeded in spinning himself around in a circle. Beautiful.

A moment later, the giant's eye spun back to Jack as its other hand descended from above. It took Jack a second to realize that the giant's other hand held something as well, but then he sighed, both from relief and frustration.

The giant was holding a broomstick with a frightened-looking princess attached to it.

"Oh, hey," Jack said to May as she reached his level. "Been a while. What's new with you?"

"What is it with our luck?!" May asked, shaking her head in disbelief.

"At least we didn't *hit* the mountain," Jack said. "Anyway, it could have been worse."

"Oh, yeah?" she said with a snort. "How's that?"

"Food!" bellowed the giant, his great voice shaking both of them. And then the monster tossed Jack up into the air and down into his open mouth, slamming it closed with a loud squish.

CHAPTER 13

Jack hadn't ever been eaten before, but the smell was just about what he would have imagined it would be like, if he ever had stopped to actually think about it.

The absolute pitch-black darkness, though, was a bit surprising.

As he passed the giant's lips, Jack had just enough time to make out a dark tunnel of a throat before the giant's mouth closed, taking all the light with it. As Jack fell straight down into the throat, he decided he was actually happy he couldn't see. After all, wasn't it better *not* to know exactly how disgusting his death was going to be?

And then, Jack smacked face-first into something warm,

slippery, and soft. Without thinking, he threw his arms out and grabbed the . . . well, whatever it was. As he hugged the slimy, soft column, his momentum sent him and the slimy thing flying forward, slapping them both up against the back of the giant's mouth. They hit with a wet smack, stuck for a moment, then fell backward again, jiggling to a stop over what Jack figured was the throat.

Unfortunately, being soft and wet, the column of skin hanging in the giant's throat wasn't exactly easy to hang on to. Jack loosened his grip a bit to shift his body, and his arms slipped on the slick surface. He began to slide down the column toward the giant's throat.

"No!" he shouted to the giant, hugging the skin flap tighter despite the fact that everything about this was making him ill. "You're not going to eat me! Do you hear me?!"

"I hear you," said a soft voice from directly behind him.

Jack almost lost his grip again from surprise. "Who's there?!" he shouted. "Who are you?!"

"Is that *really* the most important question right now?" the voice asked calmly. "Let's prioritize, shall we? To start, you seem to be in a spot of trouble."

"Trouble?" Jack said, trying to climb back up the skin flap

but only succeeding in slipping farther down it. "Nah, I'm fine over here. Everything's good. How are you?"

"A bit worried, to be perfectly honest," the voice said. "I'm not entirely sure you will survive this. And unfortunately, I can't help you." The voice sounded sad.

Jack almost laughed at the sheer insanity of that statement. "Well, thanks. That's not really surprising, considering the day I've had. Anyway, I hate to point this out, but aren't you in the same trouble I am? You're trapped here in the giant's mouth too. Maybe *I* won't help *you*! See how *you* like it!"

The voice laughed softly. "No, I'm in no danger. But you won't last very long where you are. You would most likely fare better over here."

Jack flung his head around to see, but it didn't really do much good—the dark in front of him looked exactly the same as the dark behind him. "Um, over where?"

"On the giant's tongue," said the voice. "It's more stable, if only a bit."

"Sounds like a plan," Jack said. "I'll just jump over there in the dark, miss, then fall down the throat. Watch out, I might give this guy a little indigestion, and let's be honest, I wouldn't want to be in your shoes if he burps."

"You may fall," the voice conceded, "or you may reach safety." The voice paused. "Perhaps it is safer to stay there. At the very least, slipping into the giant's throat gradually will let you live longer than if you jump over here and miss."

"True," Jack admitted. "But if I jump and make it, I might live longer than *that*, by like decades, even."

"Those *are* the two possibilities," the voice said, now sounding amused.

Jack growled again. "Stop being annoying and just tell me how far to jump!"

"No farther than is necessary," the voice said.

"Oh, I get it!" Jack shouted. "You're here to torture me!" Before the voice could respond, Jack angrily took a deep breath, pulled his feet up underneath him, then launched himself backward, kicking off the slippery column as hard as he could.

He sailed through the dark for what felt like hours, absolutely positive he'd missed the tongue completely and was now tumbling down into the giant's stomach. . . .

And then Jack splashed into something warm and wet, spit raining down all over him. He never would have thought he'd be so happy to have landed on a giant's stinking, soggy tongue.

"It looks like you made it," the voice said dryly from behind him.

"Well, after all your help, how could I not?" Jack said, trying to wipe the giant's saliva off himself and failing miserably.

"What made you jump?" the voice asked.

Jack gradually made it to his feet after a few slippery attempts. "I decided that it was better to take the chance and die than live a few more minutes listening to you," he said.

The voice laughed.

"Who *are* you?" Jack said, taking a careful step toward the laughter.

"No one important." Jack could almost hear the voice smiling. "Not anymore, at any rate."

"That's helpful," Jack said, taking another step. The man—the voice was so quiet he had to guess, but it seemed more masculine than feminine—always seemed to be just a few feet away at all times, despite the fact that Jack couldn't hear him moving around. And he should have been able to hear the man moving, considering how much sloshing Jack himself was making with every step. The giant's spit didn't make sneaking around very easy.

"As I said before," the voice said. "I *can't* help you, Jack. Not here, anyway."

"Not here?" Jack asked, straining to locate the voice. "But I was really starting to get used to this place. Kinda homey, you know? We don't have to leave, do we?"

"You didn't ask how I know your name," the voice said, sounding almost proud. "You're not curious?"

Jack continued moving toward the voice. "I don't especially care," he said.

"A stranger in the mouth of a giant knows your name, and you don't care?"

Jack shrugged. "Should I? It's not exactly the most shocking part of all this."

The voice laughed again. "I like talking to you, Jack. You're quite a remarkable young man."

"I get that a lot," Jack said, "usually with more sarcasm."

"You're keeping me talking so you can find me," the voice said. "Clever. Would some light help?"

"Do you *have* some light?" This stopped Jack. If the voice had light, why hadn't he used it before Jack jumped?

"As a matter of fact, yes."

And suddenly, Jack could see. The light, a sort of long, thin, whitish glow, came from a corner of the giant's mouth. Jack quickly glanced around, taking in his surroundings, then swallowed hard as he suddenly realized how close he'd been standing to the edge of the giant's tongue.

Even worse, he saw how far the skin flap he'd been hanging from hung out over the throat.

There was *no way* he could have made that jump. It wasn't even close to possible.

"Is that better?" the voice said, suddenly behind him, and Jack whirled around. A man leaned casually against the wall of the giant's mouth, dressed in black armor from head to foot, a midnight-blue cloak covering the armor and the man's head. On the cloak, right at the man's chest, was a silver circle within a silver oval.

It was a symbol even a child would have recognized, from bedtime stories and nightmares. It was a symbol that grown men talked about in quiet tones, afraid they'd be heard. It was a symbol that made Jack's blood run cold at the very sight of it.

It was the symbol of the Wicked Queen's inner circle, her cruelest, most vicious knights.

It was the symbol of the Eyes.

CHAPTER 14

"Oh, *fantastic*," Jack said, backing away from the Eye despite his close proximity to the throat.

The Eye stood up and took a step toward Jack. "Is there a problem?"

"You really think I don't recognize that?" Jack said, pointing at the man's chest.

From underneath the hood, Jack could just make out the man's wry grin. "So you've heard of us?" the man said. "Still, you have nothing to fear. I'm a knight, nothing more."

"You're no knight," Jack said, his eyes narrowing in disgust. "You're one of them. You're an *Eye*."

"That's not exactly . . . ," the man started, then sighed.

"This is hardly the time for explanations. You're not safe here."

Jack glared at him. "That's the first intelligent thing you've said." He glanced around, looking for something to use against the Eye. Was it too much to ask for a toothpick or something?

"You're looking for a weapon?" The man gestured toward the light. "Here, take mine."

Jack glanced quickly at the light, then stopped and stared. A long, thin piece of glass pierced the giant's mouth in the corner. Inside that glass swirled a white liquid that gave off an eerie glow, the source of the light. On top of the glass was a hilt, off of which hung a dark blue scabbard.

Jack's throat went dry. The light . . . it was the Eye's *sword*. If anything was more feared than an Eye, it was the Eye's weapon—the source of the knight's power, cursed to destroy anyone who touched it other than the knight himself.

Jack tried to say something, but the words wouldn't come out.

"My sword," the knight said simply, as if introducing Jack to it. "Now do you truly think I wish you harm? I had ample opportunity to strike you down in the dark."

"Maybe you couldn't see," Jack said, his eyes still on the sword.

"Maybe I *could*," the knight said.

Jack shivered. "I'm not touching an Eye's sword," he said. "Those things are evil. And cursed. And . . . *evil*."

The man shook his head. "No, they are not. They are tools, nothing more."

"They destroy anyone who touches them," Jack said, staring at the sword.

"A convenient story to keep thieves at bay," the man admitted. "But a story is all it is."

Jack turned back to the man. "Okay, fine. I'll take your sword, and then I'll have all the power or whatever." He took a step toward it, then turned to look at the Eye again. "You're just going to let me take it?"

The knight's only response was a smile. Creepy.

Jack sloshed carefully over to the glowing sword. "I still don't trust you," he said.

"You will."

Jack stopped. "What's that supposed to mean?"

But the knight went silent, only watching him.

Jack kept his eyes fixed on the man while carefully reaching a hand out toward the sword.

"It won't hurt you," the knight said, making Jack jump.

"Could you be *quiet*, please?" Jack said. "I'm nervous enough as it is!"

When the man didn't respond, Jack reached out again for the sword. He flinched as his fingers moved closer, but the liquid within the crystal-clear sword just swirled around and around, not reacting to him at all. Just to test it, Jack barely brushed the tip of his index finger against the hilt, then yanked his hand back.

Nothing happened.

The knight didn't say anything, but Jack imagined him laughing anyway. His anger growing at this entire situation, Jack gritted his teeth, then reached out and grabbed the sword. His hand didn't burn off, his whole body didn't turn to dust, and he wasn't transformed into a frog. In fact, the hilt was even cool to the touch, despite the sword's glow.

Jack took the scabbard off the hilt and slung it over his shoulder while he considered his next step.

"You'll need to pull it out," the knight said.

"I thought you were being quiet," Jack said, and yanked on the sword.

It didn't move.

He yanked again and again, but the weapon didn't budge.

"Was I not clear on the pulling part?" the knight asked. Jack just growled in frustration. This time, he grabbed the sword with both hands and pulled on it as hard as he could.

The sword suddenly pulled loose, and Jack's effort threw him backward toward the giant's throat. He stumbled toward the knight, but the man made no move to grab him. At the last moment, Jack managed to grab a fold in the giant's cheek, stopping his momentum just enough for him to recover his balance less than a foot from the edge of the throat.

When he could breathe again, Jack looked at the knight incredulously. "Thanks for the help there!" he shouted, his heart almost bursting through his chest.

"I told you," the knight said. "I can't."

Jack nodded bitterly. "That's about what I'd expect from one of you."

The knight tilted his head. "I bear you no ill will, Jack. Remember that."

"Oh, really?" Jack said, holding up the sword. "Well, I bear you *plenty* of ill will, buddy. And what makes you think I won't attack you with your own sword?"

The smile reappeared, but this time it seemed sad. "It wouldn't be the first time."

Jack just stared at the knight. "No one likes cryptic people," he said finally. "Either way, I'm leaving and you're staying. I don't know how you got trapped here, but the more I think about it, the more I think you and the giant deserve each other."

The knight tilted his head again. "As you wish."

Jack aimed the sword at the knight and slowly walked toward the front of the giant's mouth. The knight didn't move, which helped Jack's confidence a bit, so he sloshed his way over to the giant's teeth, only stopping when the knight spoke.

"I'll see you soon, Jack," the Eye said softly.

Jack glared at him for a minute, then shook his head. "You better hope not," he said, trying to sound dangerous but failing miserably. Giving up on winning that fight, Jack instead flipped the sword around in his hand to hold it with the point facing downward.

Then he stabbed the sword right into the giant's tongue, probably the most sensitive part of the giant's entire body.

Immediately, the giant sucked in an enormous breath, sending Jack flying off his feet and into the giant's throat. He had just enough time to thrust the sword back in its scabbard and throw that over his shoulder before the air flow reversed, and the giant let out a bellow of pain louder than anything Jack had heard in his entire life.

The force of the scream sent Jack flying past the knight and straight out the giant's gaping mouth. The knight, however, never moved. As powerful as the giant's scream was, it didn't even ruffle the man's cloak.

"Yes," the knight said as the giant's scream died down. "I'll see you soon."

And then the Eye disappeared into thin air.

CHAPTER 15

Jack wanted to scream, but he couldn't find the air when he saw how high he was. This was the second time he'd been dropped from this height; how many times could one person take the same fall? And now, he didn't even have a feather to not help. Not that the giant would save him this time either, given that the monster was busy yelling loudly over the pain in his tongue.

As Jack dropped toward the trees he took comfort in knowing that at least the knight hadn't been blown out with him. Hopefully, the man had ended up digested in the giant's stomach, but even if not, he was still trapped. Scant comfort, sure, but hurtling to his death, Jack would take what he could get.

And then, for the second time that day, something stopped Jack's fall. Again, his stomach fell down around his toes, and before he really understood what was happening, he was swung up and over what appeared to be a broomstick, right behind someone with both blond and blue hair.

The broomstick made a quick circle, banking in midair, and shot back toward the giant. The monster roared furiously and made a grab for them, but May dropped the broomstick down several feet, angling them just beneath the giant's hand. A second later, they were out of the giant's reach, circling around and around, dropping with each turn, until the broomstick bumped to a stop at the monster's feet.

Jack immediately leapt off the broomstick: His first thought was that the giant would try to crush them with his feet. However, the monstrous legs just twitched back and forth a bit, nothing more. The giant's feet never even left the ground.

"What—," Jack started to say, then lost all semblance of coherence as May tackled him, squeezing the air out of his lungs.

"I was so *scared*, you idiot!" she screamed as she hugged him. "What were you thinking, dropping off the broomstick like that!" She pulled away and stared at him angrily, despite the huge grin on her face. "Then you went and got *eaten*! What's *that* about?!"

Jack, meanwhile, moved from surprised thankfulness to confused wonder. "I . . . huh?" he asked intelligently.

"Come on!" May said, yanking on his arm hard enough to spin Jack around. "You have to meet someone!"

As Jack came to a stop, he shook his head to clear it. *What had just happened?* He had no clue what was going on, though for some reason, he had a big grin on his face too. He allowed himself a moment to celebrate being uneaten, then put on a serious face to follow the princess.

He found her standing midway between the giant's feet, talking quickly to the most irritatingly handsome boy Jack had ever seen. The boy looked to be a bit older than Jack, maybe fifteen, and was wearing extremely rich clothing, obvious even from a distance. His sparkling white tunic looked unnaturally clean, and his pants, a deep golden color, seemed almost weighed down by the quality of the fabric. A deep purple cape fell from his shoulders, and every piece of clothing was trimmed in gold, much like the boy's head, where a gold circlet hid between long, dark locks of brown hair.

Jack hated him instantly.

May, who couldn't seem to stop looking at the new boy, pointed at Jack, talking the whole time. Jack reluctantly moved close enough to hear what she was saying.

"I'm so glad I went back up there like you suggested, because the giant just yelled and out he came!" the princess said, barely breathing during her story. "I'm not really sure what happened yet, but—" And then she stopped in midsentence. "Jack!" she yelled as he reached them. May grabbed his arm and pulled him closer. "This is Phillip!" She nodded toward the purple-caped boy. The princess seemed to be almost glowing, which Jack frankly found to be a little ridiculous.

Jack stuck out his hand, but Phillip only greeted him with a nod. "Sorry . . . Jack, is it?" Phillip asked, not moving from his spot. "I would normally be quite glad to make your acquaintance, but I happen to be a bit preoccupied at the moment."

"Oh, really?" Jack said, letting his ignored hand drop. "And what is it that you're doing, exactly?"

Phillip nodded up to the giant above him. "Well, presently I am slaying this monster here." He winked at May, who smiled widely at him.

Jack raised an eyebrow. "I . . . huh?" he said again.

"He's *slaying* the *monster*, Jack," May repeated unhelpfully.

Jack looked from Phillip to the giant and back. "Oh, well, of course," he said. "Any idiot can see that that's exactly what you're doing. Need any help slaying the giant?"

As soon as the words left Jack's mouth, the giant let out an enormous roar, louder than when Jack had stabbed his tongue. Suddenly, the monster's legs began to wobble back and forth, the tremors growing more and more violent until the giant completely lost his balance. Arms windmilling around and around, the immense creature toppled forward, collapsing toward the forest floor.

It felt like the giant took forever to fall, but in reality, it was *slightly* shorter than that. It did take a few seconds before the top of the giant hit the ground, and a few seconds after that for the ground to rise like a wave in the ocean and come rushing straight for them.

"Look out!" Jack shouted, grabbing May's hand and running toward the nearest tree. He hoped to get them to higher ground, but there was no time: The ground wave curled up under them and tossed them both through the air as if they were rag dolls.

Jack landed hard, but not as hard as May did when she crashed down right on top of him. As Jack struggled to breathe he took little comfort in the fact that the princess seemed to have escaped harm by landing on him.

Clearly, someone somewhere had it in for him.

As Jack sucked in air the new boy pulled the princess off him.

Phillip then offered Jack an outstretched hand and a wry smile. "I do not believe I will need help with the giant after all," Phillip said. "But perhaps you could use some?"

Jack grunted and reluctantly took Phillip's hand. The boy had a surprisingly strong grip. Of course he did.

"Is the giant . . . ?" May said, glancing over at the fallen monster.

"Slain?" Phillip asked. "Oh yes, quite."

"Okay, but how?" Jack said, wiping his dirt-covered hands on his pants. For some reason, that didn't seem to help at all, mostly because his pants, his tunic, and every other part of him was completely covered in dirt and dust from the ground's tidal wave. Glancing over at Phillip, Jack wasn't at all surprised to see that the boy's white tunic and golden pants weren't even smudged. Of course they weren't.

"Quite simple, my friend," Phillip said in answer to Jack's question. "Before you and your delightful friend here happened along, I had hunted the large fellow, following him for days. I finally caught up to him here, and he, of course, tried to devour me. Before he could catch me, however, I challenged him to a series of contests to see which of us was the more powerful. I won each contest—mostly by tricking him, I must admit—then I convinced him that I could turn myself to stone, standing unmoving for a longer period than he could. He tried to do the same, but I knew he could not do so as long as I could."

"You . . . made him fall over by making him . . . stand still?" Jack asked, trying to wrap his head around the idea. His head just didn't seem to stretch that far, though.

"When fighting giants, young Jack, you must know your enemy," Phillip said. "I know, for example, that a giant's body cannot support itself when standing for long periods of time. Given his extreme size, a giant's bones simply cannot hold his own massive weight, not without equal hours of rest. I also know that giants view humans as their inferiors, and therefore this one would not let himself be beaten by me. In effect, all I had to do was defeat him several times to force him to move beyond his natural limits in an effort to humiliate me. His stubbornness was the true cause of his death here, as much as I might like to take the credit."

"So he just tired himself out and fell over?" May said. Jack was glad to see that she was beginning to question Phillip's story, too.

The prince nodded. "In essence. The bones in his legs could no longer support his enormous size. A fall from such a height tends to jumble what little brains they have, killing the monsters. I knew that the creature must topple sooner or later, and fortunately for my own legs," he said, smiling wryly, "it was sooner."

"How long did it take?" Jack asked, not able to contain his curiosity despite his already intense dislike for Phillip.

Phillip looked up to the sky, as if he had to think about it. "Hmm," he said. "Not longer than four or five days, I would say."

"Four or five *days*?!" May said.

Phillip shook his head. "Killing giants is not for the easily fatigued, my friends."

"Or anyone with a real job," Jack said.

Phillip's face clouded a bit. "Pardon me?" he said.

"I asked why were you hunting it," Jack said.

Phillip's face grew solemn. "That is my quest. I hunt down the few remaining giants in our lands, ever since my father was killed by one."

May stepped over to Jack, her eyes on fire. "Right, his father!" she said to him. "Didn't I tell you?"

"Tell me what?" Jack asked.

Phillip smiled politely, then stepped away to a corner of the clearing where a large purple bag waited. He sat down and reached into the bag, then pulled out some bread and began eating it. Jack noticed that Phillip bit into it far too politely for someone who hadn't eaten for five days.

"Phillip's father won a *kingdom* for himself by killing giants!" May whispered to Jack. "Can you imagine? Supposedly, his dad took down seven giants with one hit or something. How crazy is that!"

"Okay, his dad killed giants. So?" Jack said, knowing where this was going but not willing to help it get there.

"Don't you get it?" May whispered, a smile spreading over her entire face. "If his dad was a king, that means Phillip is a *prince*!"

CHAPTER 16

"Jack," Phillip called to him, politely waiting until his mouth was clear to speak. "I quite forgot to mention something. While I was slaying the giant, a bag that I would hazard a guess to be yours fell from the sky and landed right at my feet, if you can believe such a thing." At that, he held up Jack's grandfather's bag.

Jack nodded, not able to contain a dirty look. "Right," he said. "Sorry about that. I couldn't hold on to it while falling to my death. How completely rude of me. May I have it back?"

"Of course," the prince said, tossing the bag over to Jack. The bag landed perfectly in Jack's hands, then dropped to the ground when Jack fumbled it.

May laughed. "Nice catch," she said.

"I've had a rough day," he replied moodily, grabbing the broomstick and stuffing it into the infinitely large bag.

"Not many men could live through a giant swallowing them, Princess," Phillip said, as he carefully chose a piece of fruit from his sack. "You have my respect, young Jack."

"Princess?" Jack whispered to her. "So you're only denying that to peasants now, huh?"

She actually blushed at that. "Okay," she whispered back, "I know it's stupid and ridiculous and all, but come *on*. You have to give me this. He's a real live *prince*! And besides, like you said, if Snow White's my grandmother, then I'm sort of royalty too, right?"

"Of course," Jack said, "but . . ." Suddenly he froze, his eyes widening. "May, you didn't tell that idiot about your *grandmother*, did you?!"

She snorted. "I'm not stupid. I know I'm supposed to keep everything a secret. No, I just told him that I've got some royalty in the family. And quit judging me, I know I'm a poseur!" She smiled at that like it was a joke.

"I'm assuming that doesn't mean what I think it does," Jack said, his eyes narrowed to slits as he watched the prince daintily break off another piece of bread. "This guy just irritates me. So he slays giants . . . who doesn't?"

May started to say something snarky in reply, then stopped and looked at Jack closely. "Jack," she said, "are you . . . you *are*, you're jealous!" She seemed shocked.

He managed to pull up an equally shocked look. "Jealous? Of what, a prince?! You must have hit your head. Royals are completely self-absorbed and make life a nightmare for the rest of us. Have I been unclear about how much I dislike them?"

May gave him a suspicious look. "Then you'd be okay if Phillip and I go it alone from here? After all, if I've got a prince who can slay giants to help me, that's all I need, right?"

Jack rolled his eyes. "Maybe . . . if you want to die horribly. Trust me, I'm not letting the two of you handle what's probably the most important rescue in history."

May smiled that little half smile that Jack was beginning to despise. "Whatever you say, *hero*," she said, then twirled around and lightly ran over to Phillip, waving her hands delicately at her sides. She spun around when she reached the prince, curtsied to Jack, then sat down and stuck out her tongue.

Jack never hated her more.

Gradually, he forced himself to walk over to the two of them.

"So," he said to Phillip, "it's good that the giant fell forward, eh? Otherwise, he might have landed on us. You know, killing us all. *That* might have been bad, huh?"

The prince waited until he was done chewing as Jack tapped his foot impatiently. "No, he would not have fallen on us," the prince said finally. "I *do* know what I am doing, after all. But you are quite right: If he had landed on us, it might have ended badly."

"Yes, quite right," May said, imitating the prince. "We might have been crushed into little gooey pancakes, which very well could have ruined tea."

"Do you mock me, Princess?" the prince asked with a raised eyebrow and a gentle smile.

"Why would I do that when you're doing so well on your own?" the princess replied sweetly.

Jack eyed them both, then sat down between them. "I'm pretty sure there's enough mocking going on for everyone," he said. "Let's all just scoot over and make some room here, all right?"

May started to respond, but something behind him caught her attention. "Hey, um, Jack?" she asked as she stared at whatever-it-was.

He glared at her. "What, Your Highness?"

"So . . . where'd you get the sword?"

Jack threw a look over his shoulder. There, plain as day, was the hilt of the knight's sword, sitting securely in the scabbard strapped to Jack's shoulder.

"What sword?" Jack asked.

The princess stared at him. "Are we really going to play that game?"

Jack frowned. "*That* sword? I got it inside the giant."

One of her eyebrows raised. "Of course you did," she said. "I take it there was a shop just behind his teeth, then?"

Jack stared pointedly at the ground in front of him. "Not exactly," he said. "I just found it. It probably got stuck in there, you know, in the giant's mouth . . . when he ate someone."

"That is *quite* a sword, young Jack," the prince said, leaning back to examine it. "In fact, it looks almost familiar. . . ."

Jack gritted his teeth. "How old are you?" he asked Phillip.

"Pardon me?" the prince said, leaning forward again.

"How *old* are you?!" Jack repeated.

"I am fifteen years old," the prince replied.

"Then you're not much older than me, Your *Highness*," Jack growled. "Can you try *not* calling me 'young Jack'?"

The prince looked surprised. "I meant no offense, my friend!"

Jack started to protest the "friend" part too, but May reached over and put a hand on his arm to calm him. He swallowed his comment and glared at them both.

"So how did you two find yourselves here?" the prince asked, apparently oblivious to the hostility emanating from Jack.

"We're on our way to the Black Forest," May said, before Jack could elbow her to keep quiet. He elbowed her anyway, so she elbowed him back, a lot harder than necessary.

"The Black Forest?" Phillip asked, a look of concern crossing his face. "That's hardly the place for a princess!"

"It's a secret quest," Jack said dismissively. "We can't really talk about it."

"We're looking for my grandmother," May said.

Jack dropped his head into his hands. "What part of 'secret quest' were you not clear on?!"

"*Whose* grandmother is it?"

Jack threw her a dirty look.

"Exactly," May said, then turned back to Phillip. "My grandmother was kidnapped from my . . . my castle. I was taken too, but I escaped, and here we are. She told me to go to the Black Forest to find help, so that's where we're going."

"A worthy quest!" Phillip said, his eyes burning with passion. "For such a goal, I cannot help but offer my full assistance." The prince paused, his eyes sparkling. "That is, if you'll have me."

"Oh, we've already got too much assistance as it is—," Jack started to say, but May quickly interrupted him.

"Of course we could use your help!" she said. "Jack seems to have forgotten about the enormous guy chasing us." She smiled sweetly at Jack, which just made things worse, then turned back to the prince. "Besides, you seem pretty useful, your prince-itude."

"I welcome the opportunity to exhibit more useful behavior," the prince said, bowing low at the waist.

Jack rolled his eyes. "No, seriously, we wouldn't want to take you away from whatever it is you're doing," he said.

The prince shook his head. "This giant is slain. And since I cannot return . . . I mean, since my only task is to avenge my father by slaying the giant who murdered him, I must seek out more giants. That means I may travel where I will, and with whom I would."

"Maybe you just found that giant," Jack suggested hopefully, nodding toward the huge body in the distance. "Maybe you're done now and can go home."

"Unfortunately, no," the prince said. "I had a chance to converse with this giant over the last five days. He was not the one for whom I search."

"Yet you killed him anyway," Jack said. "How noble of you."

"That thing *ate* you!" May said to Jack, who just shrugged that off.

"All giants deserve death," Phillip said matter-of-factly. "The more I slay, the less there are to devastate the world. My quest only benefits mankind."

"That's nice of you," May said.

"Oh, come *on*," Jack said, but he had a difficult time being appropriately indignant, given that the giant *had* tried to eat him.

"So, the Black Forest, eh?" Phillip said, though he didn't seem too enthused over the prospect.

"Do you know where it is?" May asked him.

"Of course!" he said expansively. "It is no more than a day's travel from here. We should perhaps wait out the rest of the day here, then get a fresh start in the morning."

Jack's stomach chose that moment to rumble loudly. May looked at Jack, then smiled at Phillip. "We're both a little hungry," she admitted.

"Say no more," the prince said, reaching for his traveling bag. "I never leave home without preparing."

He untied the bag, then upended it over a blanket he set on the ground. Fruits of varying sizes and shapes tumbled from the sack as he shook it, all looking as fresh as if they had just been picked from the tree or vine. Next came bread, followed by several round cheeses. It was as if the previously thin-looking bag was now overflowing with food.

May's eyes widened. "A magic food bag!" she shouted, grabbing for an orange. "*Sweet!* Ours is only magically roomy."

The prince smiled with a royal smugness. "Please," he said, "eat all you can. The bag cannot be emptied. It was one of my father's rewards for his giant-slaying."

May tore into the orange, then proceeded to stuff her face with bread and cheese. Jack marveled for a brief moment at her feeding frenzy, then threw himself on the food with even more enthusiasm than the princess was showing. The prince seemed a little taken aback by the display in front of him, especially when half a peach landed on his shoe. May reached over to grab it back, glanced at the prince, blushed, and let it go.

"I see that you are quite hungry," the prince said, sounding a bit sick now.

"Yup," Jack responded through a mouthful. "We haven't eaten for a while."

"Oh, my friend," the prince said, shaking his head. "How could you take this beautiful young woman out into the wilds without proper provisions?"

May looked up, her face covered with seeds and fruit juices. "We haven't really slowed down enough to eat."

The prince nodded. "Such is life at times. Still, anything that I have, consider it yours."

May dropped a plum. "That's so nice!" she said, her eyes soft as she looked at him, purple juices running down her chin.

"I will do my best to live up to your trust," the prince said, for once not interested in staring at her. "Do you know what we are looking for at the edge of the Black Forest?" he asked, moving his gaze to the sky.

Jack and May both shook their heads. "My grandmother just said there would be someone in the forest to help," May said through a mouthful of a tasty deep-brown bread.

The prince raised an eyebrow. "Someone *in* the forest? But that does not make sense, Princess. Nothing lives within the Black Forest. And no man that travels into the accursed place emerges alive. Why, everyone knows that!"

CHAPTER 17

May chewed twice more before Phillip's statement hit her. After it did, Jack had to dodge bits of flying bread. "*What* was that again?" she said.

"Nothing lives in the Black Forest," Phillip repeated. "And no man has ever emerged alive from its depths."

May turned to Jack. "What's he talking about?!"

Jack shrugged. "I don't know what to tell you. I mean, everyone knows it's cursed, but—"

"Cursed?!" May said, her voice going up several octaves.

"Friend Jack is mistaken, Princess," Phillip said.

May seemed to calm down a bit at that. "Well, good," she said. "I'm telling you, I'm not sure I can handle much more creepiness."

"The forest is not cursed so much as haunted," the prince finished.

May just looked at Phillip with disappointment, then sighed heavily and turned to Jack, throwing him a truly evil look. "You knew this?" she asked in a quiet voice.

"Well, kinda," Jack said, backing a bit away from her just to be safe. "No one *really* knows what's in the Black Forest. I knew it wasn't going to be fun, exactly, but that was it."

"And *why* doesn't anyone know what's in there?" the princess asked, her voice still dangerously low.

Jack inched even farther away. "Because no one's ever made it out alive . . . ?" he squeaked.

May stared at him for a good minute, then turned to Phillip. "So. You two were going to let me just walk in there?"

Phillip put his hands up to calm her down. "I believe this is the first I have heard of the plan to actually go *into* the forest. And I did bring up my concerns immediately upon hearing of our destination."

"Okay, that's true," she said to the prince. "*You* are off the hook."

Slowly, both of them turned to look at Jack.

"What?" he asked, but May just glared at him.

"You really should have mentioned this to the princess," Phillip told him, shaking his head.

"Thanks," Jack said sarcastically. "You're a *big* help." He turned back to May. "It's not like we had anything else to go on, so we didn't exactly have a choice. Besides, who knows what's in the woods? All we know is that no one's made it out. Maybe that means there's some kind of paradise in there, something no one wants to leave!"

"Or something doesn't *let* them leave," the prince said quietly.

"Hear that?" May asked, nodding at the prince. "We're all gonna die in there, and when we do, guess who I'm going to blame."

Jack's mouth dropped open. "Listen, May, none of this was *my* idea! It was your grandmother who said—"

"Don't you *dare* blame this on her!" May exploded. "You're supposed to be my *guide* here!"

"Is *that* what I'm doing?" Jack shouted back. "I thought I was just here to get eaten every ten minutes!"

"If I may," Phillip said, but both Jack and May ignored him.

"If I'm so little help, maybe you two should just go in alone!" Jack yelled.

"Maybe we should!"

"Fine!"

"Fine!"

Jack stood up and May turned her back to him. Neither said a word.

Phillip finally broke the silence. "I, uh—"

"So go already!" May shouted at Jack, interrupting the prince.

Jack growled, then grabbed his bag from the ground and stomped over to the edge of the clearing. "Enjoy your little royal expedition here, Your Majestic Highnesses," Jack said bitterly. "I'm so glad you found a *prince* to help you, Princess!"

"Now, Jack," Phillip started, but again, May shouted right over him.

"You have no *idea* what you're talking about!" she yelled, jumping to her feet and following Jack to the edge of the clearing. "And your kiss was *pathetic*!"

"Kiss?" Phillip asked, as Jack abruptly froze in place.

"Trust me, *Princess*," Jack said without turning around, "the feeling's *completely* mutual."

Behind him, May growled in frustration. "I can't believe I ever wanted your help!" she screamed.

Jack didn't answer. He just started walking, so mad he couldn't even think of a reply.

"Oh, good one!" she shouted after a pause, and Jack's anger doubled, as did his pace. As soon as he was out of sight, though, Jack stopped and threw his grandfather's bag to the ground, mumbling and shaking his head about the stupidity of the princess.

How moronic *was* she?! How was *he* supposed to know exactly what was going on in the Black Forest when no one else did? Sure, he'd heard stories, just like everyone else, but who knew which of those were true? Just because the war with the animals had ended there didn't mean the whole forest was cursed, after all.

Still, he might have said *something*.

But why? It's not like he hadn't taken care of her up until this point. They'd done just fine on their own so far, and how could things get any worse than a man-eating giant—or a man-eating witch, for that matter?

Jack picked up his bag and took a step back toward the clearing he'd just left, then turned and threw his bag down again, shaking his head in disbelief at himself. She didn't need him anymore. She had her prince now, and obviously preferred him. After all, the *prince* could kill a giant just by standing still for a few days! All Jack had been able to do was make it yawn.

Again, he picked up the bag, but something occurred to him, and he turned to walk back down the path toward the royal pains. As he did, he caught a glimpse of someone standing just behind the trees. As he glared the person took a step out, revealing herself.

"I *saw* you there the whole time!" Jack lied.

May took a step toward him, her look not quite as hostile as it had been. "I was just checking to see if you'd left yet," she said, not looking directly at him.

Jack narrowed his eyes. "Sorry, Princess, I haven't gotten that far. I dropped my bag."

"I saw that," she said, then paused. "Well?"

"Well, what?"

"Are you leaving?"

Jack shook his head. "I was. I am. But I forgot about this thing," he said, reaching into the bag to pull out the broomstick. He held the stick out to her. "It obviously likes you better, so . . . here."

May took a step forward, her mouth open slightly, like she wanted to say something, only nothing came out. Jack didn't say anything either. He just stood in place and shook the broomstick. May sighed, then grabbed the front of the broom. For a second, they both held it, and Jack almost found himself apologizing. Instead, he dropped his end of the broomstick. "That's it, then," he said. "Good-bye, Princess. Good luck rescuing your grandmother." With that, Jack turned around and started walking into the forest.

"Jack . . . ," May said from behind him. "What do you want me to say? That I need your help? That I want you to stay?"

"I don't want you to say anything, Princess, other than 'good-bye,'" he said, then stepped into the woods, leaving May and her quest behind him.

CHAPTER 18

The rising sun shone through Jack's eyelids, irritating him just enough to wake him up. As he separated his nightmares from reality he realized with a groan that far too many of the bad parts were actually happening. The rocky ground he'd slept on didn't really help things, but even sleeping on a bed of the softest linens wouldn't have kept dreams of a knight in a blue cloak away.

Jack stretched, then pushed himself to his feet, groaning again as he did. Everything was sore, but at least he wasn't waking up in a witch's house. He picked up his bag and started walking, suddenly regretting not taking any of Phillip's food when he had the chance. After one night, his hunger had returned, and this time brought friends, some relatives, and even a few pets.

As the sun rose higher in the sky the forest began to come alive around him. Birds, both natural and magical, sang out their songs, each competing with its neighbor. Jack smiled at this, watching the regular birds futilely attempt to overwhelm their supernatural cousins. A few everyday birds gathered on a branch, trying to outsing one particular bird with silver wings and a golden head, its body as big as a crow's. The regular birds chirped away in a pretty, offbeat sort of rhythm, but they had nothing on the three-part harmony that emerged from the mouth of the silver-and-gold bird.

As Jack walked he stayed to the trail, since he wasn't exactly sure where he was going. Apparently this trail wasn't very well-traveled, as the local animals and creatures didn't seem too afraid of humans. He thought he spotted a fox at one point, and another time, he definitely saw a magical snake, shimmering like an underwater candle as it spiraled through the air, just a few inches off the ground. Jack actually found himself enjoying the walk, despite his mood.

Unfortunately, soon enough clouds blocked the sun, causing the day to grow more and more overcast as the morning moved on. Gradually, the graying light threw the path into shadow, and the pleasant magical creatures around him began to take on a more sinister appearance. Red eyes that previously had been cute in the middle of fuzzy faces now glowed menacingly from the darkness, and Jack swore he heard a voice, tiny but clear, reciting something in a strange language.

Soon little droplets of rain fell, refreshing at first, but quickly turning into a drenching shower. The storm didn't help the dirt path much, muddying it up within minutes as the rain came down harder.

All in all, the woods were getting pretty creepy as he drew closer to the Black Forest.

The fact that he could have been well on his way home by now still bothered him, but when it came down to it, he just couldn't leave the princess to die on her own . . . and Phillip hardly counted. No, this was all her fault, and Jack promised himself he'd tell her that over and over whenever he finally did catch up with them. He couldn't be too far behind, not when he'd only walked an hour last night before stopping to make camp, turning back toward the Black Forest at daybreak.

It was pouring as he turned a corner and discovered he'd reached his destination. As it turned out, the Black Forest was, in fact, just about a day's travel from where the giant had fallen; Phillip was right, as much as it annoyed Jack to admit it. There wasn't even any warning—one step, the path was just dark and depressing, but the next brought Jack to a sudden halt.

The trees along the path behind him had all been alive, even green in places. The trees of the Black Forest, though, were gruesomely dead, each and every one of them. This was no gradual change, either: It was as if an arbitrary line had been picked, and from that point on, there were only shivers and chills.

Not a hint of green showed through, just dark and twisted wood. Despite the lack of leaves, the blackened trunks and fingerlike branches filled in all gaps, making the forest a huge ruin of impenetrability. And if light couldn't fight its way into the forest, it sure couldn't make it out, either.

As the rain poured over his face and spilled down his neck Jack decided that he should get moving, if only to escape the storm. After all, the floor of the Black Forest looked as dry as a bone.

Instead, he just stared at the entrance, his eyes wide as he started having trouble breathing.

After a few minutes of this, Jack blinked. This was ridiculous! It was only a bunch of dead trees! What was there to be afraid of, some rumors with no proof to them? Centering his entire will on his foot, he forced himself to take a step forward. Though his leg shook, he finally managed to do it. That was it, one step at a time! But still, why was this so hard?! They were just trees!

Did one of them just *move*?!

Jack's blood ran cold as his foot paused in midstep, suspended in the air. Suddenly, he realized that he was sweating despite the chilly rain. The stories of this place could *not* be true. Common sense said that if no one made it out alive, then there *couldn't* be any stories. Who would tell them? So the stories had to be just rumors. Sure, the forest was ugly and intimidating, but that was it. After all, an entire forest couldn't be cursed.

Despite his logic, Jack's foot didn't move, still hanging in midair.

Though the day had been warm back along the trail, now Jack shivered all the way to his toes. The sun from earlier in the day seemed miles away now, like it had abandoned this part of the world, never to come back.

Finally, Jack's foot came down—in the wrong direction. He took a step backward, then another. Inwardly, he yelled in frustration. He had to beat this! Even if the forest was haunted, cursed, and everything else; even if the forest made it rain and blocked out any sunlight; even if the trees all moved and killed anything that was stupid enough to go in; even if all that, the princess and Phillip were in there. They must be, or Jack would have passed them on the trail.

If May could go in, then Jack could, simple as that.

And yet, he still couldn't move.

And then he heard something from deep within the forest. A voice. A girl screaming.

May.

Without a thought, Jack yanked his sword out of its scabbard and took off at a dead run right into the heart of the Black Forest, the sword's glow lighting his way.

CHAPTER 19

Branches tore at his arms, legs, and head as Jack pushed through the forest, chopping what he could with the sword, plowing through the rest. After May's scream, the Black Forest had gone dead, not a single sound escaping, not even the pattering of raindrops on the canopy of branches.

"*May!*" Jack yelled, not knowing or caring who or what else might hear him. "*May!* Can you hear me?" Whether she did or not, there was no response. Jack barreled on anyway, following the barely visible path straight into the forest. Without any further sound to guide him, all he had was the path, but he comforted himself with the idea that Phillip and the princess would have had to follow the same route.

Although, maybe whatever had made May scream had also pulled her off the path . . .

"*Mayyyyyyy!*" Jack screamed at the top of his lungs. "Yell out if you can hear me!"

A low groan answered him from just a few feet ahead. Jack skidded to a halt, almost tripping over a pair of legs covered in expensive gold fabric. Phillip groaned again, looking like someone had tossed him bodily against one of the dead trees. Jack straddled Phillip's legs, reached down, and yanked the prince to his feet.

"Phillip!" Jack said. "What happened?!"

Phillip's eyes fluttered open. "Jack?" the prince asked, his eyes slowly focusing on the face in front of him. "Jack? But I thought you left . . ."

Jack gritted his teeth at the delay. "I changed my mind and followed you two here," he said, barely holding himself back from shaking the prince for answers. "I *knew* I couldn't leave her with you. I knew something like this would happen!"

"Leave her . . . the princess?" Phillip said, then took a deep breath. "Where is the princess?"

This time Jack didn't hold himself back. He banged the prince hard into a tree trunk, then jerked him back to his feet.

"Listen to me, Phillip," Jack growled. "I don't *know* what happened to her. That's why I'm asking *you*. You were supposed to protect her. *Now tell me where she is!*"

"Something attacked us from the side," Phillip said, shaking his head in confusion. "I did not see it."

Jack wanted to scream in frustration, but contented himself with dropping the prince. "You're beyond useless. I should have known."

Phillip shook his head again. "No. I just . . . need a moment. My head aches like nothing I have ever felt!"

Jack bent down to look the prince right in the eye. "If you got the princess killed, a headache will be the least of your worries, *believe* me."

Phillip narrowed his eyes. "Threats are not necessary, Jack. I—" The prince stopped, frowning as he glanced at the glowing sword in Jack's hand.

Jack stood up quickly, torn between hiding the sword and just ignoring the prince's look. "Get up, Phillip," Jack said, going with the latter. "We need to go after her."

"Where did you get that sword?" Phillip asked, rising to his feet gracefully. Did the prince have to do everything well?

"I told you before, I found it," Jack said, the explanation

sounding pathetic even to his own ears. "Can we focus on one thing at a time here? Right now, all I care is that the sword's giving us light, which we're going to need to find May."

Phillip nodded toward the woods. "There," he said. "The branches are displaced. Whatever took her, it must have carried her through there."

Jack swung the sword around to light up a small hole between the trees. Unfortunately, the sword's glow didn't illuminate much beyond the hole itself. "May!" Jack screamed into the trees. "May! Answer me if you can!"

"I do not think she is able to," Phillip said, then laid a hand on Jack's shoulder. "Now, please, silence may be the wiser choice. We do not wish to warn whatever took her that we are hunting it."

Jack shut his mouth, then threw himself through the small hole and into the dead trees without another word, leaving Phillip behind. Branches clawed him as he ran, scratching with every surge forward, while the roots under his feet seemed to be trying to trip him on purpose, succeeding far too often.

After crashing to the ground for the third time, Jack shook off the pain and started to pick himself up, only for something to hit him in the back, shoving him face-first into the dirt. The air whooshed from his lungs with the force of the hit, and claws sharp as needles cut into the skin on his back.

"Well, well," growled a voice more animal than human from on top of him. "It takes a bit of thrill out of the hunt when the prey comes to you."

Jack gritted his teeth and tried to throw the creature off his back, but his struggling only pushed the thing's claws deeper into his back. Jack shouted in pain, and the air around him began popping as he gasped for even the tiniest breath. Was this how he was going to die? Crushed by some creature in the Black Forest?

Apparently he really *did* fail at princess rescues.

And then out of nowhere, the pressure on his back lifted. Without stopping to wonder why, Jack breathed deeply, the air never having tasted quite so good. He managed to push himself a bit off the ground, though his vision still wavered alarmingly in front of him. Whatever it was that had held him down must have stepped off his back. Stepped off, or—

Phillip extended a hand down to Jack, even while staring off into the dark woods. "Get up, Jack," the prince hissed. "That creature has not gone far, and we will have to catch it if we are going to find May."

"Did you . . . hurt it?" Jack asked.

The prince shook his head. "It ran as I came up, not that I had much to hit it with. I could barely follow you as it is. If I had not been able to see the light of your sword . . ."

Phillip glanced down at the sword lying on the ground, then back up at Jack, and Jack could see it in his eyes: Phillip knew what the sword was. He *had* to know. "Are you hurt?" the prince asked. If he did suspect about the sword, apparently he was keeping it to himself.

Jack shook his head and got back to his feet. The forest swam in front of him for a brief moment, and he found himself leaning against the prince for support, but the dizziness soon passed. Jack pushed himself away from the prince a bit too hard, then led the way after the thing that had attacked him, slicing with his sword in every direction as he pushed through the brambles and branches.

The sword cut through the growth as easily as it swung through air, a fact that Jack hadn't really noticed during his mad dash through the woods, but both of them noticed it now.

"You curse us all, using that thing," Phillip said quietly from behind Jack, but Jack ignored him. Right now, they needed to find May.

Every so often, Phillip would stop Jack, look around, then

point them in a new direction. Jack had no idea how the prince could possibly be tracking the monster or the princess, but that didn't matter as long as the prince knew what he was doing.

The slashing quickly grew tedious, taking all of Jack's attention just to clear their way, and he soon lost track of how far they had come. His world narrowed down to cutting the branches away, moving forward, then cutting again; that was all he could think about. His sword cut this way and that, taking out a gnarled limb here, a large branch there . . .

And suddenly a pair of red eyes floated in the darkness directly in front of him. Jack heard the same growl as before, except this time, the growl came from behind teeth of pure white that glowed eerily in the light of the sword, each as big as one of Jack's fingers.

With a great roar that shook the forest, the teeth came flying right toward Jack's throat.

CHAPTER 20

Just before the monster bit into him, something yanked Jack backward. The teeth, head, and entire body of a gargantuan wolf passed within an inch of Jack's face as Phillip pulled both himself and Jack to the ground and out of harm's way.

Even before Jack hit the ground, Phillip had bounded back to his feet, almost faster than Jack could see. Jack followed suit as soon as he could, standing with much less grace than the prince had, though at least he had his sword ready.

The wolf creature, if that's really what it was, stood almost completely still in front of them, the only movement coming from its chest as the creature breathed. The wolf was *enormous*, its size so unnatural that the creature couldn't possibly be anything but magical.

The wolf's head came up to Jack's chest, and its body was at least as long as Jack was tall. Yet the creature had moved silently, without even a whisper of wind. Its fur almost glowed in the light of the sword, black as a starless night. In fact, the only color on the wolf were its eyes, which burned a fiery red as they stared at Jack's sword. For some reason, the wolf actually seemed to shy away from the sword's light, baring its teeth as its eyes locked on Jack's weapon.

"You have that sword," the animal growled, its voice like gravel scraping over rock. "And you kidnap the princess! Betrayers! Villains! Neither of you will live to boast of your deeds!"

Jack glanced in surprise at Phillip, who looked at least as confused as Jack felt. A talking wolf? Hadn't all the intelligent animals been put to death in the Black Forest decades ago? But even more odd was what it had said.

"Kidnappers?" Jack asked, keeping the sword between him and the wolf at all times. "Us? *You're* the one who stole the princess."

The wolf growled again, his voice even lower. "You took the girl from her *home*. Little did you know that this child is under *my* protection!" It took a step toward them, forcing Jack to swing the sword in a large arc, just to remind the creature of the weapon. The wolf still seemed wary of it, though less so than it had been; the monster's anger was giving it courage.

That wasn't good. It looked like they didn't have long before it attacked, sword or not.

"You wish to protect her?" Phillip asked. "But how do you *know* her?"

"I do not explain myself to such as you," the wolf snarled. "Do not seek to confuse me. You must know me from my time with the Snow Queen. That should tell you that I mean to protect this girl with my life!"

Phillip gasped. "So *that* is who you are!" he said. "The Wolf King!"

The wolf's only response was a growl.

"The Wolf King?" Jack said, looking from Phillip to the wolf and back again. "Are you sure?"

"How many other intelligent wolves survived the purge?" Phillip said. "It *must* be him. And the time he served with the Snow Queen . . . I mean, Snow White . . ."

Jack took another quick look in Phillip's direction. "I don't hear him confirming it."

"The fact that you can hear him at all should confirm it," Phillip said. "Is the Wolf King not the last of the animals gifted with speech?"

The wolf growled again, and they quickly turned back to him.

"We don't want to hurt you, Mr. Wolf King, sir," Jack said slowly. "You know, despite the fact you already tried to eat me."

"You are foul betrayers!" the wolf roared. "And you were *fool-ish* enough to bring the princess here to the Black Forest! No human may depart this place alive, not without my say. The forest will not allow it! Your deaths shall be a lesson to any who dare—"

"We're not kidnapping May!" Jack shouted. "We're trying to *unkidnap* . . . rescue her grandmother! You know, the Snow Queen?" Jack waved the sword around to emphasize his point. "May and her grandmother, Snow White? Her grandmother told the princess to come here for help. . . ." Suddenly, everything clicked into place for Jack, and his eyes went wide. "She must have meant for us to find *you* here! That explains why . . . forget it. Either way, we need your help! Snow White's been taken by the Wicked Queen, and we're rescuing her!"

Jack noticed Phillip staring at him with a stunned look, and it occurred to Jack that neither he nor May had ever really explained to the prince who May's grandmother actually was. Still, that could wait. The wolf had stopped growling during Jack's explanation and was now staring thoughtfully into space.

"Snow White," the wolf said slowly, "was taken by the Wicked Queen? And this girl, and her grandmother . . ." It slowly padded toward them. "The girl's grandmother was taken?" The wolf eyed Jack closely, as if watching for Jack's reaction. "If what you say is true," he growled, "then I can help you. Then I *will* help you."

"First," Jack said, "we need to know where the princess is."

"She is safe," the wolf responded as he sat back on his haunches, his eyes twinkling. For some reason, when the wolf spoke now, it almost seemed to be smiling, probably due to the curve of its jaw. "You will see her when I've become satisfied with the truth of your tale."

"And how shall you do that, exactly?" the prince asked, shaking off his shock over the revelation about May's grandmother.

The wolf licked his lips. "Blood never lies," he growled.

Jack wanted to laugh at the sheer insanity of what the wolf was suggesting. Unfortunately, the animal looked completely serious. "You want to *bite* us?" Jack asked incredulously. "Are you kidding?!"

"A bite isn't necessary," the wolf said. "I only need to taste your blood. Cut yourself, if you prefer. Or I will do it. I care not."

"He *is* kidding, right?" Jack said to Phillip, looking for a voice of sanity.

Unfortunately, the prince let him down yet again. "Shall we use your sword, then?" Phillip asked calmly.

Jack sighed. "Really, Phillip? This sounds like a good idea to you?"

"If that's the only way to gain his trust," Phillip said, "then I shall do it. The princess"—he paused, then swallowed—"and her grandmother, Snow White, require our help. For them, I would gladly give my life."

Jack rolled his eyes. "You know, May's not here. You can tone down the whole noble prince thing. Besides, you're probably a *bit* more useful to them alive than dead."

The prince smiled. "I didn't realize you considered me to be of help."

Jack grimaced. "Don't let it go to your head. Either way, we don't have to use my sword. Hold on." He reached into his grandfather's bag and produced the knife he and May had discovered back at the witch's cottage, then handed it to Phillip. "You first."

"Ready, wolf?" Phillip said, grasping the knife in his palm.

The Wolf King licked his lips and nodded.

The prince closed his eyes, took a deep breath, then yanked the knife through his hand. He let out the breath explosively, then opened his hand.

There wasn't a scratch on it.

CHAPTER 21

The prince blinked at his uncut hand. "How curious!" he said.

"You must have done it wrong," Jack said. "Gimme your hand. I'll do it."

"Oh, no," the prince said, backing away. "The last thing I will do is give you a knife along with permission to cut me."

Jack grinned. "You seem to forget I've been carrying around a sword since I met you," he said.

"Yes, but you have not been trying to draw my blood with it," Phillip said, then paused. "At least not that I know of."

Jack sighed. "Just give me the knife back; I'll do my hand first." The prince handed over the knife, and Jack held it steady in his right hand while grasping the blade with his left. He jerked his left hand over the blade with a grunt, then opened his palm.

No blood.

"What's wrong with this thing?" Jack said, shaking the knife.

"Let me have it again," Phillip said, and ran it along his inner arm. Again, nothing happened. "I believe it is defective," he said, then thrust it at a nearby tree.

The blade sank into the dead tree up to the hilt.

Jack and Phillip both swallowed hard, while the wolf smiled slightly, saying nothing, watching everything. "Looks like it works," Jack said, his voice wavering just a bit. They'd been so quick to cut themselves with it . . . he was suddenly *very* glad they stopped experimenting when they had.

"It must be magical," the prince replied, his voice a tad shaky as well. "Perhaps it is charmed against cutting flesh."

Jack stepped over to the tree and pulled the knife out. It slid free with no resistance. Experimenting, he ran the blade along the tree, and sure enough, the barest cut separated the wood like it was slicing bread. He shivered. "I guess I should have known that it'd be charmed," Jack said. "We *did* find it in a witch's cottage."

"You *what?!*" Phillip said.

Jack grinned at him. "Why do you think I let you go first?"

The prince narrowed his eyes, but let it drop. "Either way, we still need blood," he said.

The two of them looked at each other, then down at the sword Jack had laid on the ground. It wasn't until just now that Jack realized that the wolf was closer to the sword than they were. Fortunately, the animal didn't seem to care. "The princess awaits," the wolf growled, still almost smiling. "*Surely* you can provide a few drops of blood without my help?"

That was enough to get them moving. "Right," Jack said, grabbing the sword from the ground. He held the blade out to the prince. "Ready?"

Phillip nodded. He repeated the process he'd tried with the knife, and with a quick jerk followed by a flinch, they finally had blood. Jack pushed the sword into the dirt a bit to support it, then cut himself in the same manner as Phillip had.

"If you please?" the wolf said, padding over. He opened his mouth to release a red tongue about the size of Jack's hand.

First Phillip, then Jack, squeezed a drop of blood onto the wolf's waiting tongue. The animal swallowed both with a smile, then went still for a moment, his eyes half-closing. Finally, he turned back to Jack and Phillip.

"You speak the truth," the wolf confirmed. "Therefore, I will take you to the princess."

"Thank you," Phillip said, using Jack's knife to cut a bit of his cape off to bandage his hand, then did the same for Jack.

As it turned out, May wasn't much farther down the trail. When they found her, she was lying on the ground a few feet off the path, her eyes closed. The fairy in her hair was asleep as well, though that wasn't exactly new.

As soon as they spotted the princess, Jack and Phillip ran to her, and both gently tried to wake her, but nothing worked. The wolf waited patiently for them to exhaust their efforts, then said, "I placed a simple spell on her. If you allow me a moment, I shall wake her."

Jack stared at the Wolf King. "But why?"

"She did not know me," he replied, padding over to the sleeping princess but keeping his red eyes locked on Jack. "And she screamed. I could not let her reveal our position to her kidnappers." The wolf managed to look a bit sheepish, which must have been difficult for him. "I did not yet realize that you were her servants."

"Servants?!" Jack repeated indignantly to Phillip, who didn't look thrilled with the label either.

The wolf meanwhile moved up alongside May, then stopped and closed his eyes. As Jack watched, the air around the animal seemed to shimmer, wavering in the light of the sword. Beneath the shimmer, something was happening. Something unnatural.

The wolf's hind legs stretched out grotesquely while his front legs shortened. His front paws unfolded into hands while his back paws pushed out, narrowing as they went. The wolf's snout shortened as they watched, shrinking back into his face, while the black fur all over his body receded, disappearing entirely in places. The shimmering abruptly stopped, and where the wolf had stood, now knelt a human.

A shaken Jack glanced over at Phillip, who just nodded. Apparently the prince wasn't surprised that the Wolf King could take human form.

As the wolf—no, man—stood up, the remaining fur on his back fell loose almost to the ground, covering most of the man as a cloak. Underneath the cloak were a black tunic, trousers, and boots—all the same color as the fur had been. The man's face was covered in hair, from a very shaggy head to a full beard. Though his eyes were sunken into his head, Jack noticed that the man's pupils were the same fiery red as the wolf's eyes had been.

The man knelt at May's side, then waved his hands over the

princess's face. And just like that, the princess woke up.

"*Help, Phillip!*" May screamed as she came to, apparently not realizing that time had passed. As the princess sat up the slumbering fairy tumbled from her hair to the ground, where she woke up as well, only a lot less scared and a lot more irritated.

The princess started to scream again, then noticed the hairy man kneeling at her side. She stopped abruptly and took a look around, then caught sight of the prince, mostly because Jack had taken a few steps backward.

"Phillip?" May said, confused. "What happened? The last thing I remember is some gigantic animal attacking me! And who's this?" she asked, nodding at the large, hairy man at her side. She started to say something else, then saw Jack.

Instantly, she was on her feet, her mouth open in surprise. She took a step toward Jack, but the wolf's spell must not have fully worn off, as her legs didn't support her. She fell forward, but Jack was there, throwing his arms under her shoulders to catch her.

"Jack!" she whispered, a huge smile on her face. Jack noticed a bit uncomfortably that their faces were just inches from each other.

"Um, right," he said, looking down. "I, uh, came back."

Instantly, the princess's eyes iced over. "Um, right," she

mimicked. "You, uh, came *back*. You came back after abandoning us to go into this freaking *possessed* forest alone—" She stopped abruptly and swayed a bit. "Why am I so dizzy?" Jack and Phillip both reached for her, but May made a point of ignoring Jack's arm to take Phillip's.

"Do you remember the Wolf King I mentioned in my story?" Jack asked her, trying to ignore the look she was giving him. He nodded at the huge, hairy man behind her. "This is him."

May turned around and looked the man up and down, then turned to Jack. "I don't know how to break this to you, but I'm pretty sure that being hairy doesn't make him a wolf."

The man bowed low. "I am the King of the Wolves, Princess," he said with a smile. "I've learned a few tricks in my years, turning human being but one of them. It made carrying you quite a bit easier than it might have been."

Jack stepped back while Phillip explained what had happened to the confused princess. She took it all remarkably in stride, even going so far as to try to cut herself with the knife. "Huh!" she said when it slid off her palm.

"I also learned the identity of your grandmother," Phillip said slowly. "I do not know what to say."

May shrugged. "You learn to live with it. Trust me, I have less reason to believe it than you people, but with everything that's happened, it's the best explanation we've got."

The wolf smiled, showing far too many teeth. "I served your grandmother for many years, and she trusts me implicitly. For this reason, she directed you to me. After all this time, she knew I could be trusted with your safety, and with her own. If she is in danger, we must rescue her with all possible haste."

"The thing is," May said, "we don't exactly know where she is."

"That should not be a problem," the wolf said. "I can track anything once I have its scent, and I know your grandmother's scent by heart. However, if she were anywhere in these kingdoms, either east or west, I would have sensed it already."

"Wait, what?!" May said.

Jack tended to agree with that sentiment. This was *not* good news. "Well, where is she, then?" he asked.

"Do you think I would keep it from you if I knew?" the wolf asked, sneering a bit.

Jack ignored him and took a step toward May, who was shaking from the news. The look she threw him, though, set him back. "Okay, fine, hold your grudge," Jack said. "But there still might be a way to find your grandmother."

"How?" Phillip asked.

Jack reached over to May, hooked a finger under her necklace, and pulled it out. "We could use the Magic Mirror," he said softly.

CHAPTER 22

he Mirror?" Phillip said, a look of confusion on his face. "But the Mirror was destroyed!"

The wolf growled, baring his teeth. He was intimidating, even in human form. "Not destroyed, little prince," the wolf said. "Only . . . broken. Without the crown, the Mirror is useless. With it, we will have the Wicked Queen's most powerful weapon in our paws!"

"But . . . we *cannot* restore the Mirror!" Phillip pleaded. "There must be a way to find May's grandmother without unleashing its power!"

The wolf sneered. "Do *you* know where the child's grandmother is?"

Phillip shook his head. "Of course not," he said. "But I do know what evils the Mirror wrought during the war. We have to ask ourselves if . . . well, if it is worth the price."

Once again, the wolf's teeth came out. "I would do *anything* to save my queen, little prince." He took a step forward, his eyes locked on the prince. "And I will *do* so whether I have your approval or not."

May quickly stepped between them, raising her hands to hold off any violence. "I agree with the Wolf King, Phillip," she said.

Phillip's face fell. "But, Princess, you do not know—"

She smiled a very small smile. "You're right," she said. "And I don't care. All I want is to find my grandmother, and quick. You think the Wicked Queen put her up in a nice room and is keeping her comfortable?"

"I would not think so, Princess," Phillip said sadly.

"That's right," May said. "So we find the Mirror as soon as possible, and we use it." She turned to the wolf. "And after we find my grandmother, then we *destroy* the Mirror. Deal?"

The wolf smiled. "I would have it no other way, Princess."

"So where is the Mirror?" Jack asked. "How do we find it?"

"One of the evil one's minions, the Red Hood, stole the Mirror after the crown was removed," the wolf said. "Unfortunately, the Hood's cloak for which she is named is magical. It keeps her invisible to my senses, or else I would have found her long ago. However . . . there might be another way to track her now." He reached his hand out toward May, palm up.

The princess stared at his hand for a second, then realization dawned. "Oh!" she said, and slowly removed her necklace, placing it into the wolf's outstretched hand.

The wolf brought it to his nose and inhaled deeply. His eyes closed halfway, just as they had when he tasted Jack's and Phillip's blood in wolf form, and he paused for a moment. Then the wolf turned his face up toward the ceiling of dead trees, his mouth hanging open. As he did, a strong wind rose from all around them, pushing Jack, May, and Phillip back against the trees. Within seconds, though, the wind stopped, and the wolf lowered his head.

He was smiling.

"Your necklace, Princess," he said, and handed it back to her.

"So, do you know where the Mirror is?" Jack asked.

The wolf nodded slowly. "I know which direction it is in. I will take you there."

"We have little time," Phillip said. "We should take the quickest route possible."

The wolf laughed. Strangely enough, his laugh was creepier than his growl. "I will carry you," he said simply. "I must do so if you wish to leave the Black Forest. Already, the trees hunger for human blood; they speak to me, beg me to leave you with them." He smiled almost evilly. "Don't make me regret my decision."

At that Jack, Phillip, and May all quickly took a step away from the nearest trees.

The fur-covered man shimmered again in the light of the sword and morphed back into the enormous monster of a wolf. The animal's red eyes opened, then glared at the three of them. "Climb onto my back," he growled. "There is little time to waste."

Jack took a step back. "Um, you know, this doesn't really seem like the best idea, all things considered."

"What?" May said, her tone mocking. "Don't tell me you're afraid of the big bad wolf, Jack."

Phillip forced a laugh. "Yes, Jack," he said. "What is there to fear? He's an ally of Snow White. He will keep us safe." As he spoke, the prince slowly inched up next to the animal. He put one hand on the beast's fur, then took a deep breath and vaulted onto wolf's back.

All three of them braced themselves, but the wolf didn't react at all.

"Ah, see?" Phillip said with a relieved smile. "There is nothing to fret about. Come, Princess, I shall assist you."

May smiled cruelly at Jack. "It's nice to have a big, brave man along, isn't it? You know, someone dependable?" With that, she turned and walked over to the wolf's side, where Phillip helped pull her up.

After the two of them were seated, the wolf turned his gaze to Jack. "Well, boy?" he growled. "What are you waiting for? I won't hurt you."

Jack swallowed hard. "You know, I'd like to believe that—"

"*Get on!*" the wolf roared, then leapt forward, landing just in front of Jack, his teeth only inches from Jack's face. The wolf's breath puffed out of his nostrils, sending Jack's hair flying.

"Okay, but only because you asked nicely," Jack said, sliding his sword into its scabbard and climbing up behind May. "I have a bad feeling about this," he told her.

"You have a bad feeling about everything," she sent back.

Jack started to respond, but before he could, the wolf leapt forward, sending them all airborne. All three grabbed fur and managed to keep themselves on the wolf's back as he loped off into the woods.

Wind and branches flew by as the wolf ran, threatening to

knock them all off the wolf's back if they didn't lean forward and hold on for dear life. Between the howling wind and their faces being pushed into each other's backs, all conversation was effectively cut off.

Riding the wolf was nothing like riding a horse had been. While Samson had a rhythmic gait, the wolf's loping seemed to change every few seconds as he adjusted his stride for the terrain. Sometimes, they'd be just about shaken off their perch from a short tear through a clearing, only for the wolf to leap forward at other times, taking to the air like an enormous furry bird, the wind just about pushing each of them right off his back. If Phillip hadn't locked his arms around the wolf's neck, with May holding on to him and Jack holding on to May, all three would have fallen off after the first leap.

Gradually, Jack began to notice that the trees rushing by on either side looked different. Instead of black, dead wood, the trees now had leaves; brown, living branches clawed at them as the wolf ran. Eventually, Jack started to see birds and even some animals, magical and otherwise, in the underbrush, a sure sign that they'd left the Black Forest behind.

The wolf loped on for what seemed like days. In actuality, it wasn't more than one night, as when Jack was about to yell to the wolf that they needed a break, he saw the sunrise poking through the trees up ahead.

The sunlight turned out to be a small clearing. Jack barely noticed, though, he was so intent on the natural sunlight after seeing everything by the glow of the knight's sword. In fact, he was so focused on the sunlight that he didn't realize the wolf had abruptly screeched to a halt.

While May and Phillip managed to stay on the wolf, Jack flew off to land in the dirt, skidding to a stop just before the clearing, his sword shooting off his back to land even farther away.

"*Shh!*" May shushed from behind him, still safely mounted. "You could be a little more quiet!" She laughed softly, then stuck out her tongue at him. The wolf let out a sound that sounded eerily like a chuckle. Even Phillip had a smile on his face as he helped May get down off the wolf's back.

Jack sighed, quietly promising to wipe the dirt on his clothes all over the others at the first opportunity, then joined May, Phillip, and the wolf at the edge of the forest to see what they'd found. With one of the Wicked Queen's minions, anything could be waiting for them.

Anything turned out to be a small house of white brick with a bright red roof.

"That's where the Mirror is?" May asked the wolf, who nodded.

Jack glanced at the animal. The wolf's teeth were bared, which couldn't be a good sign. "What's wrong?" Jack asked him.

The wolf's eyes narrowed. "After so many years, I have the Red Hood in my paws." He smiled, licking his lips. "Wait here," he said, then loped off into the forest. A few seconds later, they caught sight of him slinking low to the ground across the clearing, moving silently to the cottage's nearest window. The wolf pulled himself up ever so slowly, then peered within. After a moment, he sank back down to the ground, turned around, and returned the way he came, surprising all three of them when he appeared behind them a moment later.

Before they could ask the animal what he found, the wolf cursed several times. "She is not there!" he growled, his eyes as red as fire.

"How would you know?" Jack asked. "I mean, you said you couldn't track her . . . how can you be sure?"

The wolf stared at him, a furious look painted across his long face, making Jack take an involuntary step backward. "I cannot see or smell her," the wolf spat out. "But I could hear her if she was there. There is nothing alive in that cottage."

"But the Mirror?" May said, holding up the necklace. "You know for sure it's there?"

The wolf nodded. "It is in there somewhere," he said. "My senses do not lie."

"Perhaps the Mirror is there, but the Red Hood is simply out," Phillip suggested.

"Maybe we should check," Jack said. "We might be able to just sneak in and take the Mirror. That'd be easier than dealing with one of the Wicked Queen's monsters."

"Agreed," said Phillip.

"No," growled the wolf quietly. "I have waited much too long for this moment. I will not leave until I have dealt with the Red Hood once and for all! Go fetch the Mirror. I will keep watch for the Red Hood."

May nodded and started jogging off toward the cottage, so Phillip and Jack had no choice but to follow. As Jack passed the sword he grabbed it from the ground and returned it to its scabbard on his back, a scabbard that clearly wasn't holding it tightly enough if it could just fly out like that.

May reached the cottage first and tried the door, only to find it locked. Jack and Phillip both tried it as well, while May rolled her eyes at their need to confirm the obvious.

Instead of wasting any more time, Jack took out the witch's knife and used it to slice through the lock, which it cut through as easily as it had the trees in the Black Forest. As he finished Jack took hold of the knob and gently opened the door, its loud squeaking startling a large blackbird from its perch on the roof. Inside, the little cottage was filled with shadows despite the sunlight outside, so Jack reached back and pulled out his sword: Its glow gave them enough light to see by.

The cottage had just one room, though it was much larger than Jack's cottage back home. Flowered curtains hung over the windows, obscuring the outside light, while wooden furniture overflowed the cramped space, the biggest piece of which was a four-poster bed covered with linens that matched the curtains.

Jack rolled his eyes. "This whole place just *stinks* of evil," he said sarcastically.

"Do not be fooled by appearances," Phillip said. "Pleasant exteriors sometimes mask the worst interiors."

"I agree," May said. "Flowers on the curtains? This place hurts *my* interior."

As the three of them entered the cottage Jack raised an eyebrow. "So, where's the Mirror?" he asked. They all took a quick look around, searching under the bed, through a closet, even in a chest of drawers. Then, almost at exactly the same time, they all looked up from what they'd been doing, up to the wall next to the door. . . .

Looked up at the mirror hanging on the wall.

Three mouths dropped open at the same time. "She's using the most powerful magic item of all time . . . as a regular mirror?" Jack asked.

"That *cannot* be it," Phillip said, also shocked. "For her to be so . . . *open* with it . . ."

Jack nodded. Phillip seemed to have identified the problem exactly. How could she be so unconcerned? Granted, the mirror on the wall really didn't look like anything special, apart from what looked like gold in the frame. Age had worn down many of the elaborate lines in the mirror's frame to the point Jack couldn't tell what they had originally looked like. Other than that small design, however, the whole thing looked completely ordinary. This certainly wasn't the all-powerful evil item of doom they had all been expecting. Maybe hiding it in plain sight wasn't such a bad idea.

May moved in, followed closely by Jack and Phillip. The princess peered at the top of the mirror, then turned around and pointed. Sure enough, there at the top where the worn-down lines came together was a small indentation in the shape of a crown.

It really was the Mirror.

Jack cleared his throat, feeling that this was too important a time not to say something, something to impress upon the other two just how momentous their find truly was.

Unfortunately, May beat him to it. "How lame!" the princess said, tapping the Mirror's glass with her fingernail. "The glass is even cloudy! What a letdown!"

Jack and Phillip both looked at her, trying subtly to make the point that maybe such a comment wasn't the most appropriate reaction for such a significant moment, but she steadily ignored their questioning glances. Instead, May pulled the necklace out from beneath her tunic and held up the crown at the end of it. "Should I put it in?" she asked them. "Or should we wait till we find the Red Hood and, you know, beat her up?"

"One thing at a time," Jack said quickly, yanking May's hand away from the Mirror. The whole idea of unleashing the Mirror's power again turned Jack's toes cold, but they didn't really have any choice. Still, it could wait until they were safely away from the Red Hood's home, if nothing else.

"How do we handle this?" May asked. "What if she comes

in? If she's as powerful as the Wolf King says, she could kill us all—"

Just then a very feminine shout of surprise came from the path leading into the clearing. "Who's there?" the voice yelled out.

Instantly Jack, Phillip, and May turned to the front of the cottage to find the front door still standing wide open.

"Whoops," May said softly.

"*Hide!*" Phillip hissed, and, not having a better plan, all three ran and slid underneath the oversize bed. The bed's linens overhung the side, giving them some cover, if not nearly enough. Unfortunately, they had no other choice.

No, they were just going to have to hide beneath the bed and hope that May's big, bad wolf protector would come in and save them all from the Red Hood.

CHAPTER 23

Jack couldn't see much from beneath the bed. The frilly quilt that covered the sides of the bed and subsequently hid them also did a great job of obscuring what was happening. All he could make out was a pair of black shoes stepping carefully through the open door of the cottage.

"Who's there?" the owner of the shoes asked again quietly, just as a thunderous noise exploded outside. The shoes immediately turned and ran toward a wall . . . no, to the window in the wall. "What *is* this?" the voice asked softly.

Another huge crack, almost like a tree splitting in half, erupted outside the cottage. Phillip, closest to the Hood, looked over to Jack, then nodded. Phillip wanted them to take the Red

Hood by surprise while she was distracted. Jack nodded back, then pushed himself toward the edge of the bed, shaking his head as he went. How had a nice, normal boy like him gotten caught up in such an idiotic adventure?

Jack grasped the edge of the bed, his hand on his sword, but he stopped. The sword would be too large if he planned on sneaking up on her. There was the knife, of course, but it wouldn't actually be able to hurt her.

But maybe he didn't need to.

With the beginnings of a plan, Jack reached into his bag and pulled out the knife. The shoes still seemed to be intent on whatever they were looking at out the window, but that wouldn't last for long. There weren't any further noises from the forest, so the wolf had given them all the distraction he could. Jack pushed himself out from under the bed, then grabbed the linens and pulled himself up so he could see over the top of the bed.

Directly above the shoes stood . . . well, no one. Yet someone was clearly in them; as Jack watched, whoever it was nervously lifted one foot, then the other.

Even invisible, the Red Hood was panicking. Now or never . . .

Without another thought, Jack threw himself forward, directly at the spot where the Red Hood should have been. Right above the black shoes, he smacked into something solid, something that screamed in surprise and fell over beneath him.

Jack lifted the knife and slashed over and over at the invisible screaming woman beneath him. He couldn't actually hurt her this way, but she didn't know that. Besides, though the knife couldn't cut flesh, it did cut something pretty important to her.

Just as Jack hoped, everywhere he cut the Red Hood's cloak, the woman became visible. In fact, he quickly found himself lying on top of two arms and what looked to be a leg.

Then the leg pushed its knee up into Jack's chest, kicking him back against the bed. As the knife flew from his grip he marveled that his plan could both work so well and fail so miserably at the same time.

"You *cut* me!" the arms and leg screamed indignantly, rising into the air as if by magic. "I can't . . . wait, I'm not—whoop!" The last bit came as Phillip yanked the Red Hood's visible leg out from under her and she crashed back down.

As the Red Hood hit the cottage floor May jumped up from the other side of the bed, grabbed the knife, and leapt at the Hood. "Hold her down!" Phillip shouted as he tried to get out from under the bed while still holding tightly to the Red Hood's exposed leg. May kneeled down on the Hood's arm and held the knife over what might have been the woman's neck. As she did so the arms and leg stopped struggling. The princess must have put the knife against *something* important, neck or no.

Jack carefully stepped past May and made his way to what he figured was the Hood's head. He reached down and felt around until he touched something wooly, then pulled on it. Instantly, the Wicked Queen's monster finally became visible.

Only the woman on the ground wasn't some grotesque creature of the night. Instead, she was actually quite pretty, her eyes a deep blue, wide open with fright and anger as they flashed between Jack and May. Raven-colored hair flooded down the woman's back, while her well-lined face still managed to look young, especially in the blue eyes.

As he'd figured, the wooly cloth Jack had pulled turned out to be the Hood's namesake, a red cloak that covered almost all of the woman's body, despite now having several large slashes in it. Beneath the cloak, the Hood was dressed entirely in crimson from her blouse to her silky pants. Apparently she had a thing for the color red.

"Who are you!" the Red Hood demanded. "What do you want!"

May shook her head. "Oh no, lady," she said. "*You* are gonna answer *our* questions. Where's my grandmother!"

"Your . . . what?" the Hood asked, sounding confused. "What are you talking about?"

"Not good enough!" May said, and she pushed the knife against the woman's throat. As May put on a threatening face the Red Hood just looked more confused. "You know that doesn't hurt, right?" the Hood asked.

"I do know that, yes," May said, a bit annoyed. She glanced down at the knife, then tossed it aside and yanked the Hood up by her tunic. "You have the Mirror, so you have to know something!" May yelled. "Tell me where my grandmother is!"

"You want to find your grandmother?" asked a voice from the door. As Jack spun around to see who'd spoken something enormous flew through the open doorway and plowed into the four-poster bed, practically breaking it in half in the process.

It was the Wolf King. And from where he stood, Jack couldn't tell if the animal was still alive.

From the doorway, the Huntsman smiled. "You could have just asked me, you know. Oh, and Red? I took care of that little wolf problem you've been having. You're welcome."

CHAPTER 24

That is a huntsman!" Phillip said in surprise.

"You're a huge help, Phillip," May said, not taking her eyes off the man in the doorway.

"You picked up another stray, girlie?" the Huntsman said, smiling at Phillip. Without warning, the Huntsman's left hand flew out and grabbed the prince, locking around Phillip's throat even while the Huntsman's right hand pointed a crossbow at Jack's face.

"This seems like old times, doesn't it, kids?" the Huntsman said, laughing heartily. At the end of his arm, Phillip struggled to break free of the Huntsman's grasp, but the man's grip was like steel, cutting off the prince's air.

"Let him go!" May shouted furiously. "Just leave us *alone* already!"

The fairy in her hair aimed a dirty look at the Huntsman, muttering something to herself in her own language. Strangely enough, Jack thought he could almost make out a word here or there. He shrugged it off, though, and brought his attention back to the Huntsman.

In answer to May's command, the Huntsman just squeezed Phillip harder, turning the prince's face purple.

"Let him go *now*, or she's dead," May said as she dragged the Red Hood to her feet and held the knife against the woman's throat.

"The knife doesn't cut flesh," the Hood said calmly, then threw her head back into May's face. Their two skulls smacked against each other with a hollow clunk, sending May to her knees holding her forehead.

The Red Hood, meanwhile, leapt for the Mirror on the wall. Before she could reach it, Jack threw himself backward between the wall and the Hood, then yanked his sword from his back.

For an instant, no one moved as the sword's glow lit up the room.

"That's—," the Red Hood said with surprise.

"That's the sword of an *Eye!*" the Huntsman said.

"You're not getting the Mirror," Jack said, his voice calmer than he felt.

"Take it," the Huntsman said to the Hood, his eyes locked on Jack. She nodded and went for the Mirror. As she did Jack swung the sword out and smacked her in the head with the flat of the blade. The Hood crumpled against the wall for a moment, then crept back to the protection of the Huntsman, clearly in pain.

"Nicely done," the Huntsman grudgingly admitted. "But I knew you didn't have the guts to kill her."

Jack just shrugged as casually as he could. "There was no need," he said. The truth was that he hadn't even really intended to hit her at all, just scare her. Still, it wasn't as if he'd been in many swordfights in his life, so he took his victories where he could get them.

"Believe me, killing is *always* necessary," the Huntsman said, smiling bitterly. "I learned that the hard way. Now . . . why don't I pass that lesson along?" With that, he took aim at Jack's head, then shot the crossbow.

As the arrow launched out toward Jack's face the sword glowed brightly, and time seemed to slow down. Someone screamed out, though Jack couldn't tell who—he was too intent on watching the arrow fly toward him. It was moving so slowly, actually, that he wondered if arrows always took this long to get where they were going.

"Why not deflect it with your sword?" asked a voice in his head that sounded surprisingly like the knight in the giant's mouth.

For some reason, that struck Jack as a perfectly logical thing to do, so he swung the sword up, almost in slow motion, and swept the arrow right off course so it missed him entirely.

And just like that, time resumed its normal speed, though no one else seemed to have noticed. What they did notice was the fact that Jack had just deflected an arrow with his sword, moving faster than anyone had a right to.

This clearly surprised the Huntsman, but only for a moment. Before Jack had a chance to make a move, the Huntsman threw Phillip into Jack, knocking them both backward. As Jack fell to the floor he thought he saw the Huntsman grab the Red Hood and go for the door, but that was all he could make out before the prince's purple cloak covered his eyes.

"Get off!" Jack yelled, pushing the gasping prince off him and running to the door, but both the Huntsman and the Red Hood had disappeared.

Jack sighed, then turned around to help the prince up, but found that May had already done so. "That could have gone better," Jack said, but neither of the other two responded. In fact, they didn't seem to have even heard him; their attention was caught up with something that he couldn't see. "What are you two looking at?" Jack asked, stepping around them to get a look for himself.

When he saw what they were staring at, all the adrenaline of the moment drained from his body, and he almost fell over. He steadied himself on the bed and stared at the wall in front of him, right at the spot where the Magic Mirror hung.

In the exact center of the Mirror was a hairline crack, a crack that split off in all directions from the spot where the arrow had struck the glass.

By saving himself, Jack had broken the Mirror.

CHAPTER 25

No," Jack said, holding tightly to one of the bed's posts so he didn't fall over. "No, no, no, no, no!"

"You hit the arrow . . . ," May said, staring at the Mirror.

"It flew right into the Mirror . . . ," the prince said, doing the same.

May gradually turned around to look at Jack. "How were you able to do that?" she asked, sounding a bit dazed. "I barely even saw you move."

Before Jack could explain what happened, a difficult task considering he didn't know himself, the prince saved him. "The Mirror can wait," Phillip said, then turned around and stepped over to the bed.

"The Mirror can *what*?" May said, snapping out of her shock. "The thing's *broken*, and it was our only way of finding my grandmother!"

"We have a more pressing problem right now," Phillip said, then pointed down at the bed. Jack stepped over to join him, and after a pause, May did the same. The princess started to say something, then caught sight of what Phillip had been pointing at.

The Wolf King lay in the middle of a huge pile of quilts, covered in blood and bruises. The animal's closed eyes fluttered wildly and his feet shook every few seconds. He did seem to be breathing, at least, but each breath sent a shudder through the wolf's entire body.

"I think he is dying," Phillip said softly, reaching out to touch the animal's paw.

The wolf's whole body flinched at Phillip's touch, despite the fact that the animal was unconscious. The wolf was bleeding in multiple places, his pale skin showing through in patches where his fur had been torn off. Phillip grabbed some of the bed's extra linens and started to cover the wounds, while Jack and May helped where they could. Finally, the prince stopped, glancing over his work to make sure he'd caught everything.

"That will hopefully help a bit," Phillip said. "But we will need to find help. I don't know if it will make a difference, but we must try. We can use your broomstick to bring a healer."

May nodded, then looked over at the wall. "What about the Mirror?"

Jack frowned. "We can't touch it, not broken like it is. We have no idea what would happen if you put the crown back in now. Magic's a tricky thing . . . it might be dangerous. We'll have to figure out a way to fix it before using it."

Phillip nodded. "He's right, Princess."

"Right," May said, her voice quiet. "So we need a doctor, then. Or healer—whatever you said, Phillip. Who's going to go?"

Before Jack could respond, the prince stepped forward. "Me, Your Highness. I have encountered devices like the broomstick before. It shall not take me long to learn its specifics." He smiled. "Besides, once airborne, where would either of you go? I know where to find a healer, if I can but figure out our location. I will return shortly."

The prince saluted them both with a hopeful smile, then strode purposefully out the door and back to where they'd hidden their belongings in the brush outside the clearing.

May followed him as far as the door, smiling sadly. "You

know, if our history is any indication, he might kill himself on that thing," she said.

"He might," Jack said diplomatically.

"Should we stop him?"

"He's royalty," Jack said with a shrug. "I doubt we're allowed to tell him what he should and shouldn't do, regardless of the inherent stupidity."

A moment later Phillip hovered easily on the broomstick just outside the door. "I will return as soon as I can," he said, then smiled, turned the broomstick, and flew off at top speed into the distance.

"Or he'll have no problems whatsoever," Jack said. "Figures."

May laughed, then let out a deep breath. "This isn't how things are supposed to go, you know," May said softly, twisting the crown around at the end of her necklace. "This isn't how fairy tales work."

Jack glanced at the fairy in May's hair, who had started braiding a few of the princess's hairs together, humming softly to herself as she did so. "I hate to go over this again, Princess, but I'm pretty sure they *still* don't have tails," Jack said.

May rolled her eyes. "That joke never gets old. You know what I mean."

"Stories about fairies," he said.

"Stories where people live happily ever after," she said, staring at the crown. "Stories that make you think there's magic in the world. 'Once upon a time.' Heroes who do the right thing and villains who never win. The heroes always know they're right and always know what to do. They never have any doubts."

"That sounds like a good story," Jack said. "It'd be nice if the world really worked that way."

May snorted. "Where I'm from, that's exactly what's wrong: It *doesn't* work that way. Here, though, it's like . . . it's like you've got all the parts right. You've got princes, monsters, Snow White, all these fairy tales come to life . . ." She sighed. "But this isn't once upon a time. It's like the opposite . . . half or something."

"Wouldn't the opposite be 'never'?" Jack asked, but the princess ignored him.

"The story's not right, Jack. This shouldn't be how things go. Everything's so mixed up, and we're barely holding on. We're not . . . we're not winning, are we."

Jack reached over and took the crown out of her hand. May glanced up at him, letting the necklace fall back against her chest.

"Maybe not now," Jack said, "but we *will*. We're the good

guys, and we're doing the right thing. It *will* be just like your sto-ries. We'll win in the end."

"Will we?" she asked. "Look at this, this whole place! Magi-cal things happen here, but other than that, it's . . . it's just the same as where I'm from." She shook her head in frustration. "In my world, no one is safe, Jack. *Especially* not the good guys." She nodded toward the wolf. "I thought here, of all places . . ."

"You said heroes don't doubt themselves," Jack said, forcing a smile. "The prince will be back with a healer soon, and the Wolf King will be fine. Meanwhile, we have the Mirror, and—"

"The Mirror?!" she shouted, then blushed and lowered her voice. "The Mirror is broken!" May whispered, pointing at it. "And with it goes any hope I had of finding my grandmother." She dropped her head into her hands and stared at the floor. "But not only that. We were . . . we were going to do something *magical*, Jack. We were going to rescue Snow White! How amaz-ing is that? I mean, my grandmother is Snow White! I still can't wrap my head around that. But don't worry, real life won't let me go on too long like this without crashing down. And now, here we are, waiting for the ambulance to pick up one of our friends." She gritted her teeth, then smacked a hand against the wall hard enough to turn her palm red.

Jack thought about asking what an ambulance was, but decided to keep his question to himself. Instead, he took the princess's hands in his. "Princess . . . May," he said. "Listen to me." She glared at him for a second, then sighed deeply, the anger draining from her face.

"These are *challenges*," Jack told her. "That's it. We *are* going to win. You know why? Because it doesn't matter if you're in a fairy tale or here in real life, doing the right thing still counts for something. We're going to win because we're good, decent people trying to accomplish something noble."

She flashed her half smile at him. "You didn't have to get all melodramatic there," she said, then bumped him with her shoulder.

He grinned. "Just following your example, Your Highness."

She gave him an indignant look. "I was *not* being melodramatic!"

"Oh, of *course* not."

"I wasn't!"

"Did you listen to yourself? You were half a second away from saying we're the villains in our story!"

May stuck out her tongue. "Maybe not me, but I've got my suspicions about you."

He laughed out loud. "I'm pretty sure there's not a villain out there who would put up with you for this long."

This time she pushed him hard, and he fell to the ground, still laughing. May rolled her eyes, then leaned over and offered him her hand to pull him up, but Jack grabbed her and yanked her down to the floor next to him. Jack then sprang to his feet and put his hands on his hips, striking the classic hero pose. "No princess is a match for Sir Jack!" he said majestically.

"*Sir* Jack?" May said from the floor, raising an eyebrow.

He nodded toward his back. "I've got a sword, don't I?"

She laughed. "If that's all it takes, I'm going to be Sir May in about two seconds. . . ." She jumped to her feet and launched herself at him. Jack backpedaled away from her, but May was too quick. She threw both her arms around him and grabbed for the sword, even as he backed away, trying to keep her from getting it.

May moved with him, though, so Jack kicked himself backward, laughing the entire time. He kept moving backward until he bumped into the cottage wall, May's momentum pushing her right into him.

It took him all of a second to realize that she had her arms around him, he had his arms around her, and their faces were only inches apart.

Suddenly, Jack had no clue what to do. What had just happened? The wolf was hurt, and they were playing around? Plus, May was a princess, and Jack hated royalty . . . didn't he? Okay, maybe right now he had a hard time remembering why, but still. . . .

May seemed as surprised as he was to find herself in this position. Still, she recovered quickly and started to say something, but stopped and looked down toward his mouth. She looked back up at him, and her eyes softened.

A low growl from the bed interrupted whatever May's eyes were about to say. "If . . . you're not too busy," the wolf said.

May instantly blushed and jumped backward, slamming Jack hard against the wall. As Jack slid down to the floor, grunting in pain, she literally leapt to the wolf's side.

"*Yes!*" May shouted. "We're here! Not doing anything, just waiting! For a doctor! A healer, whatever! What can we do? Want some water? Something to eat? Are you all right?" She stopped to take a breath, giving the wolf a chance to jump in.

"No," he growled, "I need nothing . . . I will be fine. I heal . . . quickly. Just tell me what happened."

Jack pushed himself to his feet and walked over to the bed. "Not to disagree, but it doesn't really look like you'll be fine," he told the wolf. "You're barely able to move, and you've lost a lot of blood, but I think we've got it covered. Phillip went to get a healer."

The animal picked up his head to stare at them. "Leaving you two . . . here to do what, watch over me?" He started to chuckle, but the laughter turned into a coughing fit.

"Calm down!" May said, pushing the wolf's head back down onto the bed. "We're here to take care of you. And we will. We'll make sure nothing happens to you until the doctor gets here."

"Doctor?" Jack said. "You keep saying that. What's a—"

"You really gotta do that every time?" May interrupted without looking at him.

"I must know *now*," the wolf said, his eyes dark with pain, but also filled with determination. "Tell me what occurred here. Where is the Red Hood?! What happened to the Mirror?!"

"The Red Hood escaped," Jack said. "The Huntsman—this guy who's been chasing us down—he threw you in here and then helped her get away."

"*What!*" The wolf shouted, then struggled to push himself up, but quickly fell back to the bed and into another coughing fit.

"That's not all, either," May said in a voice tinged with anger.

"They broke the Mirror." She pointed to the wall. "More than it already was, I mean."

The wolf sat up enough to see what she was pointing at, then dropped back to the bed with a sigh. "Clearly, you do *not* take after your grandmother, Princess. She never would have let this happen."

May's mouth dropped open, the wolf's comment leaving her at a loss for words. Jack found himself filling in for her, though, far more passionately then he would have thought. "May did everything she could!" Jack shouted. "We all did! Maybe if we hadn't been surprised by the Huntsman, we'd have the Red Hood and the Mirror right now!"

The wolf's paw flew up and grabbed Jack's head, then yanked it down to within an inch of the animal's teeth. "And what, pray tell, are you implying?" the wolf growled softly.

"I'm implying," Jack said, ignoring the animal's heavy breathing, "that *you* were supposed to be watching our backs!"

The wolf glared at him for a moment, then released him. "You speak the truth," he said, lying back down on the bed, looking paler than ever. "I . . . I failed. I was not aware of the Huntsman's approach. I sought to hide my presence from the Red Hood, cloaked as a man. But in man form, I cannot use as many of my senses as I can as a wolf. I was taken unawares, and reverted to my regular form when I lost conscious control over my aspect." The wolf winced, though in pain or just at the memory of his failure, Jack couldn't tell.

"Well, it's not really your fault either," Jack said, much more eager to forgive now that the wolf had apologized. "None of us knew he was there, and we're all dealing with it now. So just get some rest, and try not to move until the healer gets here."

May nodded in agreement, and the wolf settled back into the soft bed, closing his eyes. They let him rest for a minute, then moved back to the wall.

As Jack slid down the wall to the floor a little laugh escaped the wolf's lips. "One more thing," he growled. "I hardly care what you do, but *try* not to wake me with your courting rituals again."

Jack's face turned bright red as he slipped and fell the rest of the way to the floor.

CHAPTER 26

Jack didn't plan on falling asleep; too much was happening, and happening much too fast when it did. Still, he hadn't slept in a while, what with finding the Black Forest, riding on the wolf's back, and breaking the Mirror. After all that, the quiet comfort of the cottage was just too hard to resist.

Jack propped himself up against the wall with some bed pillows, then leaned back to settle in. On his right, May was doing the same, only she'd already closed her eyes. Jack smiled slightly as he marveled for the hundredth time that her hair could really be blue like that. How had she done that? Was there magic involved?

And then Jack opened his eyes, not exactly sure when he'd

closed them. When he fell asleep, his mind always seemed to wander to the oddest places. Places where magic didn't work, and there wasn't any royalty . . . places where everyone was equal, no one was better than anyone else just because of who their parents were. That'd be nice, a place like that. That'd be some kind of dream world. . . .

And maybe it'd look something like the place Jack saw when he opened his eyes. Somehow, surrounding him on all sides was a wide field with tall, golden grasses blowing gently in multiple directions from the slightly chilly wind. The meadow seemed empty, at least from where he was sitting. As he turned to take it all in, though, he noticed an oak tree behind him. In fact, he was leaning against it. How odd . . . Had that been there a minute ago? Hadn't he just been in sunlight, whereas now he sat in the tree's shade? Jack thought so, but didn't really put too much effort into worrying about it. The tree was here now—that was the important thing.

He snuggled against the tree's trunk, sighing with contentment as his back fit into the wood just right. The gentle breeze still managed to find him under the tree's canopy, and the air blew his hair almost playfully. Jack smiled. This was actually really nice!

"It *is* quite nice," said a man at his side, a man who Jack could have sworn wasn't there a minute ago, a man whose voice was familiar.

A man who was also dressed entirely in black armor, covered by a blue cloak.

Somewhere deep in Jack's head, a small voice cried out that this was the Wicked Queen's Eye, that Jack was in danger, but the voice was too small to listen to, so Jack just ignored it and smiled. "I agree, it is nice," he said. For some reason, his voice sounded dazed, even to him, but Jack didn't let that bother him.

The knight returned Jack's smile. "Sometimes I sit here for days, you know," the man said, leaning his head back against the tree. "It's very peaceful. Also, I must admit, it's quite pleasant to think, to hear your breath moving in and out without the distractions of the outside world."

Jack nodded in agreement. "I haven't had much chance to sit still in a few days," he said. "It's been pretty strange."

The knight leaned over. "It's going to get stranger," he whispered. At that, the knight waved his hand, and an image appeared in midair. It was of a girl with both blond and blue hair, checking to make sure the boy next to her was asleep before standing up and removing a chain from around her neck.

"You're in for quite an adventure, actually," the knight said to him as Jack dreamily watched the scene unfold in midair. "You really have no idea how deep you'll be going."

"Well," Jack said thoughtfully, "we *are* going to rescue Snow White. That much I know."

The knight's eyes twinkled. "Are you now, Jack? That *would* be a grand adventure, and certainly a worthy one."

In the image, the girl snuck quietly over to a nearby wall upon which hung a mirror.

A thought occurred to Jack, one that seemed to penetrate the fog currently filling his mind. "But you . . . the Eyes serve the Wicked Queen. . . ."

The knight sighed and leaned back against the tree. "I think that you will find that much of what you previously believed, young Jack, may not be as true as you thought."

That answer didn't seem to help at all. "But you *do* serve the Wicked Queen, right?"

The knight paused as if trying to word his answer carefully. "I served the Queen in the past, yes," he said finally. "However, unlike many in my order, I pledged my allegiance to another. My allegiance . . . and more."

"More?" Jack said, looking closely at the knight next to him.

He realized with a start, though a gentle one, that the knight wasn't wearing his hood, as he had been in the giant's mouth. The hood had been hiding a rather pleasant face, wrinkled with worry lines, but also quite a few lines from wide smiles. The knight's hair was almost a bronzed brown, a color that accented his green eyes. For some reason, the man's face looked familiar, as if Jack had seen him in paintings or something.

And then the realization of the knight's identity suddenly hit him, almost as if the knowledge had come from somewhere else, somewhere outside Jack's head. "Wait a second," Jack said slowly. "You're the one who—"

"I *was*," the knight corrected, his eyes twinkling again, though there was also a hint of sadness. "But now all I am is a shadow of my former self, a hint of what was. Or for some," the knight said, a small grin sneaking onto his lips, "a hint of what might come?"

At that moment the girl in the image slowly held the end of her chain up to a small space at the top of the mirror, then pushed it into place.

An ear-splitting scream filled the air, and the floating image began pulling at Jack, yanking him bodily into it and away from the field, the sunshine, and the knight, straight back into his waking body and the cottage.

The scream had come from a tall, thin woman who now stood in the doorway wearing a vibrant blue dress, full, platinum-colored hair framing her long face. Phillip stood behind her, and both he and the woman looked completely shocked; the woman's mouth was still hanging open from her scream. Across the room, the wolf was also awake and glancing around with the same confusion that Jack felt.

With a sinking feeling, Jack quickly looked over to the wall, over to the Mirror.

And there was May, having placed the crown of her necklace into the Mirror's frame.

"Princess!" Phillip screamed.

"You must not do that!" the woman in blue shouted.

"May, don't!" Jack said, but he was far too late.

May smiled guiltily. "I know I wasn't supposed to, but you gotta understand, I need to know if it will work! I *need* to know." With that, she stepped away from the Mirror, bracing herself for what might happen, as they all did . . .

Except nothing did happen, and after a few more seconds of nothing, Jack, Phillip, and May all breathed a collective sigh of relief. Phillip reached May first, as Jack was farther away, but Jack wasn't far behind.

"What were you thinking, Princess?!" Phillip asked her.

"May," Jack said, pushing Phillip aside, "you have *no* idea what might have happened with the Mirror broken like that. We don't even know what it would have done if it was still in one piece!"

"I . . . I needed to know," May said, sounding almost confused. "I had to see what would happen. It might have been able to give us one last piece of information, even if it was broken!" As she spoke, her eyes began to moisten. "Don't you guys get it?" she said. "How are we supposed to find her *without* this? We needed the Mirror! It can't be broken! I won't accept that!"

Jack and Phillip both reached out to touch her, but she jerked away from them and strode back over to the Mirror. She stared at it in despair for a moment, then reached up to take the necklace back.

"The damage has been done," the woman in blue said from behind them, her voice sad. As if in response to her words, a small glow appeared behind the crack in the center of the Mirror. Slowly, the glow grew in intensity, filling the Mirror, shining forth at odd angles from every fracture in the glass.

Then an even stranger thing began to happen. The glow, the actual light in the Mirror, began to trickle out of the hole in the middle of the Mirror, just like smoke rising out of a chimney.

CHAPTER 27

U h-oh," May said, backing away from the Mirror.

"That pretty much covers it," Jack agreed, yanking her back more quickly. Whatever was pouring out of the Mirror looked like some kind of bright, greenish-yellow smoke, though Jack hadn't ever seen smoke that glowed.

"This way!" the prince yelled then gestured for Jack and May to get outside. Jack couldn't really argue with that, so he pushed May toward the door, then ran to the bed; there was no way the wolf could move on his own. Jack put a shoulder under one of the animal's injured legs and heaved . . . only, he didn't move the animal an inch.

"Whoa!" Jack said. "He must weigh like a hundred stone!"

"You," the woman in blue said, pointing at Jack, "out. I'll take care of this . . . this creature."

Jack started to object, then looked into the woman's eyes, eyes that were completely white. The woman, whoever she was, had no irises or pupils whatsoever. "Right!" Jack said, knowing better than to argue with a woman with no eyes. He lowered the wolf's leg back onto the bed, then ran for the door, leaping over a small cloud of whatever was coming from the Mirror.

It might have been his imagination, but the cloud almost looked like it grabbed for him as he jumped.

Phillip caught him on the other side and pulled him out the door, which slammed shut behind him. May was waiting a short distance away at entrance of the clearing, so the two joined her there.

"Who is that woman?" Jack asked the prince when they'd gotten a relatively comfortable distance away.

"We call her Merriweather," Phillip said, watching the cottage, "though I do not know if that is her real name."

"She's not human, is she," Jack said.

"No," the prince said. "She is a queen of the fairy folk. My father saved her life when I was very young, and she has watched over me ever since. She called herself my godmother, actually, when I was young." He frowned. "I wonder what the delay is."

"I am here," said the fairy queen from directly behind them. All three spun around to find her standing calmly with the Wolf King lying in the grass at her feet. The wolf was breathing hard, but it wasn't as labored as it had been. And he wasn't bleeding; in fact, his fur had grown back, and he seemed to be completely healed.

Jack's eyes went wide. "That's amazing," he said breathlessly.

The right side of Merriweather's mouth turned up the slightest bit. "Hardly," she said. "And I'd rather see the animal dead. Still, I did as my young prince requested. The animal will be fine . . . when it wakes." She bent down and picked up the wolf's chin, then let it drop back to the ground. The wolf never moved. "After healing the creature," she said, "I enchanted it to sleep, so that I'd have time to change your minds." She gave them all a hard look. "No good will come from this one, children. Its life has been one of hardship and lost love, and I do not know if it is capable of returning from such a dark place."

Jack didn't have any idea what to say to that, but before he could think of anything, Phillip grabbed his arm, spun him around, and pointed at the clearing. On Jack's other side, May gasped. As much as he knew he'd regret doing it, Jack reluctantly followed their gazes back to the cottage.

The greenish-yellow smoke was now visible through the windows, filling the entire cottage. Cracks appeared in the brick walls, and the wood in the roof began to crack, shrieking as if in pain.

The smoke continued to spread, the creaking growing louder and louder until finally the entire roof launched into the air, like a lid exploding off a pot of boiling water.

The roof spun as it shot into the air, rising in an arc that suddenly looked like it might land a bit too close to them for comfort. As the roof tumbled back down, heading straight for their group, Jack, May, and Phillip all jumped backward. Merriweather, however, didn't move. The roof crashed down a few inches from her foot, and the fairy queen didn't so much as flinch. Instead, she glanced down at it, then looked back up at the smoke and frowned. "Your Highness," she said to Phillip. "You are not safe here."

"She's quick, huh?" May whispered to Jack.

"What is it?" Phillip asked the fairy queen. As they spoke, the smoke seemed to be coalescing into some sort of shape, almost like . . . almost like a body, a torso.

Merriweather never took her eyes off the smoke as the sheer magnitude of it began to block out the sunlight. "It is a devil, plain and true," she said. "My people call them djinn, but I believe humans refer to them as genies." She narrowed her eyes. "This one is known to me. It is an Ifrit, one of the elders."

"You two have met?" May asked.

The fairy queen sighed. "I know the one who trapped it in the Mirror," she said. "Her folly invites ruin upon us all."

"An Ifrit," Jack said. "Is that more powerful than other genies?"

The fairy queen turned her white eyes on him, making him regret asking. "You might say that," she said. "The younger genies are close to being all-powerful, but are forced by their elders to learn humility through service to lesser beings, usually humans."

"How nice," May sniffed. "It's good to know where we stand in the grand scheme of things."

"Indeed," Merriweather said. "The elders, the Ifrits, are even more powerful than their young, and controlling them is next to impossible once they are let loose. Fortunately for our world, there have only been two who made their way here during my lifetime. This is the second."

"And the first?" Jack asked, watching as the genie's torso

filled in completely, the smoke now building arms the size of storm clouds. At the very top, almost too high to see, it looked as if a head might be forming.

"The first?" Merriweather said with the barest hint of a smile. "It's best that you not know, human. Your kind tends to react badly to their world almost being unmade. Fortunately, one of my fellow fairy queens tricked it into trapping itself within a kerosene lamp, then hid the lamp where no one will ever discover it."

"Bet someone finds it," May whispered to Jack.

Merriweather turned her gaze to the princess, her white eyes blazing in anger. Before May could say anything, though, Merriweather took a step back in surprise. "*You!*" the fairy queen shouted, her eyes wide.

May froze for a second, clearly just as surprised as the fairy queen. "Um, me?" she asked in a small voice. Jack inched between the two, not trusting this eyeless fairy queen at all.

"You!" Merriweather repeated, still in shock. "I *know* you! You were not where you were meant to be! I arrived at the appointed time, and you were not there!"

"Wha . . . ?" May said.

Suddenly, the fairy in May's hair sat up and waved her hands. Merriweather glanced at her.

"Little sister," the fairy queen said in greeting, and the fairy in May's hair began gesturing around, first at Jack, then at May, and back again. Somehow, Jack thought he heard her saying words, something about a "charmed one," but it must have been his imagination.

Then they all jumped as one of the Ifrit's expanding arms knocked a tree over on the other side of the clearing. "Can we talk about this later, whatever it is?" May said quickly. "'Cause, you know, I'd rather not get crushed by Mr. Smokey Pants here."

Merriweather shook her head at May. "You do not act like a princess should," she said, raising an eyebrow. "Clearly, your manners have suffered from our missed appointment. Still, there are more important matters to attend to now. If left unchecked, the Ifrit will surely destroy us all, if not this entire world."

"Merriweather," Phillip said softly. He gently took her shoulder and turned her back toward the genie, where eyes the size of small lakes stared down at them, each delving into a shade of black that Jack wouldn't have believed actually existed if he weren't staring at it. It was like he could feel the genie's eyes pulling at him, pulling at his very soul.

The face around the eyes resembled some kind of horned

mask, more than anything else, a mask that covered the front of the smoke head, while the rest of the head seemed to swirl around on its own. It reminded Jack uncomfortably of the witch with the broken eggshell for a face.

"I shouldn't have put the crown in, should I," May said. It wasn't a question.

"Merriweather," Phillip repeated, taking a few steps back, "I know that this creature is powerful, but are you able to . . . to fight it?" The perfect prince sounded nervous, and Jack wished they weren't all about to die so he could have enjoyed it more.

Merriweather looked at Phillip, then sighed. "I am sorry, Phillip. You promised to release me from my service if I healed this . . . creature," she said, pointing at the slumbering wolf. "And my debt to your father is paid. Still," the fairy queen said, glancing at May, "I do owe *this* one. If she wishes it, I could try to defeat the Ifrit. But that would then fulfill any responsibility I have to you as well, Princess."

Phillip glanced at May, looking for some kind of answer, despite it being clear that the prince had no idea what was going on. May didn't seem to be following any better, and jumped as if she were surprised to be called on. "Oh! Right!" she said quickly. "Yeah, go ahead and save us, that's great! You don't need to help me any more—saving our lives from the genie is enough. So . . . thank you?"

Merriweather smiled. "You obviously have no knowledge of what was meant for you, child. Someday, perhaps I shall tell you. However, if this is your wish, I shall grant it. Now, you three must flee while you can. I will make sure you have the chance."

Phillip nodded, then pulled the other two back toward the wolf. All three grabbed the animal's legs, and together they managed to pull him back a few feet into the dubious safety of the woods, as Merriweather boldly strode forward to stand on the fallen roof.

"*Ifrit!*" her voice rang out, startling Jack with its force. "*One of my kind imprisoned you long ago, and now I am here to send you back where you came from! Face me, coward!*"

And with that, she grew.

Her form grew slightly transparent as if she were also made of smoke, and she spread out more and more until she was the same size as the Ifrit. Then she solidified back into her normal, opaque body.

For its part, the Ifrit didn't seem to care about Merriweather's taunt. "*Little fairy,*" it said to her in a completely monotone yet booming voice, "*you do not know what you are attempting to do.*"

"Oh, I do," Merriweather said. "*I realize that you may destroy me, and if that is my fate, I welcome it. Come now, let us see if the vaunted reputation of the djinn is well deserved!*"

"Oh, what have I done!" Phillip said, fear filling his eyes as he looked at Jack and May. "She . . . I did not . . . I thought she could . . ."

Jack grabbed his shoulder and shook him, trying to either comfort the prince or shake some coherence back into him. "She's probably bluffing!" Jack said. "She wouldn't just throw her life away, no matter what she thought she owed May. What would be the point?"

Phillip shrugged off Jack's hand and took a step toward the cottage. "I do not care! I will not allow her to die for us! No one will die if I can help it!"

Jack jerked him back toward the woods. "That brings up an interesting question, Phillip! Namely, how are you supposed to help?! You're not going to do much good by standing there really still, are you?!"

Phillip struggled against Jack's grip, but Jack locked his arm around the prince's. "We have to *do* something!" Phillip cried.

Jack nodded. "That's right," he said, grunting at the effort it took to keep the prince from running off. Whatever else he might be, Phillip was *strong*. "We have to run, to get away," Jack continued. "If not, Merriweather might be sacrificing herself for nothing! We have to get out of here, and *now*, Phillip. Tell him, May."

When the princess didn't answer, Jack abruptly released Phillip, who fell forward in surprise.

"May?" Jack asked in a small voice. He looked all around the forest path, but the princess was gone.

"There!" Phillip shouted from the ground, pointing out toward the clearing. Jack glanced up to see May running as hard as she could, heading straight for the remains of the Red Hood's cottage.

A cottage that was going to be the center of the battle between a genie and Phillip's fairy godmother.

CHAPTER 28

May!" Jack screamed after her, but either she didn't hear him or didn't care, because she didn't even slow down. As he watched, May barreled into the roofless cottage, plowing right into the thick of the genie's smoke.

"What is she doing?!" Phillip yelled, but Jack didn't wait for the prince. Instead, he took off after the princess, sprinting as fast as he could. He barely heard Phillip swear from somewhere behind him, then race to catch up to Jack.

Running through the genie's body felt like pushing through heavy fog. It was much more solid than Jack would have expected. He threw a brief look above him as he passed through the smoke, just in time to see the Ifrit raise its hands, a tornado forming at the end of each.

Merriweather had her eyes closed, and seemed to be humming . . . only she was humming in harmony with herself, effortlessly voicing different parts of the same tune. As she hummed a long, silvery wand flickered into existence in her hand, and she pointed it at the genie.

And then both disappeared from view as Jack entered the cottage. As he skidded to a stop, a bit of the genie's smoke broke off from its body and clung to Jack's legs. Panicking for a moment, he frantically dusted it off him until he realized it wasn't trying to kill him.

Outside, a brilliant light lit up the windows, brighter than the sunlight had been before it was blocked out by the genie. Another flash, and the remaining smoke inside the cottage began to swirl around as if it were caught in a tornado.

And right at the eye of that tornado was May, running toward the cottage's door clutching the broken Mirror in her hands. She threw Jack a worried look as she blew past him, not even pausing on her way back out the cottage door. Jack threw up an arm to catch her, but she ducked under it, not stopping until she barreled right into Phillip, knocking both of them over.

"What are you *doing!*" Jack yelled to her over the wind, which was now strong enough to make him grab at the doorway to stay on his feet. May leapt up from the ground, but immediately almost lost her footing again in one of the stronger gusts. Jack caught her and steadied her, then reached out to help Phillip up, as well.

May screamed something at him, but he couldn't make it out over the wind. "What was that?!" he yelled back.

"I said, I'm *not* going to let her die for me!" May screamed in his ear. The princess then grabbed the Mirror from the ground where it had landed, pushed past Phillip, and ran off into the middle of the clearing, Jack right behind her.

Above them, tornadoes raged throughout the clearing, but they weren't just air: Somehow, the tornadoes seemed to be tugging at the edges of the sky, the land, everything, pulling it all in . . . at least, the tornadoes not aimed at Merriweather. Those seemed to be pulling the fairy queen apart from several sides, and everywhere they touched her, she turned transparent again as bits of her were pulled away from her body.

Merriweather snarled, her eyes glowing a blinding white, and her song grew louder. Now what had been one wand became ten, a hundred, maybe a thousand wands, all dancing faster than Jack could follow. The Ifrit burst into flame, and the sudden fire lit up the clearing. Merriweather's wands continued their dance through the air, conjuring up her next spell . . . only, the genie didn't give her the time. It reached out with its enormous hands and locked them around the fairy queen's throat, its masklike face contorted with rage.

On the ground, May skidded to a stop near the middle of the battle. Stray bolts of magical energy from the wands were flying around her on all sides, along with several small trees and huge clumps of earth that had been sent into flight by the tornado winds.

May planted her feet firmly, then quickly ducked under a bolt of energy that came within inches of splitting her head open. Just as Jack reached her, the princess pulled the crown out of the Mirror frame and held the Mirror aloft, its glass face pointed straight at the genie.

"*Hey, Ifrit!*" May screamed. "I pulled your plug. Time to say *good night!*" With a triumphant smile, she braced herself under the Mirror and waited for the genie to be sucked back in.

Of course, that didn't happen.

May, clearly frustrated, brought the Mirror down and stared at it, even shaking it a bit. Finally, she turned to find Jack and Phillip both staring in horror at the incredible chaos swirling around her. She ducked under a flying tree and took a step toward them. "It didn't work!" she yelled. "I took the crown back out, but the genie's not going back into the Mirror!"

Another bolt of magical energy crashed into the spot where she'd just been standing. May looked up, and the realization of what was going on all around her finally seemed to sink in. She threw the Mirror up over her head as if to cover herself from rain, but almost dropped it as Jack grabbed her arm, practically yanking it off in his effort to pull her to cover.

"What were you thinking?!" he yelled at her as he pulled her toward the forest.

"Don't act like you *knew* it wouldn't work!" she shouted over the wind, following closely behind him. "It made sense that he'd be sucked back in there!"

"Princess," Phillip shouted, struggling to be heard on her other side, "we have no idea what kind of spell imprisoned him within the Mirror. It was not necessarily logical that removing the crown—"

"You say that now!" May yelled. "But where were you when I was coming up with the plan?!"

Suddenly, the wind completely stopped; the remaining airborne trees and dirt crashed to the ground like deadly rain.

As the energy bolts continued to strike all around them Jack glanced up to see what was happening, and found himself looking straight into the burning white eyes of Merriweather. The fairy queen looked dazed as her hands struggled to free herself from the genie's grasp, yet she wasn't putting as much energy into it as she had been. She was losing her strength, and it looked as if the tornadoes had ripped off giant pieces of her body.

If the fairy queen failed, they were all dead. So why was she turning her attention from the Ifrit to look down at him?

Unless it wasn't him she was looking at.

As if she could hear his thoughts Merriweather smiled faintly, even showing some perfectly white teeth. Apparently she *did* know what he was thinking. Jack nodded up at her. If she could see him, she'd know he was ready.

Thinking the battle was almost over, the genie doubled his efforts. Magical energy from Merriweather's wands crashed into him—a last-ditch effort on Merriweather's part—but the Ifrit just shrugged it off. With a triumphant yet eerily monotone cry, it released Merriweather, letting her slump over. The genie then brought its hands up above its head and formed a circle with its fingers. An enormous ball of pure, burning light formed in the middle of that circle, which the genie held in his hands for a moment, savoring his victory.

Then it launched the light ball straight at the fairy queen. . . .

Except, she wasn't there. Jack blinked and looked again, but Merriweather was completely gone. The ball of light passed right through the spot where she'd been, incinerating a swath of forest at least a mile long in its wake.

Above him, the genie didn't seem to know where Merriweather was any more than Jack did. It glanced around, searching for its missing opponent, but found no one. Finally, as if to eliminate all options, it looked straight up. . . .

Just as blue cloth the size of the sky fell straight on top of the genie.

The blue cloth covered the Ifrit's head first before settling over its body and its arms, the sides of the cloth coming together at the bottom of the genie's smoky base. Within seconds, the Ifrit's entire body was enclosed by the blue covering.

First one, then the other of the genie's hands cut through the cloth, while its head pushed furiously against the top of the cloth, trying to break out. Before the genie's head could break through, though, the cloth began to shrink—slowly at first, then faster and faster. Even as the genie endeavored to free itself,

Merriweather steadily reduced both their sizes, shrinking as quickly as she'd grown.

And Jack was ready. He grabbed the Mirror from May's hand, then ran back to the spot where the princess had stood just a minute ago, a spot right beneath the steadily shrinking Ifrit and fairy queen. There, he lifted the Mirror above his head, just as May had. "*Merriweather!*" he shouted as loudly as he could.

What might have been an ethereal laugh from the fairy queen floated into his ear. The genie seemed to realize what was going on now, and frantically tried to escape, but it was too late. With a rush like the tornadoes of a moment ago, the Ifrit and Merriweather began swirling around and around, the point of their combined cyclone aimed directly at the Mirror.

When the tip of the genie-and-fairy-queen tornado hit the hole in the Mirror's glass, Jack almost fell over. The Mirror suddenly weighed dozens of times its usual weight! Jack's legs buckled under him and his arms strained like they never had before as the Mirror pushed down on him harder and harder.

Above him, the fairy queen couldn't do anything to help, as she was struggling to keep the genie in place while she pulled them both into the Mirror. And Jack knew he couldn't afford to drop it. One misstep would give the genie the distraction it needed. But there was no way he could hold the Mirror up for much longer.

And then May was at his side, grabbing one side of the Mirror. Phillip took the other side with a curt nod, and suddenly, the weight was bearable. All three braced themselves as Merriweather slowly pulled the shrieking genie back into its prison, the Magic Mirror.

To Jack, the process felt like it took hours, the two majestic creatures swirling around in an endless cyclone of rage and supernatural energy, the genie fighting for its freedom, the fairy queen struggling to save the lives of three teenagers. But in reality, it wasn't more than a few seconds before the genie let out one final shriek, and Merriweather sucked them both back into the Mirror.

And just like that, the Mirror was its normal weight again. Without the heft to balance against, all three of them lost their footing: Phillip tumbled to the ground while May and Jack both fell to their knees. Jack managed to hold on to the Mirror as he fell, narrowly saving it from further damage by hitting the cracked and broken ground.

After taking a deep breath, Jack rose shakily to his feet, then brought the Mirror up to his chest and held it so that they could all see what was happening. All the cracks had disappeared as if they'd never existed, while the hole from the crossbow's arrow had been filled in with what looked like a small piece of blue stained glass.

"Oh, Merriweather," Phillip said softly, dropping to his knees and bowing his head.

May, though, stared deep within the Mirror, her brow furrowed. She squinted her eyes a bit, then reached down and tapped the prince on his shoulder. "Look," she told him, pointing into the Mirror. "There's . . . there's something in there." And then, as if she didn't even realize she was doing it, May reached into her pocket, took out the crown necklace, and pushed it back into the top of the Mirror.

The now familiar green smoke filled the glass, but before it could cover the entire Mirror, blue bands of light shot out from behind it and wrapped themselves completely around the green smoke in several rings.

"She got him," May said softly. She looked up at Jack, and he saw that her eyes were wet.

Jack nodded. "She really did," he said, finding that he suddenly had no energy. "But it's not like she's gone, right? Maybe we can still get her out."

"That's right," Phillip said, gently touching the glass. He stared into it for a moment, then raised an eyebrow. "Merriweather?" he said, then cleared his throat and repeated her name in a voice that was loud enough to have been heard across the clearing.

The Mirror swirled, blue ribbons fighting with green smoke as both tried to push toward the front. Then, for the briefest of instances, Merriweather's face appeared. The fairy queen looked awful: Her beautiful face bubbled in and out of focus, and the look in her eyes made it clear that she was in pain as she continued her fight within the Mirror. The fairy queen locked eyes with Phillip for a brief moment and mouthed one word, but Jack couldn't recognize it. And then she was gone, the swirling green surrounding her and pulling her back into the Mirror's depth.

Phillip winced, then slowly pulled May's crown necklace off the Mirror. He handed her the necklace, then turned to face them, the Mirror hanging limply from his hand. The fairy in May's hair silently cried, her little body racked by noiseless tears.

"I heard Merriweather," the prince said. "I heard her within my head. She told me . . . she told me a name."

"A name?" Jack said. "For what?"

"Someone to help her?" May asked.

"I believe so," Phillip said, and then shook his head. "Though why this individual, of all the beings in the world . . ."

Jack waited for him to finish, but the prince just trailed off. Impatiently, Jack cleared his throat. When that didn't work, he whacked Phillip on the arm. "The name?" Jack said, his irritation growing.

Phillip sighed, his eyes haunted as he looked at Jack. "Malevolent," he said. "The name she told me was Malevolent."

"Malevolent?" May said. "Who's that?"

Jack shook his head. He'd never heard the name either.

"She's dead," growled a voice behind them. They all glanced over in surprise to find a very healthy-looking Wolf King staring at them with his glowing red eyes. "At least, she will be once I get ahold of her."

CHAPTER 29

Malevolent is a fairy queen," Phillip said after a hesitant look at the wolf. "A distant relative of Merriweather, though that could be the only thing they have in common. The stories I have heard of Malevolent's horrific deeds . . ." He shook his head sadly. "Still, if she is the only one who can save Merriweather, then to her we shall go."

"Wait a second," May said. "There are *evil* fairies? That doesn't seem right." She reached up to her head and patted the still grieving fairy sympathetically.

"It is *not* right," Phillip agreed. "But let us hope that the rumors of her wickedness are just that."

The wolf laughed, a sound like gravel rubbing against meaner gravel. "That creature is as evil as they come," he said. "She betrayed your grandmother, Princess, turning on her in her hour of need. She's most likely the reason your grandmother fled in the first place."

May's eyes went dead. "What did the fairy queen do?" she asked the wolf.

The animal just growled in response, shook his head, then turned and padded away. May and Jack turned to Phillip with a questioning look.

"I . . . do not know to what the Wolf King refers," the Prince said, "but I will tell you what I know of Malevolent. As you know, Merriweather watched over me for a great many years. During that time, I heard stories about the other fairy queens, often told to me by candlelight as I drifted off to sleep. However, there was one of her kind that she would not speak of, no matter how much I begged—a fairy queen of perfect features, every bit as cruel as she was beautiful."

"I knew girls like that," May said. "I'd trip them in the halls sometimes."

Phillip paused, threw her an odd look, then continued. "I learned about Malevolent from others, however. Stories of her vanity, her evil deeds. They say only one person has ever come close to matching her, and that's the Wicked Queen."

"Perfect," Jack said. "We could use a few more all-powerful enemies. Wouldn't want to get bored."

"I am afraid there is more bad news," the prince said, looking a bit embarrassed. "Malevolent . . . she despises my family in particular. The following events happened when I was but a baby, so I learned the details later: A neighboring kingdom to mine had just been gifted by the birth of a baby daughter. Seeking to unite our kingdoms, my father betrothed me to this girl—"

"Betrothed?" May repeated in surprise.

"It means engaged," Jack said, grinning widely.

May glared at him.

"Arranged marriages are quite common in our region, Princess," Phillip said, frowning disapprovingly at them both. "This royal family asked for the blessing of all the fairy queens at the birth of their children, hoping that each child would receive gifts beyond any that nature might bestow. However, at the birth of the king's first daughter, he erred, asking for the blessings of all the fairy queens except one."

"I think I see where this is going," May said, and Jack nodded in agreement. This sort of thing happened so often, you'd think people would learn.

"Yes," Phillip said. "Malevolent, enraged at what she perceived to be a lack of respect, stormed the castle during the baby's celebration, then cursed the child to die the day the baby girl turned fifteen by pricking her finger on a spindle."

"Nothing good ever comes from sewing," May said, shaking her head sympathetically.

"Indeed," Phillip agreed. "Still, Merriweather had yet to bless the child, and was able to transform Malevolent's curse from one of death to an eternal sleep instead. Meanwhile, the king attacked Malevolent for cursing his child, which enraged the fairy queen even more. Just as Malevolent was about to destroy the entire kingdom, Merriweather blocked Malevolent's spell. The two began a great battle that ended with Malevolent holding the upper hand over Merriweather. Before she could strike the final blow, however, my father stepped in."

"Brave guy," Jack murmured.

Phillip smiled. "You have no idea, friend Jack. My father struck Malevolent over the head with a spinning wheel, of all things, a gift for the king's daughter. This distraction gave Merriweather time to banish Malevolent from the castle. It was then that Merriweather vowed to watch over my father's family in thanks, promising to someday return the favor."

"So what happened to the baby girl?" May asked.

"No one knows," Phillip admitted. "The good fairy queens consulted with the king and my father, then disappeared with the child. No one has seen her since. We assume she's being protected from Malevolent, hidden away from spindles and curses."

"Sleeping babies aside, it sounds like Malevolent wouldn't be too thrilled with you just showing up," Jack said. "Or with helping Merriweather, for that matter. But why would Merriweather have given you Malevolent's name, then? It sounds like she's almost the *worst* person we could ask for help."

Phillip shrugged. "That, I do not know," he said. "Perhaps Malevolent is the only one with enough power to save Merriweather?"

"Maybe," Jack said. "First we have to find her, though."

"Do not worry," Phillip said. "All children in my kingdom know of the fairy queen's castle. It sits atop an island in the sky on the eastern shore, formed of lava and maliciousness. Parents told us stories to scare us into eating our vegetables."

"Vegetables *can* be scary," May said, frowning. "This castle, though, sounds pretty much par for the course for us. So, I guess we know where we're going next."

"But how do we get there?" Jack asked. "We don't have time to

trek across the world, not with Snow White most likely being—"
He stopped and glanced at May. "Being, uh, held prisoner," he
stammered. "She needs to be rescued *now*."

"We passed a river on the way here," May suggested. "If the
castle's on the shore, maybe we could build a boat or something,
float down the river to the ocean?"

Phillip and Jack just stared at her.

"What?" she said, raising an eyebrow. "You two aren't afraid
of water, are ya?" She smiled mockingly at them.

"Afraid of water?" Jack said. "No. Afraid of the things that
live *in* the water? Terrified."

"What," May said, "like fish?"

"On the bottom half, yes!" Jack said with a shudder.

"Princess," Phillip said, stepping between them. "Jack is right:
Traveling by water would be suicide."

He was right. After all, giants, witches, and genies were one
thing. But mermen? Those things were something else *entirely*.

"Worry not, children," the wolf said. "I know the location
of Malevolent's castle, and I can carry you three once more. I'm
healed enough for that." The animal smiled, showing far too
many teeth. "I can even protect you from the fish-men, if that is
your worry."

"Mermaids?" May asked incredulously. "You're afraid of mermaids?!"

"Mer*men*," Jack corrected. "No one's seen a mermaid in like fifty years. Since that day, the mermen have been hunting down anything that goes within five feet of the water's edge. I know people who won't even go outside if it rains."

"I give up," May said. "I'm just gonna have to see one, I guess."

The wolf smiled again. "By the time you saw one, it would be far too late. Now, are we finally ready to run?"

CHAPTER 30

The ride to Malevolent's castle combined at least three of Jack's top ten least favorite things. Between holding on to the wolf for dear life, infrequent stops for too little rest, and stopping for those rests on the riverside and catching glimpses of yellow eyes and hideous looking claws in the water, it all blended together into an unholy nightmare that Jack was only too glad to put behind him.

The only problem was, by putting the ride behind him, he was forced to look ahead to dealing with Malevolent. That reality hit hard when they finally reached the castle right as the sun giant in the sky began to lower his burning orb to the ground, giving up for the day.

Malevolent's palace sat atop a large island of land hundreds upon hundreds of feet in the air, supported by a fragile rock base rising out of the ocean. The castle itself had been built in the shape of a snarling dragon, with the head directly across from what looked to be half a bridge jutting up from the forest. Jack wondered if the dragon's lower jaw might actually be a drawbridge; it certainly was in the right place.

On either side of the head, the dragon's front legs were raised in the air as if ready to clamp down on intruders. The dragon's claws acted like ramparts, perfect for defense. Rock spines covered the back of the dragon, the larger ones creating towers that rose above the main castle-body. At the very back of the castle, the dragon's tail stuck straight into the air, with the end of the tail forming yet another tower, this one with a lit window at its peak.

All in all, it was very creepy, very intimidating, and *very* high up.

"First problem," Jack said, nodding at the castle. "Anyone have any ideas how to get up there?"

"We could fly up on the broomstick," Phillip suggested, which seemed logical enough. The logic only held until the part where they dropped like a stone from five feet in the air, the broom not able to hold all three of them.

"Phillip," May said sweetly from the ground, "if you ever make another suggestion like that, I'm going to have to hurt you."

"Could we climb up the side?" Jack asked dubiously. The island's overhang would most likely make it impossible, but for some reason, Jack didn't see Malevolent lowering the drawbridge for them.

"Whatever we do," May said, "I think it's going to have to wait until morning." She squinted as darkness fell over the beach. "I can barely see you guys, let alone a way to get up there."

"If we flew up now, Princess, we could use the dark to our advantage," Phillip suggested.

"Honestly, Phillip," May said. "I'm going to shove the broomstick right up your—"

"I think we should wait too," Jack agreed quickly. "It's too dark to see what we're doing, and it's definitely too dark to be breaking into *that*," he said, pointing at the castle. The whole thing was much too real-looking for Jack's taste. The dragon's fangs even glistened in what sunlight remained, while its claws, some kind of lava stone like the rest of the castle, looked lifelike enough to skewer a giant through the heart.

All in all, waiting until daylight seemed like a good idea.

They didn't dare light a fire, not this close to Malevolent's castle. Instead, they ate fruit from Phillip's bag and tried to make themselves comfortable on the beach. The Wolf King left them to hunt for his own food, promising to keep watch over them. For some reason, that didn't make Jack feel much safer.

"He's really not into the whole protecting thing, is he?" May said.

"He did lead us to the Mirror," Jack said. "Without that, we'd have had no idea where to find it . . . you know, to break it."

"Sometimes I can't believe any of this is real," May said, lying down on her side with one arm supporting her head, staring into the distance. "I mean, I can't even believe my grandmother is trapped somewhere, maybe hurt, maybe . . ."

Jack and Phillip glanced at each other, and both moved closer to May to offer what little support they could.

"She's the sweetest woman," May continued, still staring at nothing. "She taught me to be my own person, but she was still there to support me when I needed it. And her laugh . . ." May smiled at the thought. "Such a beautiful laugh. So full of life."

The fairy in her hair patted May's head, and May absently patted her back.

"I know how you feel, Princess," Phillip said. "I miss my father every day. I miss my mother as well, though she is safely back in my kingdom. Still, I couldn't just stay there, not with my father's death to avenge." Phillip sighed. "Besides, my mother kept pushing me to hold a royal ball to find a wife."

"Ah!" Jack said. "So the real reason comes out finally!"

"Not true!" Phillip said. "Justice comes first, of course! It . . . it was just a convenient time to go. Still, once I find the giant that murdered my father, I will be ready to settle down and marry." He gave May a meaningful look, which she didn't see. Jack, however, saw enough for everyone, and moved the conversation back to a safer topic.

"So what happened to your father?" Jack said quickly. "Who is this giant? Where did he come from? Tell us *everything*, Phillip."

"There is little to tell," the prince said. "My father was known far and wide for his giant-slaying skills. Therefore, when a giant began rampaging in a kingdom miles from home, word came to my father requesting aid. He bravely set out to slay the beast, but the creature was too much for him, and he was slain. To this day, I know little more about the giant than what details were in the message my father received."

"What were the details?" May asked.

"The giant apparently lived in a castle in the clouds," Phillip said, "and a thief broke into his home and stole some items of great worth."

Jack suddenly froze in place, but Phillip didn't notice. "In chasing the thief," the prince continued, "the giant rampaged across kingdom after kingdom, killing many, including my father, before escaping to parts unknown."

"So," Jack said as calmly as he could, "what kinds of things did the thief steal from the giant?"

"Priceless trinkets and such," Phillip said. "A harp that sang the most perfect melodies. A bag of gold bigger than the thief's head."

"And a goose that laid golden eggs?" Jack said, almost off-handedly.

Phillip's head shot up. "Why, yes! How did you know?"

Jack cringed. "I think I know who the thief was."

"How?" Phillip said. "I would as soon bring him to justice as the giant, for both were equally to blame in my father's death!"

"Good luck with that," Jack said very softly. "No one's seen my father for years."

The entire camp went silent, and Jack found that he had some trouble breathing.

"Your . . . father?" Phillip said, a torment of emotions flooding his face.

"My father, yes," Jack said, avoiding Phillip's gaze. "Believe me, you can't hate him any more than I do."

"I think you might be mistaken," Phillip said softly.

"Uh, let's all calm down," May said, moving between the two boys. "How could anyone know who did what so long ago?"

"My father broke into the castle of a giant who lived in the clouds," Jack said. "He stole a magical harp, a bag of gold, and a goose that could lay golden eggs. The broken harp is still at my grandfather's house, May. It was him."

"Because your father stole from this giant, my father was murdered," Phillip said, his voice very quiet.

May looked between them quickly, then laid a hand on Phillip's arm. "Listen, how could Jack's father even get up there? I don't know if you've ever looked at them, but the clouds aren't exactly close. Not to mention that they're just water vapor, so you can't exactly build a castle on them, let alone walk—"

"He climbed up," Jack said. "He climbed up a magical plant."

"A what?" May and Phillip said together, their confusion harmonizing nicely.

"He climbed a beanstalk," Jack said. "He traded the family cow for some magic beans that were supposed to make him rich. Turns out they could have, given that one giant bean could feed a family for years. My grandmother tossed them out the window, though, pretty annoyed at her son for trading away their only cow for some potentially normal beans. The next morning, there it was, a beanstalk ladder to the clouds."

"So the giant pursued your father, ravaging whole kingdoms to find him while he hid like a coward?" Phillip sneered.

"Pretty much," Jack admitted. "And 'coward' is putting it lightly. Still, that was probably the smartest thing he ever did, as it at least saved my grandmother."

"At the price of my father's life," Phillip said, rising to his feet.

"Whoa!" May said, standing up too. "Phillip, none of this is *Jack's* fault. And Jack, stop telling him all this!"

"Why?" Jack said, standing up as well. "He deserves to know. And if I were him, I'd beat me up too."

"No one's beating anyone up!" May said.

Phillip growled. "Of course not. Jack, I formally challenge—"

"No formal challenges, either!" May yelled. "Besides, I think you're all missing the big picture here!"

Both boys turned to her while May grabbed Jack's grandfather's bag and rummaged through it. Finally, she pulled out what looked like a tiny round seed.

"Don't you see?" she said. "We've got a way to get to Malevolent's castle!"

"But—," Phillip said.

"May, you don't know—," Jack said.

"Shut up!" May shouted. "I'm not going to let you two fight over something this stupid! Phillip, you can't blame Jack for something his father did. Jack, stop trying to work out your father issues through Phillip."

"Wait, what?" Jack said, but May didn't let him continue.

"My grandmother needs our help, and this is how we're going to do it!" May said, handing Jack the last of his father's magical beans. "Now, help me dig a hole; we're going to need to aim this just right."

CHAPTER 31

It didn't very take long for the bean to take root in the sand below Malevolent's castle. It took even less time for the first sprout to break through the dirt with a loud pop, startling a nearby blackbird from its sleep.

"Wow!" May said as she bent over to stare at the sprout. "That was quick! How long do you think it'll—"

A second sprout interrupted her, popping up right between her feet. "Whoops!" she yelled, jumping backward. Jack and Phillip both stepped back a few paces as well, giving the plant more room. That turned out to be a good thing, as five more sprouts immediately broke through the sand where the teenagers had just been standing.

"How many shoots will it grow?" Phillip asked suspiciously. "The bean did not appear to be that large. . . ."

"Four beans went all the way into the clouds," Jack said, eyeing the shoots. "One bean should be plenty to get us up to the castle."

"I'll never get used to this," May said as the sprouts grew under the moonlight. "I mean, shouldn't it need sunlight? Right, sorry. Magic."

As the first bean sprouts grew larger, more and more popped up through the sand, each one inching up toward the sky. Proving it was only a matter of time, the first sprout tipped over and curled right into its neighbor. Without even pausing, the two sprouts spiraled around each other, then branched off together in a third direction.

It didn't take the other sprouts long to push their way into the mix as well, and soon a relatively thick vine made up of dozens of smaller shoots rose into the sky. Other individual sprouts still grew on their own, but most seemed to gravitate toward the larger vine.

"Maybe we should give it more room?" Jack said nervously, glancing down at the ground beneath them. There was no telling what was forming underneath the sand and might burst out at any second.

"It's not *that* big," May said, reaching out to touch a leaf on the larger vine as it rose quickly beyond her grasp. "Do you think we should grab on at some point?" she asked. "It'd save us the climb."

"Perhaps we ought to wait until it has finished growing?" Phillip asked nervously, looking a bit green himself as more and more shoots twisted and wrapped themselves around the larger vine, moving like the grotesque tentacles of some foul squid.

"Why wait?" Jack said. "You're not scared of a little plant, are you, Phillip?" He tossed a challenging look back at the nervous prince.

Phillip just glared at him. Jack smiled in response. "Fine, you wait down here," he said. "I'll go save Merriweather." Quickly checking to make sure his bag and sword were secure on his back, Jack readied himself, waved to Phillip and May, then took a running jump straight at the vine.

He slammed into the plant a bit harder than he would have liked, considering he was going for an impressively easy sort of look, but at least he managed to find a fairly secure shoot to grab ahold of before he lost his grip. Jack's feet kicked around for a brief moment before finding a shoot strong enough to stand on, but that was all he needed to hold himself up.

By the time Jack secured himself and looked back down to the beach, he found himself ten feet above May's and Phillip's heads. "Come on!" he shouted down to them. "You'll miss your ride!"

May shouted in excitement, then took a running leap onto the beanstalk as well, landing much more gracefully than Jack had. Phillip hesitated, then took a deep breath and followed the princess. Jack noticed with more than a little annoyance that the prince landed on the rising vine absolutely perfectly, as if he did this sort of thing every day.

"Should we have told the wolf what we're doing?" May shouted up to Jack.

"I think he'll be able to figure it out!" Jack yelled. He glanced down past May and Phillip to see if he could locate the wolf from this height, but he was already higher than he'd thought and couldn't make out much on the ground in the dark. Suddenly, Jack felt dizzy, and for a brief moment, he almost lost his grip. He quickly shook off the feeling and threw both arms around the vine, resolving not to look down again for the rest of the trip.

Unfortunately, up wasn't looking much better, as Jack quickly realized.

"Uh-oh!" he shouted.

"What!" May said.

"I think we aimed badly!" Jack shouted back.

"Did we miss the castle?" Phillip yelled up.

"Oh, we're going to hit it all right," Jack said with a wince. "Just hold on! Make sure you're secure down there!" Without waiting for a response, Jack quickly followed his own advice, wrapping stray shoots around his arms and kicking his legs through some other loops. It wasn't much, but it was all he could do under the circumstances. Feeling a bit more secure, he glanced upward again.

As they'd seen from the beach, the castle sat on an island in the sky, an island supported by a very narrow column of stone. That meant the sides of the island hung far out over the ocean and beach, nowhere close to the supportive stone column in the middle of the island. When planting the magic bean, they'd tried to aim for the very edge of the island's overhang, considering they would have to jump from the beanstalk to the castle.

Unfortunately, aiming a magical beanstalk wasn't the easiest thing in the world to do. Instead of pulling up *next* to the overhang, it appeared as if the beanstalk was headed straight for it.

As Jack watched with growing apprehension, the first shoots reached the bottom of the overhang. Pushing up into the rock, the shoots curled back over themselves when they couldn't move the stone. Fortunately, those first strands didn't have the support of the main shoot, which itself was about two seconds away from reaching the overhang.

"*Brace yourselves!*" Jack shouted down as the main beanstalk connected with the cliff. Instantly the entire stalk shuddered sickeningly, shaking and vibrating all over the place. Even worse, the shaking was soon followed by a rather horrifying cracking noise from the overhang.

Small rocks began to tumble down all around Jack. He held on to the vine as tightly as he could, his eyes firmly closed as he desperately hoped that the beanstalk would just push up and around the overhang, leaving the rock intact.

Instead, the overhang decided to kill Jack's hopes by cracking right in half with a sound like thunder. The shock of the break sent the beanstalk into brutal convulsions, shaking Jack right off the plant. As he tumbled backward his eyes opening wide in shock, his heart pounded louder in his ears than the rock breaking above him.

Fortunately, the loops around his legs held firm, and instead of falling completely off the beanstalk, Jack found himself suspended upside down over nothing. He quickly threw a hand back into the vine, grabbed the center stalk, and jerked himself back in, just as the broken half of the overhang plummeted down past him, right through the spot where his body had been a second ago.

As Jack's toes went numb at the thought of what had almost just happened he managed to scream out a warning to May and Phillip, knowing in his heart that he was already much too late. A second later he heard the rock explode as it hit the sand below.

"Are you *kidding* me with that?!" May shouted up at him. "Could you maybe not drop anything else?!"

"To be fair, Jack was not at fault," Phillip said in response. "Not *this* time, at least."

"She knows that, idiot!" Jack yelled down. "Stay close to the vine. It's not done!"

After the largest piece broke off, smaller but no less deadly bits of rock tumbled down past Jack, each one falling with enough force to split his head open. The deadly rock shower soon slowed, then stopped completely, fortunately leaving him with nothing more than some bruises. The beanstalk, though, hadn't stopped growing, and was pushing right up through the newly created edge of the overhang. As he rose toward it Jack watched the rock carefully, making sure he knew exactly when to jump.

"The edge of the island is on May's side, Phillip!" he yelled down. "Both of you, watch out for it!" As he said this it occurred to him that he himself had to get to the other side of the beanstalk. Unfortunately, the thing was growing so fast, he didn't have very much time to decide how exactly to do that. He threw a leg around to the other side of the beanstalk, quickly located a sprout that hopefully would support his weight, and stepped down.

It held. He sighed, then moved his other leg around. The first step had taken him halfway around, but the overhang had just passed right by him. As he frantically searched for another foothold with his right foot he watched the overhang fall away as the stalk continued growing.

There really was no choice. Jack sighed, closed his eyes, and threw himself off the beanstalk.

His fall ended with a shoulder-crunching landing on the overhang. The pain caused him to bite down hard on his lip, but overall, he counted himself lucky. After all, if he had missed, it was a long way down, and frankly, he had already taken far too many falls from great heights in the past few days.

Jack pushed himself to his feet just as May's head popped up past the edge of the overhang. She smiled as she rose up and easily stepped off the beanstalk onto the overhang.

"That wasn't too bad," May said. Jack couldn't bring himself to return her grin as he felt around his body to see if anything had broken. A few seconds later Phillip rose up past the overhang, stepping off just as neatly as May had.

"Quite a nice way to travel," the prince said. Jack just shook his head and wondered what kind of supreme being would allow this sort of injustice. He started to say something, then noticed that Phillip had frozen in place and was staring at something behind Jack.

On his other side May seemed to have seen the same thing. "Yup, that's just about our luck," she said quietly.

Jack whipped his head around to see what she was talking about, then sighed deeply. Six lumbering goblins covered in black armor strode toward them in the moonlight. All six held swords easily as long as the goblins were tall, and all six swords were pointing at Jack, May, and Phillip.

Even as Jack frantically tried to come up with a plan, May clapped a hand on his shoulder. "I got this one," she said confidently. The princess stepped past him, then raised her hand, palm out. "*Stop!*" she roared.

Immediately, the group of goblins stopped in their tracks. Jack stared at them in surprise for a second, then realized that the creatures most likely didn't know what May planned to use that hand for. After all, the goblins knew as well as anyone that palms could be awfully dangerous in the wrong hands, so to speak. If she was a witch or magician of some kind, she might be casting a spell.

"What're you doing?" Jack whispered out of the side of his mouth.

"Getting us inside," May responded in the same way. "Hear me, Creepy Little Monster-Thingers!" she shouted to the goblins. "Take us to your leader! Take us to Malevolent! We have important information for her!"

The goblins looked at one another, then smiled. One of the larger ones took a step forward. "Gladly," it said.

"Well, *good!*" May responded. "It's nice to finally meet some reasonable people here!"

"But first," the bigger goblin said, "we'll take you to the dungeon. You'll see our Lady, all right . . . in a few hundred years."

And then the goblins attacked.

CHAPTER 32

Jack slowly opened his eyes to find himself in a strangely familiar place. Behind him, the leaves of a large oak tree filled the sky, while golden grasses waved in the gentle wind at his feet. For the life of him, though, he couldn't remember what this place was, or how he'd gotten here. The last Jack remembered, the goblin guards had swarmed over them from every side. One had lifted its sword and brought it down . . .

Oh, right, brought it down straight onto Jack's head.

Jack felt around the back of his skull, then winced as he found the spot the goblin had hit. It didn't hurt, exactly; it was more like a memory of a pain. Well, at least that explained why he had his eyes closed—the creature had knocked him unconscious. But hadn't it been nighttime before? Here, the sun burned high in the sky, causing the grasses to glow a calming green.

How exactly had he gotten from Malevolent's castle to this field? And why was it so hard to think clearly?

"I see you've returned," said a man in a blue cloak on Jack's right. As Jack turned, the memory of his last dreamlike encounter with the man flooded into his foggy consciousness. Unfortunately, just as it had the last time, the situation seemed much too surreal to take very seriously.

"That's right," Jack responded, finding himself oddly happy despite a nagging feeling that something was deeply, deeply wrong.

The knight leaned over and looked closely at Jack, as if the man were peering right into him. "Your training progresses slowly," he said. "I assume there is no cause for worry?"

"Worry?" Jack asked, confused. "Training?"

"You haven't been making use of your sword as you should have, Jack," the knight said with a touch of disappointment. "That sword is a powerful tool; it can help to awaken the world around you, if you let it."

"The sword?" Jack furrowed his brow. "But the sword . . . it's . . ." He struggled with what he wanted to say, but in the end just gave up and went for the obvious. "It's bad."

The knight laughed. "It certainly has the possibility for evil, I'll grant you that. And most of the Eyes did use their weapons for horrible deeds. But the sword can be used for great good, in the hands of the right person." He glanced momentarily at Jack. "I do hope I haven't chosen wrongly. Still, you must be careful. There are those in the world who would turn you from your path."

"My path?" Jack asked. Why was it so hard for him to think here?

The knight nodded. "You walk a dangerous road, my young friend. Few have the courage to walk it, and all before you have failed, including myself. You are our last chance."

"Chance?" Jack asked. "It's . . . hard to think."

"You will get used to it as time passes," the knight said. "This is a realm of great potential, yet you haven't reached the point where you might take advantage of it. For now it provides a convenient place for us to meet. Soon, it shall be more . . . when you are *ready*."

Jack didn't even bother asking about any of that, instead going back to a previous question. "What . . . what is my path?"

The knight raised an eyebrow, then leaned in close. "Why, just what you believe it to be. You are on a quest to save Snow White, are you not?"

Jack nodded slowly.

The knight smiled. "I cannot think of a more important one," he said. Abruptly, his smile vanished. "However, you must heed this word of warning—"

Before the knight could finish, a sharp pain struck Jack in the spot where the goblin had hit him. He hissed in pain, then looked to the knight. "I . . . I think I might be waking up now."

The knight looked concerned. "Oh, you *are* waking up," he said. "Yet not nearly fast enough. And the Wicked Queen *knows* you, Jack. She has always known, and she awaits your arrival. However, she doesn't yet realize that I have found you first. And you must keep that from her, Jack, above all else. If she learns that I am training you, all will be lost. There would be nowhere you could run, nowhere you could hide from that woman."

And with that, the knight sat back against the tree. As Jack tried to fight through the fog in his head to ask something, anything, about what the knight had just said, the grass and sunlight began to swirl around in front of his eyes. Faster and faster they whirled until the bright colors drained away, leaving just the dark unknown of his unconsciousness, tainted by a throbbing pain at the back of his head.

CHAPTER 33

Jack?" someone whispered.

Jack groaned but didn't open his eyes. The pain in the back of his head pounded away, threatening to magnify dramatically if he so much as cracked his eyelids. And what if he *did* open his eyes, and he was still in a meadow?

No, that had been a dream . . . but where had the dream actually started? Had he dreamed the entire beanstalk mess? Maybe he could just go back to sleep and let this whole nightmare end on its own.

"*Jack!*" the voice whispered again, louder this time. "Wake up!"

"I knew you were gonna say that," Jack grunted, then cracked his eyes open. Instantly he closed them: Some kind of floating globe of light was shining right in his face, blinding him. More cautiously this time, he tilted his head to the side and opened his eyes again.

Not only was there a light but bars, too. Big metal bars. They'd been thrown in jail by the goblins, as promised. At least the monsters were reliable.

"May?" Jack asked, reluctantly pushing himself to a sitting position. He glanced around his cell and quickly spotted her staring at him from the next cell over, just to the left of the floating will-o'-the-wisp globe that eerily lit the cells.

"About time you woke up!" she said indignantly. "I've been sitting here for hours!"

"Did they hit you, too?" Jack asked, lightly rubbing the back of his head, then resolving not to do that anymore when new pain shot through his temples.

"Well, no," May said. "They didn't touch me."

Jack nodded. That was something.

"I'm still annoyed, though," May said, standing up with her hands on her hips. "I mean, what kind of guards don't take you to the person in charge?!"

"Yeah, evil monsters not listening to you—who could have predicted that?" Jack asked, taking a quick look around his jail cell.

Greenish hay filled one corner, probably for sleeping on. Nice of his jailers to throw him onto the hard ground in the middle of the room instead of onto the hay. An old wooden bucket sat in the opposite corner, the one nearest a barred window at the rear of the cell.

"Great," he said, shaking his head. "How do we manage to hit the worst possible outcome in every situation?"

"We'll just talk our way out," May said, though she didn't sound too convinced.

Jack raised an eyebrow. "Talk to who?"

"The guard, a judge, Malevolent . . . someone! They can't just leave us here!"

"Oh, really?" Jack said, then nodded toward the cell on his right. May strained to see what he meant, then gasped.

"Is that a skeleton?" she said, cringing.

"Yup," Jack said. "He probably should have tried talking his way out."

"Don't make me come over there," May said, banging on the bars between them. Then she gasped suddenly, jumping backward. "Jack! I saw something moving!"

"Don't worry," Jack said, following her gaze. "It's just rats. Where's Phillip?"

"No clue," May said. "I haven't seen anyone but you. Well, and now that guy. And the rats."

Jack nodded and stood up, bracing himself against the walls. The room chose that moment to sway and spin, apparently just to spite him. He shook off the dizziness and set to work.

"What're you doing?" May asked Jack as he bent over and stared into each corner of the cell.

"There's always one in these places, just watching for someone interesting," he said. "They can't resist checking out the new people. You just have to find . . . *aha*." He reached into the corner with the bucket and grabbed ahold of what looked to be a long white thread. As he yanked on it the thread pulled up a tassel, which topped a funny little red hat.

Which, in turn, sat on top of an imp's tiny, pointed head.

Jack dragged the creature out of its hiding place and held it in midair.

"*Let me go!*" the imp screamed, desperately clutching its red hat with little, white-knuckled fists as it kicked at Jack with all its strength. The imp's furious face scrunched up as tightly as it could, considering its beard was tucked into its bright blue pants, a color that happened to go nicely with its shockingly goldenrod tunic.

Jack held the imp out at arm's length, both to keep the creature from biting him and to avoid the smell. Maybe the corner with the waste bucket wasn't the smartest place to live.

"Release me!" the imp said, struggling even more viciously.

"No," Jack said simply. "You're going to help us first. I'll let you go when you agree to free the princess there."

"Oh, a princess!" the imp said, immediately stopping its struggle with a big grin. "Put me down, let me get a look at her!"

Jack smiled. "I'll put *you* down, but your hat's mine, just in case you're thinking about running." He jerked his arm, ripping the hat off the imp's head and tossing the little creature to the floor. Before it even hit the ground, the imp started screaming obscenities, its face an unnaturally bright purple, but Jack just shrugged.

"I'm keeping your hat until you get her out of here," he said calmly.

The imp stopped swearing. "I'll help her out of here all right . . ." A smile slowly made its way over the imp's beady little face.

"Again, no," Jack said. "You'll put her out there on the floor, right outside our jail cells. You will not alert the guards or do anything else to put her in danger. Also, you will not turn her into a frog or shrink her to the size of a mushroom. You will put her outside the cell without changing or hurting her in any way. Do we understand each other?"

The imp stamped its foot. "You humans have become far too clever to be any fun." Then it smiled again. "But what about you, fine sir? You said you would give me my hat back if I freed her, yet you'll still be stuck in this dank, dreary cell! What deal will you strike for your *own* freedom?"

"No deal," Jack said, his eyes narrowing. "She'll find a way to get me out."

The imp managed to look indignant. "You wound me, good sir! I could easily grant your freedom from this cell and ask nothing in return!"

"That sounds good, we'll take that!" May yelled from the other cell before Jack could stop her.

Jack groaned all the way down to his feet. "Oh, *May*," he said, shaking his head.

"Deal!" the imp said, jumping forward to seize May's hand, which it pumped furiously up and down. "And now, I shall grant his freedom, yes, and for no price! However . . ."

The imp snapped its fingers, and suddenly Jack was hanging in midair outside the castle, a few feet from the barred window and hundreds of feet above the ocean below.

Jack glanced around fearfully and swallowed hard. The rest of the castle was below him; he was hanging outside the very top of the tower in the tail of the dragon. Apparently, the lit window they'd seen from the ground had been the jail.

"*Jack!*" May screamed from inside the tower.

The imp's eyes burned with greed as they stared at the princess. "Let's just say that if you want me to *not* release him at this point, milady, we'll have to make a second deal."

May grabbed the imp by its white hair and smashed its head straight into the bars of her cell over and over. "*Get him back in here!*" she screamed.

The imp howled in pain. Outside, Jack abruptly dropped a few feet. As Jack shouted in surprise May dropped the imp, who instantly collected itself.

"That's a no-no, milady," the imp said, a cold gleam in its eyes. "Wouldn't want me to lose concentration and drop our hero boy, now would we?"

"What do you want!" Jack yelled from outside. "What's the deal?!"

The imp jumped up to the windowsill. "I'm a creature of few desires, good sir," it said. "Why, I'd be perfectly satisfied with, say, both your arms."

Jack shook his head in disgust. The imp shrugged, and Jack dropped a few more feet, making him yell out again despite himself.

This really wasn't going well at all. "What else?!" Jack said, trying to keep his voice calm but failing miserably.

The imp thought about it for a second. "You could hand over that pretty set of teeth," it said. "Or an ear . . . an ear and an eye!" Its eyes lit up all of a sudden. "*Oooh*, I'll take every other word from the princess's tongue! That would serve me *quite* well! One can never have too many words, after all!"

Jack shook his head again, and this time dropped out of sight of the window, coming to a stop about halfway down the dragon's tail. May screamed his name, but he waited to respond until he could hear her over the sound of his heartbeat. "I'm okay!" he yelled finally. "You know, relatively! I'm actually a little scared for some reason!"

"I figured that out!" May yelled in reply as the imp floated Jack back up to the tower's window.

Clearly, the imp had them. But maybe there was still a way out? Jack quickly ran through the stories he'd heard. What about . . . no, they didn't have a chicken. Or . . . wait, what about . . . "A contest!" Jack yelled.

"I know better than to fall for that," the imp said disgustedly. "A cousin of mine taught a girl to spin straw into gold once, if she would give up her firstborn child. The girl agreed at first, then reneged on the deal—typical human. Being the kindhearted imp my cousin was, he agreed to one of your foolish contests. If she could but guess his name, he'd let her keep her gold *and* her child. The girl cheated, of course, as you people always do, and won." The imp's nostrils flared as it continued. "Then the bitter little witch had her husband, the prince, rename every city in their miserable little kingdom by my cousin's name! He's a laughingstock to this day! He even had to exile himself to regain his dignity!"

May looked from Jack to the imp and back, and her eyes went wide. "Mr. Little Imp-Man, sir?" she said. "Can I *offer* something?"

"May! Don't!" Jack yelled, but the imp just waved its hand and Jack dropped halfway down the tower again.

Even though he couldn't see her, he could still hear the shake in May's voice. "Okay, *first* of all," she screamed, "you're gonna have to stop dropping him like that!"

The imp shrugged, and Jack reappeared outside the window.

"*Thank* you," May said, sighing in relief. "Now, I have something to offer you if you'll bring him back in."

"Is it your skull?" the imp said, licking its lips. "The skull of a princess is a delicacy, you know."

May stared at the thing in shock for a moment, then shook her head. "Ah . . . no," she said. "I have something much more valuable. Something I use each and every day. Something more *important* to me than my very life!"

The gleam in the imp's eye almost lit up the room. Jack started to say something to stop the princess, but she threw him a quick look that told him to stay out of it. He slowly shut his mouth, hoping she knew what she was doing.

"I'll give you . . . ," May said, then paused and leaned in close to the imp, who obediently followed suit. "I'll give you . . . my *sarcasm*," she whispered.

The imp's smile slowly faded, and it pulled back away from her. "Your . . . sarcasm?"

"Yes," May said, wiping a fake tear from her eye. "I don't know if I can live without it! I'll just have to do my best!"

"But . . . but princesses don't use sarcasm!" the imp protested.

"Oh, yeah, they *never* do," May said.

"Wow," the imp said, visibly impressed. "That's pretty good!"

"Who'd have thought a girl like me would know anything about *sarcasm*!" May continued, snorting a bit.

"You are incredible!" the imp said. It was jumping up and down now. "Such a natural!"

"It must be because I'm having so much *fun* right now!" May said, rolling her eyes.

"You've got a deal!" the imp screamed delightedly.

It snapped its fingers, and Jack instantly appeared back in the cell. The imp snapped again, and a bluish light appeared over May's head. The light shone briefly, changing from blue to green, then disappeared. A second light, this one green, appeared over the imp's hatless skull, then turned blue and also faded away.

Jack gritted his teeth and leapt for the imp, but the creature made as if to snap his fingers again, and Jack stopped short. "You little *monster*," Jack growled, more furious than he'd ever been. "If you've taken *anything* from her, I swear I will hunt you and take it out of your empty skull! And I *won't* be using magic."

"Oooh," the imp said, shivering. "I'm *so* scared!" Then it laughed. "Your sarcasm is amazing, Princess! You had a master-level talent!"

May started to say something, then paused, looking confused. "Yeah," she stammered. "I . . . um. Yeah, I . . . I used it a lot." She glanced at Jack, her eyes wide. "I didn't think it was something he could actually take!"

"You didn't know?" the imp said, grinning evilly. "Someone as *worldly* as you? I'm *so* surprised! Now . . ." It snapped its fingers. May disappeared, instantly reappearing on the other side of the cell. "My hat?"

Now that the imp had fulfilled its part of the deal, it didn't need Jack's cooperation. It snapped its fingers, and its hat reappeared on its head, leaving Jack holding nothing.

"Let him out too!" May yelled from the other side of the bars.

"That was never the deal, *genius,*" the imp said, stroking its hat lovingly. "I just said I'd bring him in, and I did. He's stuck here, I'm afraid. I'm *really* surprised you didn't figure that one out sooner, though, considering that huge brain you've got going for you."

May glared at the imp, then suddenly smiled her half smile. "If you leave him in there," she said softly, "I'll tell everyone your name. . . ."

"Ha!" the imp shouted. "You don't know it!" It went back to stroking its hat, but Jack noticed that it didn't seem quite as sure of itself.

"Oh, yeah?" May said. "Let's just say I've heard of your cousin . . . and family names are family names, aren't they, Mr. *Stiltskin?*"

The imp started to respond, then turned a very pale shade of white. "How . . . where . . . how did . . . ," it stammered, then abruptly started howling and stomping its feet. It opened its mouth to say something else, then glared at the princess, who glared back defiantly.

Finally, the imp dropped its head and sighed. It snapped its fingers, and Jack appeared outside the bars, right at May's side.

"That's what I thought," May said, turning up her nose at the dejected, sarcastic imp. "You don't mess with a princess from Punk, little man," she said. "Remember that next time."

The imp pushed itself up against the bars. "Oh, I'll remember you, Princess," it said, its smile showing all four hundred of its teeth. "You can count on that!" And then, with an unsettling wink, the imp disappeared.

CHAPTER 34

Jack grabbed May's head with both hands and stared her straight in the eye. "How do you feel?" he asked her, looking from eye to eye. She *seemed* all right, but you never could tell with magic. "Does it hurt?"

She looked at him miserably. "I don't feel any different," she said, "but it's like . . . it's like there are words I don't *know* anymore. Except it's not words. I can still say whatever I want, but when I try to use a tone, I just . . . can't. Does that make sense?"

Jack nodded slowly. "Don't worry," he said. "We'll find that thing and get back whatever it took, okay? Trust me, that little monster's not getting away with this."

She smiled weakly at him. "Since when did you care so much, huh? I thought you hated royalty and all."

Jack took a step back unconsciously. "I did," he said. "I mean, I do." He rolled his eyes dramatically. "Leave it to a princess to assume basic human decency is something more."

Her eyes narrowed, and she started to say something, then stopped, looking like she was searching for the right word. Finally, she sighed dejectedly and her face fell. "Let's just go find Phillip, huh? I'm ready to move on and forget all about this."

Jack nodded, suddenly feeling absolutely terrible. Why had he said that? May had lost a part of herself to save him, and he insulted her? And it wasn't like he really thought badly of her, not anymore. They'd gotten closer as they'd traveled, and he did think of May as . . . well, as something.

He wasn't quite sure what he thought of her, but he knew it wasn't bad, princess or no. So why had he said that, especially after what she'd just been through? He ran his words through his head over and over, each time coming across worse than the last.

"They took our stuff somewhere when they dumped us here," May said, still not looking at him. "Your sword, the bag, the Mirror . . ."

For some reason, the mention of the sword made him nervous, so he changed the subject. "Considering what good the bag's been so far, we're probably better off," Jack said as good-naturedly as he could.

May glanced up at him, and he did everything he could to smile, apologizing as hard as he could without actually saying the words.

"The bag itself was kinda cool," May said tentatively. "I mean, if it could fit everything in the world in it, it might almost have been big enough for your ego!"

Jack raised an eyebrow. "I thought you couldn't be sarcastic."

She shrugged, the hint of a smile playing across her face. "That wasn't sarcasm," she said. "I was making fun of you. Trust me, no one can take *that* away from me."

And just like that, everything was forgiven.

Opposite the jail cells, a door opened to a dark spiral stairway that sank into the dragon-tail tower. As they stood at the top of the stairs they could barely make out a light at the end. A light meant the stairway led *somewhere*, probably somewhere with people . . . or, more likely, goblins. Still, there wasn't another choice.

Jack led the way, wondering briefly as he trudged down the stairs what would happen at the end of all this. Eventually, they'd find May's grandmother and, hopefully, rescue her. Then that would be that. Jack would go back to his grandfather, while May and Phillip went back to their royal lives. Despite all the obstacles still in their way, the thought of the quest ending gave him a strange feeling in the pit of his stomach.

But why? It wasn't like he was an adventurer like his grandfather—or even his father, for that matter. Jack knew the need for this sort of thing just wasn't built into him like it was in them. In fact, the whole quest so far had been pretty miserable . . . hadn't it? He glanced behind him, up at the princess, who flicked her eyebrows twice at him. He grinned and turned back around. She was so adorable. . . .

Wait, what? Jack stopped dead in his tracks, causing May to plow straight into him. The princess's momentum pushed them both down a few more stairs before Jack caught himself against the wall, halting May's fall, as well.

"Sorry!" she said quickly. "I totally didn't see you stop!"

"That's all right," he said, his face bright red in the dark. "I hadn't really planned on stopping."

"Oh, yeah?" she said, blowing a stray hair out of her face. "What happened?"

Jack opened his mouth, then closed it, turned around, and

started down the stairs. "We're almost there," he said, his face as hot as fire. "We should be quiet."

"Gotcha," she whispered behind him, thankfully letting it go.

The light they'd seen from above shone brightly through an uneven crack beneath another wooden door at the bottom of the stairs. Jack tiptoed up to the door and carefully pushed on it, just to test to see if it was locked. The door creaked open the slightest bit, hopefully not enough to be noticeable if anyone was watching from the other side.

Now that he knew it was unlocked, Jack held his breath and listened against the door for any sounds, but there was only silence. He breathed out, and ever so slowly pushed the door open, trying to catch a glimpse of what lay on the other side in case someone was waiting for them.

Thankfully, the hallway outside looked deserted.

"Okay, let's go," Jack said. "Remember, quietly. We don't want anyone to hear us."

May nodded, so he pushed the door open the entire way . . .

And almost ran into a short, fat goblin guard.

"*I* heard ya," the goblin said. "Too bad for you, eh?"

Jack froze. Instead of a sword, this guard held a battle-axe in its stubby fingers, the blade covered in what looked like blood. Jack knew he could attack the goblin empty-handed, but that wouldn't end well. Unfortunately, there wasn't anything else in the room other than a desk and a frail-looking chair behind it— nothing to use as a weapon. . . .

And then he saw his sword and his grandfather's bag sitting on top of the desk, along with some random items from the bag. Apparently the goblin had been looking for loot. Maybe Jack could make a grab for—

"Excuse me," May said, stepping past Jack. The princess threw her nose into the air and glared down at the goblin. "I'm ready to see Malevolent now," she said. "Be a good little monster and fetch her, will you?"

"We're trying this again?" Jack whispered, but she ignored him.

The goblin snorted. "You'll not be seeing anyone. How did you get out, anyway? I bet you found that imp, right? I've been after him for months. You're the fifth group he's let out this year." The guard looked them up and down. "Though you've emerged with considerably more limbs than the others."

"I need no impish-type creature to free me!" May exclaimed haughtily. "I am a *princess*. I demand to see Malevolent!"

Jack desperately wanted to stop her, considering how well

this act had played out before, but he couldn't think of anything to do that wouldn't make things worse.

The guard laughed. "Get back in your cell, and *maybe* I'll let you keep your hands!"

May laughed back. Then she kicked the goblin in the stomach as hard as she could.

The goblin doubled over, and May grabbed his axe from his hands, then bashed him in the head with the flat of the blade. The goblin dropped to the floor, unconscious.

"See?" she said to Jack. "That's what they get for not listening to me."

It took Jack a minute to catch up, but when he did, he still couldn't think of anything to say. May just smiled sweetly at him. He shook his head, then grabbed his sword and opened the bag to see if anything was missing, beyond what had been thrown on the desk.

The only thing he could find in the bag was May's fairy, who apparently had hidden herself deep in its recesses. She seemed a bit disheveled but otherwise okay as she climbed up May's shoulder and back into her spot in May's hair.

Between the items on the desk and the now empty bag, something rather important was missing. "No Mirror," Jack said, feeling a chill. "That's not a good sign."

May scrunched up her nose, then paused. "Hold up a second," she said. "Why wouldn't Phillip be put in a cell with us? Maybe Malevolent recognized him somehow, from his father or something. She's a fairy queen after all, right? And we have to assume she would have recognized the Mirror, too. If we find Phillip and Malevolent, we'll probably find the Mirror, right?"

Jack slowly nodded as he tossed all his grandfather's prized magic items back into the bag. "Maybe," he said. "So you're saying that instead of searching through the rest of the castle, we should just save ourselves some time and fight our way through the thousands of goblins to wherever Malevolent is?"

"Pretty much," she said, "though I think you're getting cynical in your old age. We probably won't have to fight more than a hundred or so."

"Old age? I'm fourteen. That's barely middle age."

"Funny."

"There's nothing funny about the life expectancy of male peasants, Princess," Jack said, trying hard not to smile. "But fine. We'll fight our way through. They're probably in the throne room, right?"

"You're the expert."

"You're the princess!"

"You act like that should mean something."

"I'm starting to wonder about that myself."

"Funny," she said again, then punched him hard enough for him to think it wasn't that funny at all.

"Can we just get on with this?" Jack said, rubbing his shoulder.

"Of course!" May said in that high-pitched voice she used whenever she really wanted to be irritating. She batted her eyes at him, then led the way down the stairs that the goblin had been guarding. Jack watched her go for a second, then shook his head and followed the princess.

Fighting hundreds of goblin guards would still be easier than figuring her out.

CHAPTER 35

Fortunately for Jack and May, there weren't actually hundreds of guards. Really, there couldn't have been more than three dozen or so, and even then, the hallways were so narrow that the creatures could only attack two or three at a time.

Of course, the goblins found it hard to attack when Jack and May kept running off in the opposite direction. After sprinting through the halls and opening random doors to escape the goblins, Jack and May also managed to find themselves completely lost.

"You have . . . a sword . . . you know!" May huffed at Jack when they stopped to catch their breath. "You could . . . use it!"

Jack shook his head. "I'm not . . . gonna kill them! Even if

I . . . could . . . they're still almost . . . people, just . . . shorter. They're not that different from us."

"They want to eat us," May said, pushing herself off the wall she'd been leaning on. "Do you want to eat them? *That* makes them different."

"I think you'd be surprised how rarely monsters actually eat people," Jack said, standing up as well. "It's mostly a myth. Besides, I don't know that I trust the sword."

The princess stared at him for a second. "Trust the *sword*, huh?" she asked. "The strangest stuff upsets you, you know that?" She glanced around the hallway, trying to determine where they were, something Jack had stopped bothering with. All the halls looked exactly the same to him. In fact, the only reason he'd felt like they were on the right track was due to the obscene amount of guards they'd found. And now the complete emptiness of the halls just reinforced his belief that they were going the wrong way.

He started to say that out loud, but May held up a hand for him to be quiet. She cocked her head to one side, apparently listening intently . . . to what, Jack had no idea. He tried copying her, straining to catch whatever she was listening to, but he couldn't hear anything.

"What—," he said, and she shushed him. May slowly took a step, then two, down the middle of the hallway, followed by a step to the right, then two back to the left. She nodded to the left, then went for the closest door.

May didn't seem to care that the door's rusty hinges shrieked as she opened it, but Jack winced, waiting for the guards to come hurtling down the hall at any second. May didn't bother waiting for them. Instead, she grabbed Jack and pulled him through the door, then quickly shut it behind him.

Inside, he tried to speak again, but May shushed him one more time. "Stop *doing* that!" he whispered. Without even glancing his way, she reached out and covered his mouth with her hand.

Of course, this irritated him even more, but for some reason, despite his annoyance, he found himself a bit preoccupied by the smell coming from the skin on her hand. Jack would have thought after all these days on the road, the princess wouldn't exactly smell very pleasant. But there she was, giving off a fragrance that smelled like a breeze on a spring day. Probably some kind of natural magic that girls were just born with.

Jack inhaled deeply just as May dropped her hand, leaving him sucking air loudly through his nose. This got the princess's attention, at least enough for her to raise an eyebrow at him. Jack coughed to cover it. "Dust," he said, glad the room was dark enough to hide his face, which was on fire again. It was doing that far too much lately.

May looked at him oddly for a second longer, then motioned him over to an enormous fireplace easily twice as tall as Jack. The fireplace was made of some kind of shiny stone, and a large iron grate lay in its very center. To the left, a metal basket for firewood lay on its side against the edge of the fireplace. It looked as though none of it had been used in years.

And yet, voices wafted up through the grate.

May pointed down, then knelt next to the fireplace. Jack joined her on the floor and put his ear next to the grate. He could clearly make out words now—a woman was speaking to someone, her voice resonating with power, much like Merriweather's had.

"She never could stay out of my affairs," the woman said. "Always interfering where she wasn't wanted. And now, look at her. I could help her, of course. It would be easy. Therefore, it gives me no small amount of pleasure to refuse to do so."

"Please," said a male voice that rasped just a step above hoarse. "Please," the voice repeated, coughing. "She's trapped—"

"Yes, she is, isn't she?" the woman said, then laughed cruelly.

Jack was so intent on listening to the conversation that it took him a moment to realize that May was staring at him. In fact, it actually took her slapping him in the shoulder for him to notice. He glanced up at her with a raised eyebrow, and she mouthed something.

"Malevolent," her lips said. Then, "Phillip." Jack nodded. It *had* to be them . . . only, Jack hadn't ever heard the prince sound so beaten, so dejected. What had the fairy queen done to him?

"The thing that most surprises me," said Malevolent from somewhere below, "is that you would bring her here, to me! Such a wonderful present, my little human absurdity! Who could have imagined that *you* would deliver my greatest rival to me. You, the very boy destined to kill me!"

Jack pushed back from the grate, his eyes wide. "Wha . . . ?" he mouthed to May.

May shushed him, then bent over and grabbed the grate. As she yanked on it, Jack realized what she was trying to do: If the fireplaces were connected to a common chimney, they might be able to get to the throne room through the grate.

May pulled and pulled, but the grate never budged. Jack

tapped her shoulder to let him try, and she moved out of the way and gave him a chance. Unfortunately, he had no better luck.

"Kill . . . kill you?" Phillip mumbled, the sound barely reaching their ears.

"Of course!" Malevolent said. "One cannot imagine how, and yet—"

"But . . . how do you . . . how would you know?" Phillip stammered.

Malevolent laughed again. "How?! I trapped an Ifrit within an ordinary mirror, you silly, pathetic creature! I, greatest of the fairy queens, created the most powerful magical device the world will ever know! While others might have sought personal wealth, I knew better. Wealth is fleeting, yet wisdom, knowledge—these are the true hallmarks of personal power! Knowing that, I used the first question I forced from the Ifrit to learn who might possibly strip my immortality from me, who in this world could possibly destroy me."

"That is . . . sad," Phillip said, "that . . . you would even think . . . to ask that."

Then he screamed.

May quickly looked to Jack, deathly worried for Phillip, and for once Jack agreed.

"I will not take any insults from you, of all people," Malevolent said, her voice much lower. "Believe me, I fully expected the Mirror to tell me I would *never* die! Yet, when I learned that you, a human, would one day destroy me, I knew that I must escape that fate at all costs. So I asked the Mirror how I might avoid my death, and it told me!"

"Did it tell you . . . to talk and talk . . . until you kill me . . . from boredom?" Phillip said.

The prince screamed again.

"No, little human," Malevolent said. "The Mirror told me that I will be protected from you as long as a certain princess isn't around in your moment of need. I believe you know of this girl—you were at one point betrothed to her, after all." The fairy queen laughed bitterly. "I tried to kill the girl, but Merriweather interfered, as she always does. And to be honest, I believed at that moment my fate was sealed."

"You mean . . . it is not?" Phillip asked.

"The princess disappeared," Malevolent admitted, "but I have it on good authority that she will no longer be a concern. The Wicked Queen herself promised me that."

"Is that what you received . . . for betraying Snow White?" Phillip asked.

There was a brief pause, then Malevolent laughed. "Oh, my little prince, I have quite enjoyed our time here, yet all good things must come to an end."

And then there was silence.

May jumped to her feet, then grabbed Jack and pulled him up. The princess gestured frantically, silently telling him that they had to go, they had to find Phillip and rescue him *now*. But how could they? The grate was just too heavy, and there was no time to search the castle for Phillip, not if Malevolent was—

"Silly man-child," said a musical voice right in front of Jack. "You have a key, why don't you use it?"

Jack's head flew up to look for the voice, but he didn't see anyone. May, meanwhile, looked questioningly at him. The fairy in her hair also stared at him, only the fairy was pointing at something with her little hand.

She was pointing at his sword.

"You aren't very smart, are you, man-child?" the fairy said to him.

Jack's mouth dropped open. Since when could fairies talk? More important, since when could he understand them?

He looked from the fairy to May, but the princess just stared at him with confusion. Jack pointed up at the fairy, surprised that the princess, with her incredible hearing, hadn't heard the fairy in her hair. May kept shaking her head, though, just not understanding.

"Use your key!" the fairy said again, pointing at the sword.

"All right, fine!" Jack whispered back. May's eyebrows shot up in surprise, but Jack ignored her as he drew his sword. The room instantly lit up from the sword's glow, illuminating what, in the past, must have been a luxurious bedroom.

"So it's a key," Jack said to the fairy. "What do I do with it?"

"A key?" May asked, but Jack shushed her.

"Open the lock!" the fairy said, exasperated. "No wonder the Charmed One worries about you! You haven't the brains of a worm!"

Jack chose to ignore that last comment and turned his attention to the grate. Did she mean that maybe he could use the sword to lever the grate out? He brought the sword down and pushed it between the grate and the shiny stone of the fireplace.

As soon as the blade touched the iron of the grate, the metal split in half with a tiny hiss. Behind him, May gasped as Jack, realizing what the fairy had been telling him, quickly cut a circle in the iron wide enough for them to fit through, then replaced the sword in its scabbard and yanked on the grate.

The metal circle he'd cut came flying out, throwing Jack backward along with it. They both hit the ground with an ear-shattering clang, a sound that probably woke up every goblin within a hundred miles.

May paused for a brief moment in wonder, then shook her head, smiled at Jack, and jumped straight into the hole he'd just cut, even as a god-awful howling tore up through the grate from the room below.

CHAPTER 36

Jack gave May what he hoped was enough time to get out of the way below, then took a deep breath and jumped into the hole after her. Beneath the grate was a stone vent or chimney, barely large enough for Jack to fall through; his bag wasn't so lucky, banging back and forth against the sides as he dropped.

He only fell for a second or two before his feet slammed into another grate at the center of a fireplace exactly like the one he'd just left. His landing sent pain spiking up through his boots, all the way to his knees, while his bag stopped its fall right on his head.

Making things worse, he landed in a pile of soot, the remains of what had probably been an even deeper pile that May had landed in. Now soot completely blocked his view of the room he'd just dropped into, thrown into the air by the force of their landings.

Though Jack couldn't make out what was happening, he could hear Phillip screaming. "Stop, please!" the prince was yelling . . . but he wasn't the only one. A woman was also shrieking, the same woman who'd been speaking just a minute before.

Malevolent.

Whatever was happening, Jack wasn't helping anything just standing there, waiting for feeling to reenter the soles of his feet, so he hurled himself through the cloud of soot. . . .

Only to jerk to a halt barely a foot out to avoid plowing into May, who'd stopped just beyond the fireplace. Jack frantically windmilled his arms and managed to avoid knocking them both down, though he had to grab May's shoulders to keep from falling over. The princess didn't even notice, she was so surprised by something.

Jack quickly stood up straight and looked around to see what she was looking at, only to have his mouth drop open—unfortunately letting in more soot.

They were too late to save Phillip. The Wolf King had beaten them to it.

The howling Jack had heard was the wolf, and now the animal, in his human form, was holding an unnaturally tall woman in the air by her neck. The woman, dressed all in black, had to be Malevolent—she had pupil-less green eyes, just like Merriweather's white ones. Unconscious goblin guards covered the room's floor in heaps, a by-product of the wolf's entrance, most likely.

Right behind one of the larger goblin piles was Phillip. Jack quickly ran to the prince, who was chained to the wall opposite the fireplace. Phillip, his face battered and covered with bruises, hadn't stopped shouting since Jack jumped in. Except the prince wasn't screaming in pain anymore; he was pleading with the wolf, begging the animal not to kill Malevolent.

"Please stop, Wolf King!" Phillip shouted, his voice breaking. "We *need* her. She must save Merriweather!"

The wolf, though, completely ignored the prince as he slowly choked the life out of the fairy queen. Malevolent, now quiet, just stared down at the wolf, her eyes on fire with hate.

Jack swore loudly, then leapt forward and grabbed the wolf's arm, pulling with all his might. "Let go!" Jack yelled.

The wolf barely gave him a glance. "Leave me be," he growled, then turned back to the woman in his grasp.

"Jack!" May shouted from the other side of the wolf. "This might be a problem!"

"No kidding!" he yelled back. Jack backed up a bit, took a deep breath, then launched himself right at the wolf, driving his shoulder into the animal's chest. The wolf tumbled over under the force of Jack's assault, dropping Malevolent to the ground as Jack's momentum sent them both to the floor. Jack landed hard, but the wolf had barely touched the ground before he was back on his feet and heading for the fairy queen once more.

As the wolf stalked his prey the world began to slow down again for Jack. On the other side of the room, Phillip struggled futilely against his chains, his face a mask of enormous pain yet also stubborn determination. May, meanwhile, had inserted herself between the wolf and the fairy queen, trying to stop the animal's attack.

All this Jack took in as the wolf bent down, then leapt straight at the princess. The animal's arc sent him right over May's head, though, and straight for the fairy queen. . . .

Until Jack took a step forward, grabbed the wolf's flowing fur cape, and yanked down with all his strength.

Though the wolf's head came to a stop, the rest of his body continued moving forward, completely flipping him. The wolf's back slammed into the ground just past May, barely a foot short of Malevolent. This actually seemed to surprise the wolf; he lay on the ground for a fraction of a second, dazed, but even that amount of time was plenty for Jack, given how slowly time seemed to be moving.

His mind strangely blank, Jack pulled out his sword and pointed it straight at one of the wolf's glowing red eyes. As he stared down at the wolf, his face expressionless, the sword's normal cloudy white glow changed to a deep, desolate black, as if it were sucking the light out of the very room.

And just like that, time returned to its normal speed.

The wolf stared at Jack and his midnight black sword for a very brief moment, then actually smiled. "You win," he growled. "You learn quickly, Jack."

"That's right he does!" May shouted, though she didn't seem entirely sure what had just happened. Not that Jack understood either. When time had slowed, he almost felt like he had acted completely without thought . . . as if he weren't the one making the decisions. How *had* he moved so fast? And why had the sword changed color?

Except, just like that, the sword brightened from black to its usual dull white, like the sun emerging from behind a cloud.

"What are you *doing*?!" May hissed, stepping over to him.

"Do I look like I know?" he whispered back, still staring at the sword.

"That doesn't exactly make me feel better!"

"*Look out!*" Phillip bellowed from across the room. Jack immediately grabbed May and dove to the floor, barely dodging a bolt of lightning that incinerated the stones just above the Wolf King.

Jack quickly looked up from the floor to find Malevolent, her hair swirling around her as she stood in the middle of a tornado of wind and lightning. As he watched, the fairy queen's lips parted, rising into a wide grin . . . except they didn't stop there. Her mouth continued to pull apart as Malevolent's entire face bulged and stretched grotesquely, almost as if there was something inside her, fighting to break free of its prison.

"You pathetic little mortals!" the fairy queen snarled from her much-too-wide mouth, her voice deeper now. "You have no idea the power you have challenged!"

As her face continued to grow in places it wasn't meant to, two long, black claws abruptly sliced their way straight out of Malevolent's back, twitching and shuddering with wild abandon at their freedom. As her whole body shook the fairy queen's mouth suddenly unhinged, and her lower jaw dropped open far enough to almost curl up under itself. From inside her mouth emerged a black, reptilian head.

The claws on her back continued thrashing around, growing as they pushed out farther and farther until, finally, long batlike wings unfurled, spreading from one corner of the room to the other, ripping apart the rest of the fairy queen's body as they did.

And there, standing in the remains of what had seemed to be a normal human woman, was a dragon, her black skin shining like a glowing shadow.

The terrifying beast whipped her long neck first to the left, then to the right, reveling in her freedom from her human-shaped shell. The dragon reared back on her hind legs and lifted her long neck straight up, then came crashing down to the floor hard enough to shake the foundations of the castle.

Her head snapped down a second later, releasing a sickly green flame straight at Jack, May, and the Wolf King.

Instead it hit the Magic Mirror.

As May and Jack clutched the Mirror by the hanging wire on its back, the fire splayed off to either side of them, barely missing them and the Wolf King right behind them.

The dragon roared furiously and doubled the intensity of her flame.

The heat of the unnatural fire almost staggered Jack, and May didn't look much better, but neither dropped the Mirror. Phillip, still chained to the wall, pulled himself as far from the flames as his chains would allow; even on the opposite side of the room, the prince was soaked through with sweat. The whole room's temperature rose past uncomfortable, heading straight toward burning alive.

Jack turned to May and nodded, shaking the sweat from his eyes. May nodded back, her entire face glistening in the firelight. They really only had one choice. They both took an uncomfortable breath, then began to slowly push the Mirror forward toward the dragon's mouth.

The dragon redoubled her efforts, and now the green flame completely filled Jack's vision, but neither he nor May stopped pushing the Mirror steadily toward the dragon's mouth.

As they inched forward the flame actually seemed to lessen a bit . . . maybe she was running out of breath? And then the fire stopped abruptly as the dragon's head snaked up and over the Mirror, her mouth open wide to devour both Jack and May in one bite.

Instead she found herself staring at her reflection as the Mirror smashed up into her chin. The dragon let out a bellow of pain, then snarled and shot back down toward the two teenagers, her mouth open wide. The dragon latched her teeth onto the Mirror and ripped it from their grasp, realizing too late that she'd been set up. Jack and May had let go of the Mirror.

As Malevolent stared down at Jack and May with the Mirror in her mouth, both humans smiled up at her, then raised their weapons—Jack with his sword, May with the broomstick from Jack's bag.

Malevolent reared back, but she was too late: Jack and May struck in unison, each using two hands to smash their weapons down as hard as they could right on the dragon's head.

Malevolent's head smacked down against the floor, and she roared in pain, but Jack didn't wait. There was no time; they needed some way to tie the dragon down, or she'd just fill the entire room with flame and that'd be it. But how could you tie down a dragon with a neck like a snake? And there wouldn't be enough rope in the castle to keep that enormous body still. What could he—

And then it came to him. As Malevolent started to raise her head up once more, Jack threw his hand into his grandfather's bag and pulled out the reins they'd used on Samson, reins that supposedly could tame any horse, no matter how wild.

Maybe it would work on something other than a horse.

Jack dropped the bag, then leapt up onto the dragon's neck as she raised it. Malevolent began to shake her head wildly from side to side, flame shooting out in spurts, but Jack just hugged her neck as hard as he could and inched his way up toward her head.

Maybe she suspected what he was doing, or maybe she just feared what he could do from his position, but Malevolent grew even more desperate, banging her body into the stone walls and ceiling hard enough to make them crumble in places. However she moved, though, Jack just kept climbing until he reached the back of the dragon's head.

From there, he gathered the reins in his hand and waited for his moment. It didn't take long: The dragon immediately roared in frustration, opening her mouth wide. Just before she could let loose another torrent of flame, Jack grabbed the ends of the reins in both hands and swung the mouthpiece right into Malevolent's open mouth.

And just like that, the dragon's entire body shuddered to a stop. Completely shocked, the dragon teased, trying to move. Failing that, she attempted to spit out the reins. When the magic of the reins kept her from doing even that, she began shrieking louder and louder as her entire body shook and shuddered below Jack.

Each time he felt the dragon's body quake, Jack was sure that the reins' magic would give out against Malevolent's monstrous strength and rage. Yet, each time, the magic miraculously held the great beast in check. As Malevolent gradually gave up and settled down, Jack sighed deeply in relief.

Sometimes, the simplest magical charms really did work the best.

"I think I got her," Jack told May, trying to hide the surprise in his voice.

"Good job!" she yelled. "Now what?"

"I'm open to suggestions," he admitted.

From the floor, May growled in frustration. "I really miss my sarcasm right now!" she said. "So what do the reins do, exactly? I mean, Samson did whatever we told him. Maybe she will?"

"Maybe," Jack said. "Worth a try, at least." While May grabbed the Mirror and his grandfather's bag to get them out of the way, Jack tightened his grip on the reins. "What should I tell her to do?"

"Try something simple," May suggested.

"Right," he said. "Malevolent, *sit!*"

Immediately, the dragon dropped her haunches to the floor, sending Malevolent into a torrent of profanity Jack wasn't familiar with, many of the words in languages he wasn't sure existed anymore.

"That is *not* my name," the dragon growled. "My name is *Mellifluent*. My sisters gave me the name Malevolent to make your kind fear me!"

"I don't care what you're called," Jack said. "Let's try something a little more complex. Mal . . . I mean, Mellifluent! Free Merriweather from the Mirror!"

This set off the loudest bout of wailing yet, but the dragon obediently began to mumble words that Jack couldn't understand. He suspected that even if he could make out what Malevolent was saying, he wouldn't have been able to remember it to save his life.

Of course, it wasn't *his* life that was being saved right now. As Malevolent chanted Jack began to hear tones, melodies that played off one another in harsh, unpleasant ways. It reminded him of Merriweather's magic during her fight with the genie, yet where Merriweather's music had struck him as beautiful, Malevolent's harmonies sent a chill running through his body.

Despite that, the spell seemed to be working. As they

all watched, a cloud of blue mist slowly leaked out of the spot where the Mirror had previously been cracked. As the blue gradually left, the greenish-yellow mist of the genie still trapped within the Mirror began to swirl uncontrollably. The genie grew more and more wild until the last of the blue was sucked out of the glass and into the air around them.

The blue mist started to come together, looking as if it was going to form Merriweather's shape. Jack almost thought he could see a smile where the fairy queen's head would be. The fairy in May's hair even began jumping up and down excitedly. Then, abruptly, the mist began to drift apart, dissipating into nothingness.

"Wait!" Jack yelled to her. "Where are you going?! You're safe, you're all right now!"

"She's hardly that," the dragon beneath him growled furiously. "Merriweather was barely alive. She most likely fled back to our homeland to heal herself." At this, the dragon snaked her neck around until she was face-to-face with Jack, her green eyes burning into him. "Now, I did as you commanded. She is free. Release me!"

Jack started to respond, then noticed that green mist was trickling out of the same crack that Merriweather had just escaped from. "Fix the crack in the Mirror!" he shouted, tugging backward on the reins. The dragon renewed her struggle, shaking her body so hard Jack had to grit his teeth to keep from biting his tongue. Just as he thought her head was going to whip around and bite him in half, Malevolent tucked her head down and began to chant again.

This time the hole in the glass began to slowly knit itself together as if it were ripped clothing being sewn, cutting off the stream of green mist as it closed. Finally, it shut completely, leaving the Mirror's glass as seamless as they'd first seen it. What little green mist that had managed to make it through the hole quickly rose toward the ceiling, then up and out the same grate Jack and May had come in through.

"Is it . . . ?" May asked, reaching out for the Mirror with a shaking hand.

"Give it a try," Jack said, his whole body shaking both from nervousness and from the dragon's continued struggle. "You," he said to the dragon, "don't move unless I say so."

This cut out the shaking altogether, though Malevolent continued to shriek furiously every now and then. A few feet away the princess propped the Mirror up against a charred portion of the wall, removed her crown necklace, then pushed it into the Mirror's frame, both hands shaking as she did so.

Immediately, the flat face of the genie surfaced on the Mirror's glass as if it were emerging from underwater. The fire in its eyes glowed with a white-hot intensity, and the look it shot May could have burned what was left of the room.

But then, the genie turned its eyes downward with an almost respectful look.

"How may I serve you?" it asked the princess.

CHAPTER 37

S tay," Jack ordered the dragon.

The dragon let out another howl.

"And stop the screaming," Jack added absently, and the howling stopped immediately. He tossed a leg over the dragon's neck, then slid down her body to the floor. He could feel Malevolent's green eyes boring into the back of his head, but he ignored her.

"Uh, Jack?" Phillip said, still chained to the wall. "Might you have a moment to release me?"

"Phillip!" May said, turning away from the Mirror for the first time since the genie spoke to her. "Oh my God, I can't believe we didn't—"

"I've got him," Jack said to her. "Just ask the Mirror your

question before anything else comes up." He hurdled the charred remains of a chair, then pushed half a table out of his way to reach the prince.

Sadly, Phillip didn't look too good. Between the torture and the dragon's fire, Jack was actually surprised the prince was still conscious. As it was, one of his eyes was swollen shut, and the rest of his face was a mess of purple and red. His expensive royal clothes hadn't survived any better—there were more tears and rips in his tunic than there were clean spots. And beneath those rips and tears were more bruises and cuts.

"We'll get you fixed up, Phillip," Jack said softly as he carefully sliced through the prince's manacles with the witch's knife.

The prince smiled, then winced at the pain. "I would like to say I have been through worse . . . but it hardly seems the most appropriate moment to begin telling lies."

"Nice," Jack said, then gently helped Phillip to his feet. On the other side of the room, May took a deep breath, closed her eyes, and asked her question.

"Mirror," she said slowly, "please tell me where my grandmother is."

"Your grandmother is imprisoned within the Palace of the

Snow Queen," the Mirror replied in its monotone voice.

"That must be one of Snow White's strongholds," Phillip said as Jack set him down next to May. Jack then moved back to Malevolent, whose eyes hadn't left him the entire time.

Despite the success of the reins, Jack didn't like this situation at all. Magic had a tendency to fail . . . and usually at the worst possible time.

"Unfortunately, no one knows where those fortresses might be," Phillip continued. "The locations were kept secret to keep the Wicked Queen from finding them." He shook his head. "Apparently, that was in vain, if the Wicked Queen now holds your grandmother in one of her own castles."

"Where is the Palace of the Snow Queen located?" May asked the Mirror, carefully wording her question. Jack nodded in approval: The princess was learning. It was never good to be ambiguous with bitter magical creatures.

"The Palace of the Snow Queen," the Mirror said, "is located in the snowbound lands at the very top of the world, surrounded by mountains higher than the clouds."

"Uh-oh," Jack said.

"So, how do we get there?" May asked, panic edging into her voice.

"The palace is unreachable under your power," the Mirror responded.

"What?!" May shouted.

The Mirror repeated itself, and this time, Jack could have sworn the genie smiled.

"Wait, May," Jack said. "That doesn't mean we can't get to it. It's just saying we can't walk there. There's obviously another way to get there without physically traveling the distance. After all, the Huntsman's been there and back again, right?"

"Mirror!" May said. "No messing around . . . Is that right? Has the Huntsman been to the palace and back? And if so, how'd he do it?"

"The Huntsman has indeed traveled to and from the palace," the Mirror stated. "He does so through the use of magic abilities that lie beyond your power."

May growled in frustration. "I'm gonna break this thing again in about two seconds!" she yelled.

"That can't be the only way," Jack said to Phillip, since May seemed to be off on her own tangent.

"Perhaps we could find Merriweather," Phillip said. "Once she has healed herself, she might transport us to the palace."

"And how long would that take?!" May said, whirling around on Phillip. "My grandmother doesn't have that kind of time!"

From behind, a deep rumbling startled all three of them. Jack whirled to find Malevolent laughing softly to herself.

"I thought I told you to be quiet," he said, narrowing his eyes.

"You said to stop screaming, young lord," the dragon said, and laughed harder. "Poor little humans . . . can't find their way to one of their own castles."

"Jack, if you don't shut her up . . . ," May warned.

"You will what?" Malevolent said, her mouth pulling back into a smile, revealing her disgustingly sharp teeth. "Poor little princess. If only you had a way to the Palace of the Snow Queen, your grandmother might have yet lived. But now . . ."

"What do you know about it?" Jack said.

"Why, nothing, of course!" the dragon said, with an indignant hiss.

"She knows something," Phillip said, and Jack nodded.

Jack climbed onto the dragon's back and took the magic reins in his hands again. "Answer me truthfully," Jack ordered her. "Can you take us to the Palace of the Snow Queen?"

Without struggling in the least, the dragon responded. "Of course," she said. "Though I will not."

"Yes, you will," May said, grabbing the Mirror and shoving it into Jack's grandfather's bag. "Wolf, help me get Phillip onto her back."

"I tell you, I will not help," the dragon said again. Jack stared at her suspiciously. She had to know he could order her. Why give them the idea in the first place?

"Mellifluent, you *will* transport us all to the Palace of the Snow Queen," he said. He paused, then added, "Including yourself."

That did it. "There is no reason for *me* to go!" Malevolent said furiously, sounding as if she wanted to scream but still bound by Jack's earlier command. "The spell doesn't allow me to go along—"

"Are you lying?" Jack asked quietly.

". . . *Yes!*" Malevolent hissed, and her whole body shook so hard Jack almost tumbled off. "I *will* transport us all, little human, but I swear on my last breath I shall hunt all of you down, and your mothers shall cry when they hear tales of what I've done."

"Right, right, mothers crying, whatever," May said, pulling herself up behind Jack, then turning around to help pull Phillip up. After they'd secured the prince, May reached down to help up the wolf, but the animal, still in human form, hesitated, a growl rumbling in the back of his throat. Suddenly, Jack remembered the wolf's earlier words.

"You said she betrayed your mistress," Jack said to the wolf. "She betrayed Snow White somehow, didn't she?" The animal just stared at him, not responding. "That explains how she knows where the Palace of the Snow Queen is," Jack continued. "She's been there before. Is that true, Mellifluent?"

"Yes," the dragon hissed. "I have been to the palace. And I will take you. But only if you release me after I do so!"

"So you can hunt us down and make our mothers cry?" May said as the wolf slowly climbed up behind Phillip. "Not likely. You'll be lucky if you make it out of this alive."

"Oh, I will live," the dragon said. "Believe me. And we will meet again, much sooner than you think."

"Right," May said. "Whatever you say there, Puff. We're all ready to go, so let's get a move on!" And then she kicked her heels into the dragon twice. "Giddyup!"

The dragon hissed again, but didn't move.

"What's the hold up, Malleable?" May said with another kick. "I'm serious, let's go!"

"I . . . cannot . . . move," Malevolent growled furiously, "until the young human—"

"Oh!" Jack said. "Sorry!" May smacked him on the back of his head, but he let it go. "Okay, Mellifluent, you can move . . . but *only* enough to get us to the Palace of the Snow Queen. Got it?"

Then Jack kicked the dragon too, just for the heck of it. He figured that might not be the smartest idea, but frankly, it was just too tempting to resist.

The dragon hissed in rage, but began chanting quietly. The entire room started to shimmer in time to Malevolent's harmony, a rainbow of colors melting in and out of their vision.

Jack shuddered with excitement. They were finally going to rescue May's grandmother!

Except . . . it occurred to him that they'd been so focused on finding May's grandmother, they'd neglected to think about who they'd have to face to rescue her.

The Wicked Queen.

Now Jack shivered for a different reason. Jack, May, Phillip, and the Wolf King—the four of them were going to personally face down the Wicked Queen? They were going to fight the woman whose armies had conquered half the world, the woman who would have ruled over the *entire* world if not for Snow White? This was the woman whose dark spirits and demons terrified people everywhere at just their mention, the woman who controlled armies of dragons purely by the strength of her own magic. This was the woman whom the greatest heroes in the world had failed to defeat.

This was the woman who waited for them in the Palace of the Snow Queen.

As the blackened walls of the room melted into a blinding white cloud of snow and cold, Jack had just enough time to wonder if any of them would make it out alive before everything went dark.

CHAPTER 38

Jack woke up facedown in a snowdrift, and for a second— before the cold cut through his shock—he wondered exactly how many times he was going to be knocked out during this quest. Then the shock wore off, and his attention shifted immediately to the fact that he couldn't feel most of his body, and that he'd never been so cold in his entire life.

All around him the wind swirled and eddied, spinning snow into whirlwinds of wintery blankness. As a result, Jack couldn't see more than a foot or two in front of him. Beyond that, it was as if someone had dropped a curtain of pure white. More important, though, Jack also quickly discovered that besides being blind, he also couldn't move. He glanced down and quickly realized why.

He was sunk up to his chest in snow.

"*Hello?*" he screamed out to the nothing all around him, but got no reply. He tried to kick his feet, but neither of his legs would move. After a bit of shifting, he was able to pull his arms out of the snow, then free his lower body through a combination of pushing with his arms and creating toeholds with his feet.

Soon he found himself lying on top of the snow instead of beneath it, completely exhausted by the effort to free himself. "*Hello!*" he screamed again, trying to be heard over the biting wind, but again received no response.

Where was May? And Phillip and the Wolf King? If nothing else, he should have seen the dragon, as enormous as Malevolent was. How had they ended up separated?

Jack dropped his stinging hands back onto the snow, then pushed himself to his feet—at least, as well as he could in the snowdrift. Once he was sure of his balance, he stumbled forward, exposed hands buried in his underarms to try to regain some feeling. His face was also exposed, but there wasn't much he could do about that; besides, the rest of his body wasn't exactly a whole lot warmer.

"*Hello!*" he screamed a third time, but still heard nothing. Then a thought occurred to him. "*Mellifluent!*" he yelled out at the top of his lungs. "If you can hear me, *get over here!*" If she heard and was still under the control of the reins . . .

Just like that, the ground shook as a monstrous shape plowed through the snow toward him. The shape was just a few feet from him before he could fully make out that it was Malevolent . . . not that the dragon seemed to be stopping. Instead, she rushed toward him at full speed, snow flying wildly around her, a vicious smile on her face.

"*Stop!*" he screamed at her. "That's close enough!"

The dragon swore in multiple languages, but did come skidding to a stop, the snow piling in front of her as she did, knocking Jack right off his feet.

"Where is everyone?" he asked her as he worked through the tedious process of getting back to his feet.

The dragon snarled, then growled, "They are all foundering, just as you were."

"Well, rescue them, then!"

The dragon stared at him, then dropped her head and began to chant her musical magic. Just like that, Jack could hear the ever-present howling of the wind had stopped. The reason why became readily apparent: Surrounding them in every direction was a dome of green light crackling with lightning.

The dome seemed solid, yet Jack could see through it to the wind swirling on the other side. The dome wasn't just keeping out the wind, Jack felt heat emanating off it.

"Thank you," he said to the dragon, who just glared at him with murder in her eyes. He decided to ignore that for now, and started searching the area for the others instead. As it turned out, none of them had been too far away; the wolf had landed closest to Jack, just over a hill of snow from where Jack had woken up. The Wolf King was awake and had even managed to dig himself most of the way out, so Jack helped finish the job as fast as he could.

Next, Jack and the wolf found May, who had somehow managed to avoid being buried in the snow, landing on the sheltered side of a snowdrift. It looked like May's fairy had been thrown from her perch when they'd arrived, but had snuggled back up into the princess's hair to try to stay warm. Jack quickly woke May, and she seemed to be fine, if freezing.

They found Phillip, or more accurately, his shoes, at the top of another enormous pile of snow. After some digging, Phillip emerged in one piece—at least relatively, considering he was still wounded from Malevolent's torture. May and Phillip were completely numb, but the heat of the green dome quickly helped, melting the snow from their clothes and warming them up.

"We've definitely found the snow part of the palace," Jack said when they'd all regained feeling in their extremities.

"So where is it?" May said, glancing around.

"Mellifluent, show us the Palace of the Snow Queen," Jack ordered the dragon, who for once complied without arguing. She chanted a few more words, and the green dome opened on one side to allow a tunnel to stretch forth. As they watched, the green-light tunnel extended farther and farther, finally stopping at what looked to be twin tornadoes of swirling wind and snow.

"That is the entrance to the Palace of the Snow Queen," Malevolent said. "The walls are made of snow, the windows and doors formed by the wind. I have transported you here, now I *demand* that you release me!"

"Nah," Jack said absently, staring with the rest of them at the doors to the palace. How could someone open a door made of wind?

Phillip stood up and brushed the remaining snow from his pants. "Well, my friends," he said, "it appears that we have reached the end of our journey. With a few more steps, we will finally rescue Snow White, the beloved grandmother of Princess May." He smiled. "I am actually surprised we made it."

Jack almost laughed. "Me too, honestly," he agreed. "Not that we're done or anything, but . . . wow."

Even May grinned. "I can't believe we're finally here," she said, a strange look on her face.

Jack put a hand on her shoulder. "Ready to rescue Snow White, Princess?" he asked, and now he couldn't help smiling too.

She stuck out her tongue. "You've got no idea."

Jack nodded, finding himself much more excited than he would have expected. *This must be how it feels to complete an adventure.* No wonder so many tried it. It was intoxicating!

"Can you make it?" Jack asked Phillip, who'd limped over to stand next to the princess.

The prince winced a bit, and even that seemed to be painful for him. "I am hurt, I admit, but I would not miss this."

Jack stopped for a moment, then slapped himself in the head. "Mellifluent!" he said. "Heal Phillip!"

The dragon let loose a stream of obscenities, this one small act seemingly the last thing she'd *ever* be willing to do. Finally, though, the magic of the reins overpowered her will, and she chanted the spell under her breath. Before their eyes, the bruises and cuts faded from Phillip's body, and he stood up straighter, a smile coming over his face as he did. Even his clothes had been repaired.

"Those reins really are quite useful," the prince said happily.

Jack nodded, looking from Phillip to May, and suddenly he felt the need to say something profound. "You know, this might be the last time we three are together without things going crazy, so I just wanted to say—"

"You can have a good cry later, girls," May interrupted. "Time to go!" With that, she broke into a run for the green-light tunnel, leaving Jack staring after her with an open mouth. Phillip looked at him, shrugged, then sprinted after her. Jack grinned and shook his head, then ran to catch up to the other two.

As Jack reached the green dome's tunnel he could just make out the outline of the palace on the other side, an enormous castle that didn't look built so much as sculpted from snow, carved into place by whatever forces had designed it. Spirals of ice erupted from the snow walls on either side of the wind doors, gleaming with terrible beauty in the light of the green dome. The walls themselves loomed higher than Jack could see, carved to resemble stone. Besides the white color, the only thing giving away the fake stone was the fact that the snow was so dense and smooth it actually glowed.

"This place is incredible," Jack said, almost breathless from the sight.

"How do we get in, then?" May said, staring at the two tornadoes in front of them.

Before Jack could even open his mouth to respond, the tornadoes began to slowly pull away from each other, separating enough to open the way into the palace.

And there, in between the two doors of wind, stood someone dressed all in green.

The Huntsman grinned widely. "Well, then," he said. "I hope you didn't have too much trouble finding the place?"

CHAPTER 39

Jack didn't even pause at the sight of the Huntsman. Instead, he leapt forward, yanking his sword from his back with both hands as he sprinted straight at the man blocking the entrance to the palace. The Huntsman pulled out his own axe, ready for Jack to swing at him.

Except Jack never swung. Midway through his run, Jack whipped his arms forward and threw his sword end over end right at the Huntsman.

The man's eyes went wide with surprise and he ducked under the sword, bringing his head down to the level of Jack's shoulder just as Jack's momentum crushed the two together with a loud crack. Both dropped to the ground, Jack clutching his shoulder in pain but smiling, the Huntsman clutching his head in pain and moaning.

The larger man shook it off quickly and jumped back to his feet with a fierce growl, only to have Phillip slam the broadside of the Huntsman's own axe right into the man's face. The blow threw the Huntsman backward, knocking him to the ground again. He landed hard on his back, the air whooshing out of his lungs.

Before the Huntsman could even take a breath, a shadow covered his face. The Huntsman blinked and looked up to find May standing over him, the point of Jack's sword at his throat.

"We're ready to see my grandmother now," the princess said calmly.

There was a pause, and Jack briefly wondered if it could be that easy.

"No," the Huntsman said, his eyes twinkling maliciously.

"I'm sorry?" May responded incredulously, pushing the tip of Jack's sword into the man's throat until a dot of red blood appeared. The Huntsman swallowed as the sword bit into him, its white glow lighting his face eerily. Yet again, he refused.

"She'll do it, you know," Jack told him. "Is this really worth your life?"

"That's right," May said. "I'll do it!" She nodded to Jack, who nodded back.

"You have no idea what you're playing with," the Huntsman said. "If she finds out you have *his* sword . . ."

"We'll worry about that," May told the Huntsman. "You worry about the fact that this thing's getting heavy." With that, she lifted up the sword so it hung about a foot over the man's neck. Then she dropped it.

Jack could have sworn the Huntsman's eyes popped right out of his head before May caught the sword an inch above his neck. "I could do this all day," the princess said with her half smile.

The Huntsman winced. "I'll take you to your grandmother, all right?" he said. "Just let me up!"

May nodded, backing off a little to give the Huntsman some room . . . and he swept his right leg up, kicking May's hand hard enough to send the sword flying from her grasp. A second later he was back on his feet with a grin.

"You kids are so gullible," the Huntsman said, chuckling. He put a toe under the axe Phillip had dropped, then kicked the weapon up and grabbed it in midair. "Did you really think it would be *that* easy?"

Jack sighed. If only.

"I'm glad you kids finally figured out where we had your dear old gran," the Huntsman said, casually twirling his axe in front of him in a figure eight. "I thought you'd *never* get here."

"Shows what you know!" May shouted. "We *didn't* figure it out! The Mirror told us!"

"Good one," Jack murmured to her.

"I'm *useless* without my sarcasm," May said, shaking her head.

The Huntsman took a step forward. "So!" he said happily. "Who's first?"

Jack and Phillip both moved toward the giant of a man, but he kept them at bay by swinging his axe in a large arc, all the while keeping himself between May and the sword, which lay on the ground a few feet away. "Did you *really* think you could take me down like that?" the Huntsman asked incredulously. "It was just so *easy* to let you think so, thereby trapping you in the palace without all that fuss we've had the last couple of times we met."

"Trapping . . . ?" Jack said, then spun around to look behind him just in time to see the twin tornado doors whirling closed. And now, between them and the door appeared seven small, ugly creatures, the same ones that had attacked May in her home.

Each one hefted a nasty-looking pickaxe, and each one looked ready to use it.

They were trapped.

"And to think!" the Huntsman said. "I spent all that time hunting you down, girlie, when I should have just waited here!"

"We might be trapped," May said, faking confidence, "but this isn't all of us!"

"Who else . . . oh, you mean the wolf?" The Huntsman laughed loudly. "After the last time, I'd be surprised if he was fool enough to face me again!"

"Count me a fool, then," said a voice from behind them. Jack turned around again just as the wind doors exploded into thousands of little breezes. Filling the now empty doorway was Malevolent, still in dragon form, with the human Wolf King riding on her back, reins in hand.

He quickly dropped the reins, then leapt down from her back, landing directly on two of the small monsters—dwarfs, they looked like. Without even a pause, the wolf kicked those two hard enough to send them flying into the snow walls, where their helmets crashed into the snow stone with loud *gongs*.

Two others leapt for him, but the wolf jumped straight into the air, leaving the dwarfs to collide below him. He came down on top of the second pair of dwarfs, knocking both to the ground. He reached down slowly to pick up an axe in each hand, twirled them around for a moment, then launched both right at the Huntsman.

The Huntsman knocked the pickaxes straight to the ground with his own axe. "Are you *challenging* me?" the Huntsman asked disbelievingly.

"I hardly think it will be a challenge," the Wolf King said, an evil smile on his face. "You caught me unaware the last time we met. Do you dare fight me face-to-face this time, coward?"

The Huntsman returned the smile. "I think we both know the answer to *that*," he said, as dwarf arms grabbed the wolf's cape from behind, yanking the animal off balance. "You see," the Huntsman continued, "I *would* face you man to . . . well, *dog*, but why take the chance when I can take you down underhandedly?"

As the wolf fell backward he pushed off with his feet to land hard on the dwarfs behind him. The one remaining dwarf drove its axe toward the wolf's face, but the wolf kicked up, knocking the axe into the air and the dwarf off balance. By the time the Wolf King caught the axe, he'd slammed the dwarf back against the snow wall, knocking it out. "I believe it is time you took that chance," he said to the Huntsman.

The Huntsman shrugged. "I've faced worse."

"The real question is," the wolf said, a large grin playing over his face, "have you been *distracted* by worse?"

The Huntsman frowned, then spun around, his axe at the ready.

Unfortunately for him, Jack, May, and Phillip were gone, the wind door on the opposite end of the courtyard blowing wildly as it swung open.

CHAPTER 40

Behind them, the Huntsman bellowed in rage, a roar that ended abruptly as the wolf let out his own howl. Jack didn't bother looking back; whatever was happening, the Wolf King was on his own. If the wolf could keep the Huntsman distracted for long enough, the three of them might actually have a chance to find Snow White and get out alive. Of course, there was also the Wicked Queen to deal with, but Jack was trying to stick to one thing at a time.

It didn't help, therefore, that the hallway beyond the courtyard ended in a room with three different doors.

"Nothing can ever just be *easy*!" May shouted in frustration.

"Should we split up?" Phillip asked.

Jack nodded. "May, you go right," he said to the princess. "Phillip, you go straight; I'll take the left. If you don't find anything, come back and follow someone else." Jack pushed Phillip toward the center door, but grabbed May by the shoulder. "Here," he said, giving her the witch's knife. "You might need it. Just remember—"

She snorted. "Yeah, it cuts everything but people. You know, I *so* had a sarcastic comment ready there."

Jack smiled, then gently pushed her toward the door on the right. After watching the other two leave the room, he turned and ran through the left-hand door.

Jack found himself in a long passageway with multiple doors on either side, each of which he ignored for the time being, as at the end he saw a spiral staircase going down. Hopefully, Snow White had built her castle like any other civilized person would have done, putting the dungeon underground.

He took the stairs two at a time, doing his best not to slip on the snow stone the stairs were made of, despite the fact that the snow seemed as dry as rock. As Jack passed floor after floor he realized that he was so deep in the castle now, he'd be absolutely no help to May or Phillip if this was the wrong direction.

And it was. The stairs abruptly ended in a solid wall of ice, a wall he plowed right into, smacking his head against it with a loud *conk*.

"*Owwwwwwwww!*" he yelled, stumbling backward to trip on the step behind him. He landed hard on his bottom, and for a second, he wasn't sure which hurt more, his rear end or his throbbing head. And then the shock of the impact wore off, and he quickly declared his head the winner as sharp pains spread like lightning bolts through his skull. This brought on an even louder scream, one that, in his frustration, he didn't bother holding back.

As the pain gradually subsided Jack pushed himself to his feet and stared angrily at the offending wall. Who in their right mind would ever build a wall smack in the middle of a stairway?!

"You assume there *is* such a thing as a right mind," said a voice from behind the wall.

Jack instantly froze, and not from the cold. He peered more closely at the wall, and realized he could just about make out a shape on the other side: a dark, almost *human* shape.

"Who's there!" Jack called out, trying not to hope.

"Just an old woman, dear," the voice said. "Someone in need of a little help, in fact."

Jack smiled in spite of himself. "Right!" he yelled through the wall. "I'll get you out of there, just hold on!" He felt all over the wall, pushing here and kicking there, but nothing gave—there wasn't a crack anywhere in the ice. "Um . . . do you have any suggestions for how I could go about doing that?"

In response, Jack could have sworn he heard a sigh. "It's not a natural wall, dear," the voice said. "Do you happen to know any magic?"

"No," Jack yelled back. "I mean, I have some magical stuff, but if you're asking if I can do magic, as in actually cast a spell, then no."

"That's all right, dear," the woman said kindly. "Unfortunately, while *I* do know magic, I cannot use it. My captors have seen to that. Still, there is a way—"

"Great!" Jack yelled.

"Try not to interrupt, dear."

"Right!" Jack yelled back. "Sorry!" What was he doing? He could barely get a word out! And why? Because he was talking to Snow White? Well . . . yes! He was *talking* to *Snow White*!

"No need for apologies, child," the woman said. "First, let me explain our problem. Despite its appearance, this wall isn't just frozen water—"

"It's not?!" Jack blurted out. He reached out and touched it again, just to confirm that it did still feel like ice. "What is it, then?"

"Frozen ice dragon's breath," the voice said. "That being the case, I'd recommend not touching it."

Jack involuntarily took a step backward and almost tripped on the stair behind him again. "Um, right!" he shouted. "Is it a problem that I've already touched it a few times?"

"Only if the dragon is still alive, dear," the woman said. "Let's hope it isn't, shall we?"

Jack winced. "Uh, yes," he said. "And I'll just, um, not touch it again."

"A wise decision," the woman said. "Now, listen carefully, for the spell to break this wall requires a powerful will as well as absolute concentration. You must explicitly follow every instruction I give you. Do you understand me, child?"

"Pay attention," Jack repeated, shifting his weight from foot to foot in anticipation. "Got it!"

The woman laughed. "My child," she said, "you must be truly blessed to have survived this long. Now, are you ready? Listen carefully, for we shall not have another chance. To break a spell of this magnitude would normally require centuries of study.

Unfortunately, we have maybe minutes before you are discovered, so we will make do.

"There are three things to watch for when performing the spell I am about to teach you. First and foremost, you must be careful to protect yourself. This magic will open your mind to spirits beyond the natural world, and many of those spirits would like nothing more than to take over, if you let them. You must be careful to retain control at all times.

"Second, we will be breaking a dragon's spell. There is a large chance that by doing so, every dragon within a thousand miles will hear it and come running in an instant. If that happens, I suggest that you beg for mercy: Some dragons keep human pets. Not many, but a few.

"Finally, and most importantly, since you have never attempted a magic spell before, and given the forces that you will be unleashing, there is a small chance that you will simply—how should I put this?—cease to exist. By that, I mean you will completely disappear from this and every reality, both now and for all time. In this last case, I admit things would look bad. Still, you won't exactly be around to see it, so there's always that."

Jack blinked a few times, his mouth hanging open. "Ah," he said finally, snapping his jaw shut.

"Do you understand what I have told you?" the woman asked.

"Yes," Jack said. He stood up straight, sighed, drew his sword, and plunged it straight into the wall of ice dragon breath.

The blade sank in without an ounce of resistance all the way to the hilt, leaving a trail of a thick white vapor in its wake.

The entire wall shuddered for a moment, then a large crack abruptly split the ice from top to bottom. As Jack held tight to the sword more and more cracks appeared, vapor escaping from each one.

Jack kept the sword in the wall for a moment longer, then yanked it out quickly. The wall shuddered again, violently this time, cracks jutting out from the main breaks until the entire wall of ice was riddled with fractures. For a moment, it appeared as if the wall might still hold . . . then, with a sound like a sigh of defeat, the entire wall collapsed into a heap of thick, white vapor.

"Child!" the voice exclaimed in surprise. "What did you *do*?!"

Jack tried to see what lay beyond the vapor, but couldn't make out anything yet. "I *really* didn't like the sound of never having existed," he said, even now blushing as he spoke to her, "so I took a chance. And I know what you said about it not really being ice, but my sword's cut through some pretty strong stuff before, so—"

"Your . . . sword?" the woman asked. "Step forward please, young man. I must see the sword that did this."

"What about the ice dragon breath?" Jack asked warily, staring at the thick, white cloud in front of him.

"It should be quite harmless by this point," came the reply.

"*Should* be?" he asked indignantly.

The woman sighed impatiently. Not really wanting to push it, Jack quickly closed his eyes and jumped through the fog. Other than a tingling over his skin that felt like he'd been splashed with ice water, he made it through the fog in one piece.

As he emerged on the other side Jack opened his eyes. There, seated on a chair of ice was a woman, her back perfectly straight, her hands resting comfortably on her knees. Despite her captivity, the woman looked like nothing less than a queen on her throne. Even the enormous iron boots locked over the woman's feet did nothing to dispel the regal image.

She was quite beautiful, as well: The woman's jet-black hair had only a few streaks of white playing through it, and her face seemed to have been barely touched by age. That was, every part of her face except her eyes. There, Jack found a depth he didn't dare stare too deeply into, for fear of being lost. He'd seen haunted eyes before, often in the gazes of veterans of the Great

War, but this woman's eyes were far beyond haunted: These eyes held a full-blown supernatural invasion within them.

But this was her! This was the woman he'd seen in his grandfather's Story Book: This was May's grandmother! Jack almost fell to his knees in relief. He had found her—rescued her!

Only, the woman's dark eyes were focused intently on Jack's sword.

"My child, where did you get that?" May's grandmother asked quietly.

Jack shifted back and forth, far too conscious of every inch of his body. "I, uh, found it. Someone gave it to me."

The woman's gaze shifted to look Jack in the eye. His squirming stopped abruptly, frozen by her stare. "This is *his* sword, child," she said. "To be given it . . . *he* must have done so."

"Yes . . . uh, yes, ma'am," Jack stammered.

The woman's look doubled in intensity. "The owner of this sword is dead, Jack. Are you aware of that?"

Jack managed to shake his head no, almost dropping the sword to the ground while doing so.

And then the intensity in her gaze disappeared, replaced by a desperate sadness. "I apologize, dear," she said, her voice tired. "I hardly meant to scare you. It's just . . . I was quite surprised. At one time . . . but that's not important." She gestured at the iron boots on her feet. "Might you be willing to help me with these?"

And just like that, Jack was back to being the gawking boy, awestruck in her presence. He quickly tried to pull off the iron boots, without any luck. "What *are* these?!" he asked her as he yanked on them.

The woman smiled. "I think my captors fear my meager magic, dear. Iron dries out one's magical wellspring, in a manner of speaking. By forcing me to wear these boots, they have made me quite powerless." She smiled gently. "Still, at least I was not forced to dance in them."

Jack smiled stupidly at that. "Right, that would have been bad," he said, having a bit of trouble thinking clearly. "How do I get them off?"

The woman gestured slightly at his sword. "That should work as well on these as it did on the wall."

Jack nodded his head over and over. "Right!" he yelled enthusiastically. He bent down, located the locks on either side of the boots, and whacked each with the blade. One slice was all it took, and a moment later, Jack helped the woman step gently out of the boots.

"Ah," she said, stepping forward with a grace Jack would have thought to be physically impossible. "That feels wonderful." She held up her fingers, and a small red spark danced between two of them. "Truly wonderful," she repeated.

Jack just stood there, grinning like an idiot.

"Are you all right, dear?" the woman asked, looking closely at him. "I know you must have been through quite a bit on your way here to rescue me."

"A little," Jack said, toeing the snowy ground. "But nothing *you* should worry about, of course."

"You are modest. And courageous," the woman said with an approving nod. "Admirable qualities . . . as long as you know when to use them, and when other traits are called for."

"I usually do," Jack said, barely able to look at her. "But I'm having a little trouble thinking right now. I gotta say, I'm pretty intimidated."

The woman laughed. "That's sweet, dear, but believe me, you have nothing to worry about."

"You're . . . really her," Jack said to the woman, dropping to his knees and bowing his head. "You're Snow White!"

The woman smiled the smile of a true queen. "Please, call me Eudora, dear."

CHAPTER 41

N ow," Eudora said, "do get up, Jack. May will soon find herself in quite a bit of trouble, if I am not mistaken. We must hurry."

Jack picked himself up off the snow floor and dusted himself off before something occurred to him. "Um . . . Miss Eudora? Ma'am?" he asked shyly. "How did you know my name?"

May's grandmother patted his cheek, smiling gently. "I knew you were coming, dear. I've been waiting for you for a long time." She glanced down at the sword in his hand. "And yet, you still manage to surprise me." She gazed at him fondly, and he blushed. "Now," she said, "let's go rescue that granddaughter of mine, shall we?"

As May's grandmother—Eudora—moved to climb the stairs, Jack couldn't help noticing how her time in the dungeon had seemed to weaken her. He could see it in her every step, in each move she made. As they started up the stairway he silently offered her his arm, which she took with a slight nod.

"You're quite the little gentleman, aren't you, dear?" she said to him, and he smiled politely, even if he'd have normally argued the point. Though Jack never would have believed it of himself, he was completely at a loss with this woman. Her presence was just so . . . so powerful!

With Jack's help, the two managed to make it most of the way without too much delay. However fast they went, though, it wasn't nearly fast enough for Jack. "We might still be quite a distance, Your Majesty," Jack said as they paused for a moment's rest. "Maybe I should just run ahead, if May's in trouble?"

Eudora shook her head, breathing harder than he'd have liked. "You alone are simply not enough," she told him. "I need to be there, as well. But I am still weak." Abruptly, she stopped and looked Jack up and down, as if sizing him up. "It occurs to me, though, that there are other options. If you are willing, child, I could use some of your youthful strength—just enough to give me the energy to deal with these matters. Nothing you'd miss for too long, of course."

"Whatever you need," Jack said, without even thinking about it.

"Such a pleasant boy," the woman said with a sympathetic smile as she reached out a hand to touch Jack's chest.

For a brief moment, nothing happened. Then, out of nowhere, Jack almost fell to his knees. All of his strength, his energy, seemed to be flowing right out of his chest and into Eudora's hand, which burned the skin over his heart as if it were on fire. Spots began to pop in front of Jack's eyes, and the bright white of the snow walls began to blur, but just as he thought he would black out, May's grandmother removed her hand. The drain on his energy stopped immediately, and whatever was left flooded throughout his body.

Jack fell to the stairs and took a deep breath, waiting until his head stopped pounding to get back up. Within a few seconds it did, and other than a tiredness deep in his bones, Jack didn't actually feel too horrible. Everything seemed a little less bright in the palace now, but other than that, things hadn't changed much.

May's grandmother, though, looked as if she'd dropped a few

years off her age. "Thank you, dear!" she said, her eyes burning brightly. "I apologize for doing it . . . as I'm sure it wasn't pleasant, but as I said, you'll recover quickly. Meanwhile, I believe it is time to find my granddaughter." With that, Eudora strode up the rest of the stairway and down the subsequent hallway, leaving Jack out of breath and struggling just to keep up.

With Eudora leading the way, they quickly found themselves back in the room with three doors. Just as they passed through the doorway into the room, though, something very large and very green came flying past them to slam into the wall just a foot or two from Eudora. The green object slid down to the floor, still breathing, but just barely.

It was the Huntsman.

From the hall leading to the courtyard, the Wolf King walked into the room in his human form, grinning his wolfish grin. The animal was breathing hard, and his left arm was hanging limply at his side, but otherwise, he looked fine.

"*That* was invigorating," the wolf said. He approached Jack and Eudora, then dropped to one knee in front of May's grandmother. "Your Majesty," he said in a low voice. "We have missed you."

"Oh, do get up, my friend," she said to him. "You honor me too much."

The wolf stood back up, the grin still locked on his face. Jack hadn't ever seen him look so happy. "You have no idea what this means to me, Your Majesty," the wolf said to her, shaking his head as if in disbelief.

She curtsied to him. "I'm pleased to see you as well, Your Majesty. However, we're on our way to find my errant grand-daughter and have little time for pleasantries. Please, do accompany us. By the by, you have my gratitude for bringing her to me."

"It was my pleasure," the wolf said.

"And now we are three," May's grandmother said. "Which door did my granddaughter go in, Jack?"

Jack led them to the door. "This one," he said, "though she might have doubled back and—"

"No, no," May's grandmother said. "She's down this hallway; I can feel it. Shall we?" The older woman led the way, followed closely by the wolf. Jack brought up the rear, though he did allow himself a second to quickly kick the unconscious Huntsman. Such a small thing, and yet it made him so happy.

The hallway behind the door on the far right had a few doors on either side, yet May's grandmother bypassed them all, striding confidently toward a door at the far end of the hall. This door she threw open and marched through.

The room beyond the door was an opulent suite, filled with every shade of red imaginable, from the bed linens to the cushy rugs and heavy drapes. And there was May, standing in the middle of the room with her back to them. The princess was breathing hard as she whipped her head around, looking for something . . . or someone. "I know you're here!" she yelled.

"Jack," Eudora whispered, then gently touched him on the forehead.

Instantly, the whole room brightened into a sort of hyperfocus for Jack. The reds of the linens and rugs, the molten golden-orange of the flickering firelight, every color in the room grew so vibrant they almost hurt his eyes just to look at them.

And then Jack saw her: The Red Hood, invisible to the naked eye, stood right in front of the princess, preparing to strike.

"*May!*" Jack yelled out. "Go *left!*" Without waiting for a response, Jack swung his bag up and launched it right at the spot May had been standing only seconds before, the spot where the Red Hood had just thrown herself.

May hit the ground to the left, and the bag slammed into the Hood, knocking her to the floor. As she landed the Hood's head bounced against the hard snow below the red rug with a loud crack, knocking her unconscious.

May jumped back to her feet and turned to the doorway. "Jack!" she yelled in surprise. "How did you . . ." And then she trailed off, finally noticing who was with him. "Grandma?" the princess asked in a very small voice.

Eudora just smiled in response, her eyes glistening with tears.

"*Grandma!*" May shouted, and threw herself into the arms of her grandmother, almost knocking them both to the ground. The two hugged and cried, each trying to talk to the other but not making much sense through the flowing tears.

Neither seemed to care at all that they were still in danger, or that they hadn't quite escaped yet, and Jack was hardly going to remind them. After all this time, May deserved her moment.

For his part, Jack had to look away for a second to wipe his eyes. He caught the wolf looking at him, so covered his watering eyes by sniffing loudly. "Dusty room," he said, and the Wolf King just grunted.

And then Jack heard footsteps behind door to his left. "Jack?" said a voice. Jack twisted around, prepared for any-thing, but fortunately found only Phillip.

The prince stood in the now open doorway . . . well, leaned

against it actually, though he didn't look like he was in pain. Other than looking a bit pale in the face, in fact, the prince looked as healthy as the day they'd met.

"Phillip!" Jack said, smiling widely. "Look who we found!" He stepped away from the wolf so Phillip could witness the touching reunion of May and her grandmother.

"*Jack*," Phillip hissed, losing more color. The prince paused, licked his lips, and continued. "We have a very, very, *very* large problem."

"I know," Jack said, moving to block the prince from May and her grandmother; they weren't going to be interrupted if he had anything to say about it. "We're not safe yet, but we can give them a minute, right? I mean, after all they've been through—"

Phillip shook his head over and over. "It is not that," he said, still staring at May, his eyes wide open. "I have . . . I have to show you something. . . ."

"What?" Jack asked, but Phillip just grabbed his arm and pulled him back through the doorway. Before Jack could protest, the prince yanked him into an adjacent room, this one empty but for a stone table in the center, covered by what looked to be a large block of ice.

Jack looked questioningly at Phillip, but the prince just

pointed at the stone table. Jack swallowed hard, then walked over to the table.

The ice was too cloudy to see through, but there was definitely something inside it, something long and thin . . . almost like a body. In fact, the block of ice resembled nothing less than a coffin.

"What . . . ?" Jack started to say, turning back to Phillip, but the prince pointed down at a plaque on the floor in front of the stone table. Jack bent down to look.

"'Poisoned by the Wicked Queen,'" he read out loud. "'Here sleeps the fairest—'"

Back at the door, Phillip cleared his throat. "Jack," he said softly. "You *told* me—"

"Guys?" May said from the doorway, her grandmother and the wolf at her side. All three entered the room as Jack stood up. Phillip moved to stand near Jack, his face now as white as the snow walls.

May immediately noticed. "Phillip, what's wrong?"

Before the prince could answer, the entire group heard footsteps coming from down the hall. The wolf stepped into the shadows to surprise whoever it was, while Eudora pushed her granddaughter behind her.

A moment later a tall, imposing woman swept into the room, her deep blond hair longer than the woman was tall. Every conceivable method of tying that hair had been used in one place or another on the woman's head, yet it still ran down her entire body, past her feet, and back up again like an unending golden rope. The woman's thin body was covered by a luxurious gown of icy blue, while a circlet of white gold graced the very top of her head.

Behind her in the hallway, guards drew their swords and prepared to attack. "I see you've escaped your cage, Eudora," the blond woman said.

"Oh, no," Jack said as every bit of energy, every bit of hope, every bit of happiness drained out of him like water. "Oh, *no, no, no.*"

"Apparently iron shoes weren't enough," the woman said, her blazing eyes betraying her calm speech. "We'll be sure to do better this time."

"Grandma, is *that* the Wicked Queen?" May whispered to her grandmother.

Eudora smiled sadly at her granddaughter, and inside, Jack died. He wanted to yell out, to warn May, to reach out and protect her from this. However much he wanted to, though, his arms and mouth just didn't get the message. Instead, he could only watch, absolutely horrified.

"Grandma?" May repeated.

Eudora reached out a hand to brush an errant hair from May's face. "No," she said. "That's not the Wicked Queen, my beautiful little month of May. At least, not the way you mean."

"Surrender, Eudora," said the woman in the doorway. "Step away from the girl, and she won't be hurt."

"She's my *granddaughter*," Eudora said loudly to the new woman, her calm demeanor disappearing for the briefest of moments. She immediately steadied herself, though, and the calm returned. "She will be coming with me," Eudora said, quite evenly this time.

"What . . . ," May said, backing away from her grandmother, Jack, the blond woman—everyone. "What is going on, Grandma?" she asked, her voice shaking. "*Please* tell me."

"Hush, May," Eudora said, her attention elsewhere.

"This witch is not your grandmother, child," the blond woman said, "no matter what lies she told you."

"I *am* her grandmother," Eudora said, her voice rising in volume as the air around her sparked and sizzled. "And she is my granddaughter! She *will* come with me!"

May looked from her grandmother to the blond woman and back again. Finally, she turned to Jack. "You know what's happening, don't you?" she asked him quietly.

He nodded in response, not knowing what else to do.

May took a step toward him, her face a mask of puzzled concern. "Jack, *tell me* what's going on. *Please.*"

Jack licked his lips and tried to breathe. For a second, he thought he might not be able to, and he almost choked, but a moment later fresh air spilled into his lungs. He sucked air in, closing his eyes as he did.

"Jack," May said, and he felt her hand grab his. "I need to know."

Jack opened his eyes again, though he found he couldn't actually look at the princess. "I know you do, May," he said, staring at the ground. "Your grandmother is the Wicked Queen."

CHAPTER 42

Jack quickly looked up to see May's reaction, but she wasn't looking at him. In fact, she was staring at the ice coffin, her mouth hanging open slightly.

"May," he said softly, but she didn't move. "May," Jack said again, a bit louder this time. "We need to get *out* of here."

"You will do no such thing," Eudora said, taking a step toward May. "This is my granddaughter. I care little what you told her, what stories you filled her head with." Eudora held out a hand toward the princess. "May, dear, come here."

May finally moved, turning to look at her grandmother, though she still said nothing.

"Child," said the blond woman, the proper queen of the

West. "Come away from her. I have no wish to see you harmed, and I doubt she will surrender peacefully."

Eudora smiled gently. "Oh, there will be no more surrendering, Rapunzel," she said. Her eyes flashed crimson for a brief moment, and suddenly a wall of red fire filled the doorway behind the blond woman, blocking off all entry and exit. "It still galls me that you, the *least* of your pathetic little band of rebels, would be the one to capture me," she continued. "But now you face me on your own, without your precious Huntsman or those little dwarf allies of his. Do you really think *you* can challenge *me*?"

Phillip quietly stepped over to Jack and May. "Princess," he whispered, "blame me. I should have realized—"

Jack shook his head. "No, it was me who—"

May whirled around to face her grandmother. "Tell me."

Eudora's eyes narrowed as they turned toward May. "Tell you *what*, dear?" she said, her voice calm.

"Tell me what you did here," May said, just as calmly. "Tell me why they call you the Wicked Queen."

Eudora sighed. "May—"

"No words could do her deeds justice, girl," Rapunzel said, her gaze locked on Eudora. Slowly, she drew a sword from her back, where it had been held in place by a scabbard shaped out of her own hair. "The evil performed in her name would make you shudder. But if you want proof . . ." She pointed her sword at the ice coffin in the middle of the room.

"There lies the Wicked Queen's stepdaughter," Rapunzel said, her voice now shaking. "The same stepdaughter the Queen ordered the Huntsman to *kill*, child. You see, the Magic Mirror foretold that Snow White would someday help bring down her reign, so the Wicked Queen ordered her murdered. The Huntsman couldn't do it, though, thankfully . . . so the Queen had no choice but to trick Snow White, poison her. That poison still runs through her veins, and there she lies, but a hair from death's embrace."

May never took her eyes off Eudora during Rapunzel's speech. "Is . . . is that true, Grandma?" she said softly.

Eudora reached out and took May's hands in her own. "May," she said, "all I ask is that you remember the love I've shown you. Did I not raise you to be the young woman you are today? You must listen to your heart, my little May. You belong with me. We lived happily for so long, the two of us against the world!" Her voice raised, then quickly softened to the point where Jack could barely hear her. "Don't let them take you from me, May. Don't let that happen."

May took a step closer to her grandmother, her eyes wide, though with anger or something else, Jack didn't know. "Is it true?" she asked again.

There was a pause, and then the Wicked Queen nodded. "Yes, May," she said, "and much more, besides. *Every* story has a basis in truth. But you don't understand why—"

"It's enough that it's true," May said, then took another step toward her grandmother.

"Back away, child," Rapunzel said, bringing her sword to bear on Eudora.

"May, please!" Phillip said. Desperately, the prince turned to the Wolf King. "We need to get the princess out of here," he pleaded with the animal. "Get her back to the dragon. We can escape."

The wolf just smiled. "I'm not sure whose side you think I'm on here, boy," he said. And with that, the wolf stepped over to stand by Eudora.

"What . . . *betrayer!*" Phillip screamed in astonishment.

"That one betrayed us long ago," Rapunzel said, her eyes on the Wicked Queen. "Despite swearing allegiance to Snow White, he switched sides when we broke into the Queen's castle for the Mirror. If the Charmed One hadn't joined us, we'd all have died.

Since then, I've had men tracking the wolf, but he's always managed to elude them."

"He was in the Black Forest," Jack said quietly.

Rapunzel paused, then nodded. "Clever, wolf. You hid in the one place we couldn't follow."

The Wolf King bowed mockingly, then turned to Jack. "I would have you know, children, that I never betrayed you. I did exactly as I swore I would: I helped your little princess free her grandmother—no more, no less."

He then shifted his gaze to Phillip. "As for the dragon, princeling . . . I released Malevolent from the reins." He grinned widely. "She did betray my Queen Eudora after serving her loyally for many years, but how could I kill so engaging a foe at her weakest? Instead, I shall hunt her down wherever she hides, paying her back for her disloyalty." Nodding toward the room where the half-visible Red Hood still lay, he said, "I see someone already caught my last prey."

"Another one I owe you, monster," Rapunzel said, her eyes burning with rage and tears. "Not only did the wolf betray Snow White, he terrorized her sister, Rose," she said, pointing back toward where the Red Hood lay. "Rose Red gave up everything to hide the Mirror from the wolf, day after day, year after year."

Her sword raised, Rapunzel stepped toward Eudora and the Wolf King. "I will *not* let her sacrifice be in vain."

"You always were a melodramatic little girl," Eudora said with a faint smile. "I sometimes think Snow kept you around for entertainment. Still, you grow tiresome, and it's far past time that I taught you your proper place." With that, the Wicked Queen reached down, and suddenly Jack realized she was holding his grandfather's bag. She must have picked it up when he'd thrown it at the Red Hood.

And then his blood went cold. The bag still held the *Mirror*.

Eudora reached in and withdrew the Mirror, glancing at herself in the glass. "And thankfully," she said, fixing a stray hair, "I have my most powerful weapon back in my hands. Oh, don't worry, it's working quite well now, thanks to these children. You have no hope of defeating me, Rapunzel," Eudora said, her voice as monotone as the genie's. "You will *lose*."

Rapunzel smiled softly. "Isn't that what you said the last time?" With that, she lunged for the Queen, thrusting her sword straight at Eudora.

The Queen didn't even bother moving. Instead, the Wolf King leapt forward, blocking Rapunzel's blow with a sword of his own, a sword glowing with swirling white fog. Jack's feet went cold as he quickly checked the scabbard on his back, only to confirm it was empty. The wolf must have taken it while Jack was distracted.

Jack wasn't the only one who noticed the sword. "That sword!" Rapunzel said, her eyes wide as she fell back away from the wolf. "Where did you—"

Eudora smiled again. "It wouldn't be the first time Snow's late husband served me. Let this make up for his subsequent betrayal."

She took the sword from the wolf and gently waved it through the air, almost contemplatively, before pointing it at Jack. "Still," she said, "he gave his sword to another." With that, she tossed the sword handle-first to Jack, who caught it without thinking.

The Wicked Queen winked at him. "I'm sure you'll live up to his wasted potential," she said. "Tell him I said hello, next time you see him."

Jack held the sword out away from him, wanting desperately to throw it across the room in disgust, *knowing* he should . . . but instead he slid it back into its scabbard.

Eudora nodded. "I thought as much," she said. "Now, I believe it is far past time we made our exit." She whispered a few words, and a circle of red flame seared through the back wall of the palace, cutting a tunnel just like the one the Huntsman had used to kidnap May and her grandmother in the first place.

Eudora now turned to May, her face a mask of confidence, her eyes pleading with her granddaughter. "May?" she said, putting a thousand questions into that one word.

"Grandma," May replied, then stepped forward between the Wolf King and the Wicked Queen. "Tell me one thing," she said, strangely calm—much too calm for all that was happening. "Are you really my grandmother?"

Eudora smiled sadly. "I can't believe you would even ask such a question. You must never doubt my love for you, May. With you, I have everything I could ever want."

May took a step toward her. "Grandma," she said, her voice breaking.

"Oh, May," Eudora said, then held our her arms to hug her granddaughter. May hesitated, then stepped forward.

The Wolf King was the first to see it. "The knife!" the wolf shouted, lunging forward.

And then Jack saw it too, saw May pull the witch's knife from her back pocket. Too fast for the wolf to catch her, May plunged the knife into the Mirror, straight through the glass and out the other side.

May took a step back, her face completely expressionless. "I guess you don't have everything you thought you did."

CHAPTER 43

As May stepped away from the Mirror, a hideous shriek erupted from the broken glass. The genie's voice had always been very monotone, even during its battle with Merriweather, but now, pain and terror fought against fury as the creature howled in absolute agony.

The glass from the Mirror's frame crashed to the floor as the same green fog they'd seen at the Red Hood's cottage burst out in every direction, quickly filling the room to capacity. Just as it reached the walls, the fog pulled in on itself, swirling into the center of the room like a tornado.

For a moment Jack thought they'd all be sucked into the genie's vortex, but as quickly as it started, the swirling fog exploded straight up into the snow ceiling. With as much effort as a child punching water, the genie blew through the palace's roof, sending large snow blocks crumbling down into the room. As it flew up and out the genie's scream echoed back at them, gradually fading into the blowing wind and snow.

And then there was silence.

The Wolf King broke it. "Betrayer!" he growled, leaping at May. Before she could move, the wolf grabbed her by the throat and lifted her into the air.

"May!" Eudora said, shaking her head in shock while her granddaughter struggled to breathe. "How could you *do* such a thing?!"

"Shall I punish her for you, Your Majesty?" the Wolf King asked the Wicked Queen eagerly.

"*May!*" Jack yelled, and leapt forward—only to stop abruptly as the Wicked Queen pointed one long, fiery finger at him.

"Interfere, young man," the Wicked Queen said almost absently, "and you'll regret it. Now, May, I asked you a question. Why did you do that?"

Rapunzel, meanwhile, began to hum beneath her breath, her eyes closed. Behind them, Eudora's fire in the doorway began to flicker, and Jack could see the castle guards behind it, trying to break through.

The Wicked Queen glanced at Rapunzel for an instant, and suddenly every hair on the woman's head began to wrap itself around her body. Rapunzel's eyes flew open, and she struggled to slice away the hair with her sword, but she was too slow. Within seconds, she was fully encased in blond hair, unable to move or talk. She fell to the floor with a muffled bump, her hair at least cushioning the blow.

Jack turned back to the Queen, his entire body frozen in fear.

"I don't . . . know who . . . you are," May said, struggling to speak through the wolf's grasp, "but you're . . . *not* . . . my grandmother!"

Eudora sighed. "You have no idea how much you're hurting me, my darling. Destroying my Mirror? Siding with these people over me?! You have no idea what I've seen, child! What the Mirror has told me about you!" She glanced from Jack to Phillip. "Do you want to know what will happen, May? I'm happy to tell you. One of these boys will betray you . . . and the other will die."

"*No!*" May screamed, kicking at the wolf. The animal just smiled at her, licking his lips.

"It's true, child," the Queen said, almost sadly. "I've seen it in my Mirror. But *I* will never betray you, and I certainly won't let harm come to you . . . after you've been punished, that is."

At this, Jack fought through his terror and stepped forward. "Eudora . . . ," he started, though he wasn't really sure what to say next.

"What did I tell you, Jack?" the Queen said, shaking her head.

And with that, a ray of bright red fire shot from the Queen's index finger, cutting right through Jack's shoulder. He couldn't even scream as pain completely overwhelmed him, knocking him backward off his feet.

"No!" Phillip yelled, but an unseen hand knocked him against one of the snow walls, and his dazed body slid to the floor.

"Now, May," the Queen said. "You hurt me in a very deep way today."

"N-no," Jack said, struggling to speak as he used his one good arm to push himself to his feet. The pain was worse than anything he'd ever felt before, but he couldn't let it stop him. "You're . . . you're not going to *touch* her."

The Queen sighed and raised her finger again. "Jack," she said, her voice cold as ice, "be a dear and sit back down, or I'll cut out that stubborn little heart of yours and eat it myself. Are we clear?"

Jack paused, barely able to stand, then looked from the Queen to the wolf to May and back. He nodded. "We're . . . we're clear."

And with that, Jack dove straight at the Wolf King.

"No, Jack!" May yelled, struggling with the growling wolf.

"I warned you, boy!" the Queen yelled.

And a dagger of red fire exploded from the Wicked Queen's finger, flying straight for Jack's heart.

Only . . . the Queen hadn't realized that something was in her way.

Instead of hitting Jack, the dagger of fire struck the ice coffin, shattering it into a thousand pieces. And there, in the center of the stone table, lay the perfectly preserved body of a woman with skin as white as snow.

Jack crashed into the Wolf King's legs, toppling the wolf and May to the ground. Instantly, the wolf was back on his feet, but even through his pain, Jack was faster. He grabbed his sword and thrust it up, right at the wolf's chest—but the wolf managed to slap his hands on either side of the blade and toss it aside.

Unfortunately for the wolf, he'd forgotten about May. The princess used the confusion to grab one of the ice coffin shards and drive it into the wolf's leg. The animal let out a deathly howl and clawed at the wound, only to go silent as a large piece of the crumbled snow ceiling hit the wolf on the forehead. The animal collapsed to the floor as Phillip picked up a second brick of snow, ready for another attack.

For a second, Jack actually began to hope that they might make it out alive.

And then that second passed.

"Children?" the Wicked Queen said softly. And suddenly Jack, May, and Phillip hung in midair, surrounded by glowing red fire. Eudora strode gracefully over to the wolf and gestured to the stone table. The animal nodded, got up, and moved out of Jack's range of vision, while the Queen glided over to the three of them, shaking her head.

"I have had this problem before," she said sadly. "It's one of the perils of knowing the future, you understand. I learned that with Snow—the Mirror told me that she would eventually be a problem, so I tried to remove her from the equation. But that backfired, and I quickly learned that you cannot change destiny." She smiled. "Fortunately for you, that means I can't kill any of you now. Not when one of you will later realize the error of his ways and join me."

The Queen reached down to stroke May's face, but the princess shied away. This didn't seem to surprise the Queen, though her eyes hardened a bit. "Caring for you was the one thing I never saw coming, May," she said. "But even you cannot change your fate. You too will join me, in time." With that, she turned to walk back toward the red fire circle in the wall.

As the wolf entered the circle before her, carrying something, the Queen stopped and turned to look at them one last time. "Children, I shall see you all soon enough," she said, lifting a hand to wave. Then she smiled a very sweet, motherly smile. "Until then, I hope you live happily—for one of you, it will be your last chance to ever do so."

As the Wicked Queen turned to leave she glanced up at the hole in the ceiling that the genie had made. Her eyes glowed briefly with red fire, and the entire palace began to shake like a tree in the genie's tornado. "Now might be a good time to leave," she told them, then stepped through the portal, which burned itself out as the Palace of the Snow Queen began to collapse.

CHAPTER 44

A moment after the Wicked Queen disappeared, her spells broke, and Jack, May, and Phillip all dropped to the ground. As they all groaned through the pain Rapunzel pushed herself out of her mass of hair, desperately sucking in air. Her guards, now free of the Queen's spell as well, hurried into the room, far too late to do anything.

"No!" Rapunzel shouted, searching the room. "The Queen, where did she—"

And then she went deadly silent as her eyes fixed on the stone table in the center of the room. Jack followed her gaze, and noticed something chilling.

Snow White's body was gone.

Rapunzel shouted something at the guards, but was interrupted by a crack from the ceiling above them, as the rest of the palace began to shake even harder. Snow began to rain down as half the ceiling started to cave in, falling almost a foot before halting, barely holding itself together.

Another crack sent a block of stone snow crashing right through the floor of the room an inch from Jack's hand. "May!" Jack shouted, pushing himself to his feet and helping her up. "We have to get out of here!"

May looked up, and for a moment, the princess barely seemed to recognize him. Finally, though, she nodded. Before she could straighten up completely, Jack yanked her out of the path of a block of snow, which crashed down right where she'd been standing.

Phillip caught her before she hit the ground, and together, Jack and the prince pulled May past Rapunzel's guards and out of the room, Jack's shoulder screaming in pain with every movement. He glanced back into the chamber at Rapunzel, who seemed to be casting some kind of spell, but falling snow quickly obscured his view. Her guards could take care of their queen—right now Jack had enough to worry about just getting the three of them out.

The hallway back to the courtyard felt at least three times longer than it had before, with huge gaps cracking open in the floor in some places, the ceiling and walls collapsing in others. Jack and Phillip didn't bother letting May walk; instead, they carried her as fast as they could toward the end of the hall. Snow as hard as stone rained down on them the whole way, and Jack heard Phillip grunt as one large clump hit him on the shoulder. Despite the pain he must have felt, the prince never paused.

Finally, the three of them burst through the door at the end of the hallway, into the room with three doors. There, they skidded to an immediate halt.

There was nowhere to go. The entire ceiling had fallen in, blocking the way out to the courtyard.

Fortunately, some of the crumbled rock had actually formed a makeshift ramp to the roof. After a shrug between them, Jack and Phillip carried their princess up the ramp and out of the castle.

From the outside, the palace's destruction was almost awe inspiring. Most of the towers had completely tumbled down, crushing the castle below, while the beautiful spirals of ice had crumbled in several places, parts of them whipping through the air, carried by the biting wind. Only one of the palace's towers still stood, and even that one looked to be on the edge of collapse.

"We do not have time to watch!" Phillip screamed over the wind at Jack, then began moving on, forcing Jack to keep up. The ramp they were climbing sloped up to one of the ramparts, which they quickly carried May along, desperately looking for a way back down to the courtyard.

Unfortunately, there wasn't one . . . at least, none that was still standing. They found a few crumbled stairways, but nothing that even came close to the rampart. Jack threw one look over the outer wall, only to shake his head. The rampart had to be at least fifty feet up. There was no way they could jump.

"What do we do?!" Jack yelled in frustration. Phillip just stared at him helplessly, knowing as well as Jack did that there was no way out. Jack whipped his head around, desperately searching for something, anything, that would save them, but the only way out was to go back down into the palace, suicide even if the way was still open.

Already Jack's hands and feet were going numb. Soon they'd all freeze to death if the collapsing palace didn't kill them first. "It can't *end* like this!" he screamed into the wind.

"It won't," said a voice from behind him.

Jack spun around—only, there was no one there. "Who said that!" he shouted.

Two hands appeared out of nowhere. They reached up and pulled back on something invisible—a hood. Behind it was a woman's face, her black hair dashed white with snow and red with blood.

"I bet you never saw *this* coming," said the Red Hood.

CHAPTER 45

Jack glanced at the picture of Rose Red revealing herself to the three of them, and once again, he was impressed. The Story Book's magic really was amazing.

"So I take it she didn't kill you," Jack's grandfather said to him.

"Good guess," Jack replied as he settled back in his chair, staring at the fire. For some reason, his cottage seemed different now, smaller than before they had left.

"So what happened?" Jack's grandfather asked him, puffing on a new pipe made of solid gold. Apparently, the old man had found time for an adventure during Jack's absence.

"Even after all we did to her," Jack said, "the Red Hood . . .

sorry, Rose Red . . . tracked us down to make sure we made it out of the palace. She cast a travel spell that let us escape, even healed my shoulder. Thanks to her and Rapunzel, everyone made it out of the palace all right."

Jack's grandfather shook his head. "I still can't believe you mistook the Wicked Queen for Snow White! I mean, what were you thinking?!" He paged back through the Story Book—which was even now recording everything Jack said—to May's story of the original kidnapping. "I mean, look at her! How did you not recognize the Wicked Queen?! I knew who she was instantly!"

Jack sighed. "It's not like I'd seen her picture before. All I knew from the legends was that the Huntsman tried to kill Snow White. Who knew he couldn't do it, so he switched sides?"

Jack's grandfather puffed on his pipe for a few moments, then leaned in close. "What does May think of all this?" he asked. "Knowing about her grandmother now, I mean?"

"I'm not sure she knows *what* to think, really," Jack said. "I doubt any of us could handle what she just went through. Rose offered to send her home, back to wherever it is that she's from, but May refused. She wants to stay here and figure out where she came from, how she ended up with the Wicked Queen . . . maybe even find her real family, if they're alive. The only clue we have is that Merriweather, the fairy queen, said she owed May something. So that's the first step: Find Merriweather, and find out exactly how she knows May."

"Are you going with her?"

Jack shook his head. "Are you kidding?" he asked. "After the way this all turned out? We set free the worst evil our world has ever known, and it was *my* fault, Grandpa. I can't keep doing this. I'm no hero. I'm just done."

"Really," his grandfather said, raising an eyebrow. "I see you're not done with that sword you found. Keeping that, are you?"

Jack looked almost embarrassed. "I told Rose Red how I found it," he said, "how I spoke to the knight in the giant's mouth. I offered to give it back to her, since it *was* her brother-in-law's. But she got all strange and said I should keep it, that he wanted me to have it. Unfortunately, that's exactly what the Wicked Queen said too, so who knows?"

"And the dreams?" Jack's grandfather asked quietly.

"I, um, didn't mention those to Rose," Jack replied.

"Maybe for the best, for now. So what are you going to do with it?"

Jack shrugged. "I don't know. I mean, everyone says that the swords of the Eyes are cursed, but it's only been a help so far.

Still, I don't know about the dreams. Is Snow White's dead husband really talking to me? And how did Snow White even end up married to one of the Wicked Queen's Eyes?"

"You've got my sense of curiosity in you," his grandfather said with a smile. "That might just get you into some trouble someday."

"*Someday?*"

This time, his grandfather laughed. "Either way, you've got a heck of a story to tell. I'm glad you saw it through to the end, even if it goes no further from here."

Jack nodded, then frowned. He couldn't put it off anymore. "Grandpa?" he said. "One last thing . . . I lost your bag. Well, not lost so much—I know where it is: buried somewhere underneath the Palace of the Snow Queen."

His grandfather froze, his face turning the color of summer raspberries. "What was that, my boy?" he asked, his voice shaking badly. "I must have misheard you. I thought you said that you *lost* my bag?"

A moment later Jack burst out of the cottage, a large pot barely missing his head as he ran. He quickly slammed the door behind him, his grandfather's curses still clearly audible as he escaped.

The old man had calmed down by the time May knocked on the door and came inside. She forced a smile.

"I heard screaming," she said. "If it was directed at Jack, believe me, I understand."

"Princess," Jack's grandfather said by way of greeting, his face now a much healthier color. "It's always directed at Jack, and he'll pay for it, one way or another. I see you still have my little friend?" He pointed at the ever-present fairy in May's hair.

May smiled without any real warmth. "Yup, she's stubborn. Never seems to want to leave, for some reason. Is that unusual?"

Jack's grandfather puffed on his pipe. "Well, in my experience . . . yes. How are you holding up through all of this?"

She sat down in the same chair Jack had used, then dropped her chin into her hands. "Not real great, to be honest," she said. "I basically have no idea who I am, and the one woman I counted on as my family turns out to be some kind of horrible witch." She frowned. "I'm sure there's a metaphor in there somewhere."

The old man laughed. "That almost sounded sarcastic."

She smiled briefly at that. "Nah, I wish. I'm working on it, though . . . maybe I can relearn it someday. Let's hope. I'm kinda useless without it."

"That's not what I've heard," Jack's grandfather said, patting his Story Book. "So what are your plans now?"

May shrugged. "I'd like to find out if my family—my *real* family—is still alive, or if there's any hope of learning about where I come from. It's not like I have anything left back home."

"And your grandmother?"

May's face clouded. "I don't want to talk about her."

The old man sighed. "I think we all hoped never to talk about her again. Unfortunately, it sounds as if we don't have much choice. Rumor has it she's retaken her throne, and her armies are mobilizing again."

May glared at him, then stood up. "If that's it . . . ?"

"Actually, there were a couple more things," the old man said, lighting up his pipe again. May waited with her arms crossed while he puffed a few times, then looked her in the eye. "First, my grandson's operating under the delusion that he won't be coming with you on the next journey."

May's right eyebrow shot up. "Is that a joke?" she asked. "Of *course* he's coming. I need his help!"

"Sounds like you should go talk to him."

"He's such an idiot," she said, and turned to walk out.

The old man's eyes narrowed. "One more thing: The Queen

said that either Jack or Phillip would betray you, and the other would die. Do you think she was lying to you?"

May looked back at him for a moment in silence, then dropped her gaze to the floor.

"No, I don't think so either," Jack's grandfather said sadly.

CHAPTER 46

So I guess this is good-bye," Jack said, sticking his hand out to Phillip, who had been waiting with the horses and supplies Phillip's mother had graciously given them upon their return.

The prince looked at his hand for a moment, then smiled, took it, and shook it roughly. "I apologize for challenging you to a duel before, Jack," he said, "back beneath Malevolent's castle."

"That's all right," Jack replied. "I've wanted to punch you a bunch of times. We wouldn't live long enough to apologize for them all."

Phillip laughed. "Fairly put. Have you said your farewells to the princess?"

Jack shook his head. "I sent her in to calm my grandfather down first."

"Apparently she has done so, as here she is now," Phillip said, looking over Jack's head. "I shall give the two of you a moment alone to say good-bye."

"Right," Jack said again, then turned to face May.

"Well," the princess said as she walked up to him. "I'm not sure what to say."

"Good-byes aren't easy," Jack said, holding his arms out for a hug.

She stopped and gave him an annoyed look. "No, I'm not sure what to say because there are only so many ways to call you stupid. You're coming. And you know why?"

Jack sighed. "Why?"

May glared at him a moment longer, then stepped in and hugged him hard. "Because I need you to, okay?" she said. "Because together . . . we made a horrible mistake. Well, you mostly, but I helped. A little. And maybe together we can help fix it. *Help* me fix it, Jack, okay?"

May released him and stepped back, waiting for his answer. Jack's heart began beating at a normal speed again, and he tried covering his deeply red face. "I, uh . . . ," he said smartly.

She rolled her eyes. "Okay, right. It's just going to have to be the hard way, isn't it." She abruptly leaned forward and pushed

Jack hard toward the horses. *"Get on your horse, Jack,"* she yelled. "We're going, and you're coming. That's all there is to it."

With that, she walked to her horse, mounted it, and rode over to wait beside Phillip.

It took a few minutes, but Jack eventually mounted up and made it over to the other two. Though May seemed satisfied, Phillip didn't look particularly happy about his new traveling companion. "Jack," he said, by way of greeting. "I didn't realize you were coming."

"Neither did I," Jack said. "But the princess asked me nicely."

"As if I could ask any other way," May said, batting her eyes. "Everyone ready?"

"I am," Phillip said.

"Apparently I am too," Jack said, shaking his head.

"That's what I like to hear," May said. "Let's go find out who I am, then."

Acknowledgments

First, no matter how grumpy I got, my family always put up with me, so thank you to my parents, Michael and Nancy, and Sarah, Paul, Anjie, Shawn, and Thaphne. This book wouldn't be here without your support. Kate, Will, and Jack, I hope you like it.

Thanks to Irene Kraas, my own agent of hope and change, without whom none of this would be possible. The same holds true for my editors at Aladdin, Liesa Abrams and Kate Angelella . The word "perfect" might get overused, but in this case it's just what the doc ordered.

Cari DiMargo, Valaer Murray, Leah Kim, Emily Brown, and Kori Hill . . . your feedback kept the story exciting, never letting it turn into some boring, sleepy little tale.

Paul Nadjmabadi. Meghan Jolly. Angie Ottinger. Clay Dilks. Stacey Jackson. Laura Watson. Kim Millard. You all mean more than the world to me, and your support over the years has been so . . . sorry, there must be some dust in the air or something:

My eyes are watering. I'm surprised I'm not getting sneezy. There must be so much dust. . . .

Maarten de Boer, not only did you keep me from jumping off the eleventh elevator, you shared your talent of photography and made me look good, which isn't easy. You're a true friend. Don't get bashful, it's all true.

Finally, most people probably haven't heard of this guy, but I want to thank an artist from the last century by the name of Walt Disney. It's easy to overlook the man for the company now, but the sheer imaginative power of Walt Disney was easily the single greatest creative influence on me as I grew up. I know, I know, that sounds kinda dopey, but it's true.

Thank you so much to all of you. And yes, the dwarf thing made me way too happy.

Jack, May, and Phillip's
misadventures continue in

TWICE
UPON
A TIME

Turn the page for a look
at their next journey . . .

Once upon a time, Jack knew better than to do certain things. You didn't waste time trying to find the perfect temperature of porridge in a bear's house. You didn't point out to your suddenly extremely furry grandmother how big her fangs were. And you definitely didn't walk through a creepy fog while music from magical pipes drifted in eerily. These weren't even questions, you just didn't do them—not if you wanted to stay uneaten by three bears, disguised wolves, or scary old musicians.

Except here he was—fog, magical pipe music, and all, and he just wanted to find the stupid Piper and get on with things.

Unfortunately, not everyone was so goal oriented.

"Does anyone else want to follow him?" May asked, shivering in her oversize blue cloak as her head bobbed to the music.

"I hope you are joking, Princess," Phillip said, shooting her a worried glance. "Remember, we are *not* to go into his cave. That is where the children from that village went, and they never returned."

As if to reinforce the creepiness, a blackbird crowed loudly, then took to the air from some tree hidden in the fog. Jack shivered, thinking the bird almost sounded like it was calling his name.

"I know, I know, no cave," May said, rolling her eyes before swaying to the music again.

Jack sighed and stopped her. "Maybe you should wait a little distance away. . . . You don't seem to be handling this all that well."

"The rhythm isn't going to get me," May said absently. "Besides, what's the worst it could do? Tell me my grandmother is a horrible tyrant who tried to take over half the world? 'Cause, too late."

Jack and Phillip glanced at each other, and Jack could see his own concern reflected in the prince's eyes. May caught their look, and shoved them apart. "What did I say about doing that!" she shouted a bit too loudly for Jack's taste. "I'm fine! It's been three months. I'm over it!" She glared at Jack. "Either that or I'm quietly going crazy and I'll hand you both over to the next giant we come across. Care to bet on which way it's gonna go if you keep giving Phillip those stupid emo worry looks?!"

"Seems like crazy's taking the early lead," Jack said, then quickly turned and continued on ahead, trying to ignore the glare she had just thrown at him.

"If this is too much for you, we could find another way—," Phillip began, but May shushed him.

"It took us this long just to find the Piper," she said. "I want to know who I *am* already! And besides, I for one am tired of rescuing you from various invisible gnomes."

Phillip smiled. "I thought you said that we would never speak of that again."

"Yet someone keeps bringing it up," May said, her face expressionless.

"Can we concentrate?" Jack said, dragging May forward and away from Phillip. "The sooner we pay the Piper, the sooner we get to the Fairy Homelands and find Merriweather, so that—"

"So that we can find out for *sure* that I'm completely alone," May said.

Jack sighed. "I was going to say 'so that we could find your family . . . and *I* can finally go home.'"

Phillip grabbed Jack by the shoulders and shook him gently. "Go home? Why would you ever want that? Look at where you are! We stand in the middle of a dark fog drenched field. Off in the distance a figure waits, known only to us in tales told to frighten children. Enemy or ally, we will not know until it is too late, yet press on we must!" The prince shook with excitement at the idea, while Jack just sighed and waited for him to finish. "What is the point of *life* without adventures like this?!"

"See, I like to think the point of life is to be happy," Jack said with a shrug. "Also maybe not almost dying every two minutes. But I can see how we'll have to agree to disagree here."

"Maybe we can agree to go talk to the man?" May said, and pushed on ahead of the two boys. As she approached the figure in the distance, the music began to slow, eventually coming to a halt, just as they were finally able to make out a thin, stooped figure leaning against a gnarled, blackened tree stump. The man wore a tunic of dull red, belted by a green rope with several heavy-looking pouches hanging from it. And though the music had stopped, the pipes remained at the old man's lips, his eyes closed as if he were still playing.

"Good evening, sir," Phillip said.

The man didn't move.

"Um, we heard you could maybe help us," May said.

The man didn't move.

"See, typically this would be the moment most people respond," Jack said. Nothing. "This is creepy," he whispered to May and Phillip. "Maybe he wants his payment—"

"Payment?" the old man said, lowering his pipes and opening his eyes.

"I think he heard you," May whispered to Jack.

"I'm so glad you're here to point these things out," Jack whispered back.

The old man sighed. "Ah. *You* three. It's about time."

May cleared her throat. "You were . . . waiting for us?"

The old man rolled his eyes. "For longer than I'd care to admit. You think I have nothing better to do than leave my cave in one place while I sit here, playing my pipes? The longer my cave and I stay here, the more likely it is that the Queen will find me." He glared at May. "Thanks to you three, she probably will. And now you want my help."

Jack winced, trying not to make the mention of her grandmother a bigger deal by looking at May. Thankfully, Phillip stepped forward, taking a large bag from Jack's hand. "We seek passage to the Fairy Homelands, sir," the prince said.

"Of course you do," the Piper said, eyeing the bag. "And I see you've brought payment?"

"Sounds like you're not a man to let bills go unpaid," Jack said quietly, his eyes on the pipes.

The Piper smiled. "If I'm owed something, then I will collect. The Piper will be paid, children, one way or another."

"Yeah, we visited the last town who didn't pay," May said. "The youngest person there was, like, sixty."

"They promised payment if I removed their rats," the Piper said, absently sticking his pinkie into one of the pipes as if he were cleaning it out. "I delivered, yet they did not. So I took . . . another form of payment."

"Their children," Jack said, shivering from more than the fog's chill.

"None were harmed," the Piper said, standing up to grab the bag almost indignantly from Phillip. He looked inside, and his face lit up, a smile harmonizing with the sparkle in his eyes. "Yes, *yes*, whispering reeds from the Swamp of All's End! Which of you harvested . . ."

"I did," Jack said, glaring at the bag. "And I've still got the burns. No one ever told us they whisper *fire*."

"They will do nicely," the Piper said, ignoring him. "Now you've paid, and royally so. Speak your wish, and I will do what I can."

May stepped forward, a bit nervously. "We, uh, wish to travel to the Fairy Homelands. Please. Thank you. Please."

The Piper looked at her for a moment, then, almost faster than Jack could see, he raised his pipes to his lips, blew one note, and lowered the pipes. Like magic (appropriately enough), May instantly relaxed at the sound, letting out a huge breath she'd apparently been holding in.

"That's better," the Piper said. "You have nothing to fear, children. Not from me, not anymore."

"I would if I were afraid of cryptic statements," Jack murmured. The Piper glared at him, and began to raise his pipes to his lips again, so Jack quickly added, "But of course I'm not, who would be, and we have nothing but the utmost respect for you. Sir. Your Highness."

"The Fairy Homelands," the Piper said. "Not the easiest destination."

Jack snorted. "Not exactly, no. We've been searching for a way to them for the past three months. And from what we've found, there *is* no natural way to get there. We need magic. And a very specific kind of magic."

The Piper smiled, then held up his pipes. "Music," he said. "It's true. The fairies don't think in words or pictures like you and I do. They think and talk in music . . . so that's how they perform their magic as well. That's why most humans can't understand the little ones, though the fairy queens are able to speak our language easily enough."

Jack glanced over at the golden fairy in May's hair, and the fairy winked at him. "He's right, stupid human," she said. "If your kind were smart enough to understand music, you might have fewer problems."

"We might have had fewer problems if *you'd* known where the Fairy Homelands were!" Jack whispered back at her.

"NO fairy knows!" the golden fairy shouted. "We're sent away at birth! But if we live by the code and spread more good than ill, we might eventually be allowed back in! YOU are the ones trying to take shortcuts!"

"So that humming is her talking?" May said, then turned to Jack. "And would *you* stop yelling at her? It's not like she can understand you."

"Yeah, stupid human. It's not like I can understand you!" the golden fairy shouted, sticking out her tongue.

"I hate you," Jack said to her, turning away. "So, so, *so* much."

"Regardless," the Piper said. "My music can take you to the Fairy Homelands."

"*And* bring us back, right?" Jack added quickly.

The Piper's eyes twinkled. "If you wish. For that you'll need something more." The Piper reached into a pocket and produced a wooden whistle, which he handed to Phillip.

"Nice catch," May whispered to Jack.

"I'm sure the fairy queens are nice and all, but I'm not spending the rest of my life stuck in a whole city of these things," Jack whispered back, glaring at the golden fairy, who made a face at him.

"Blow into this whistle when you are finished," the Piper continued, "and you'll return right to this spot."

"*Return* to this spot?" Jack asked. "Are we leaving soon—"

The Piper brought his pipes to his lips and blew a melody so quick and intricate that it sounded like three or four Pipers playing all at once. The mist began swirling around faster and faster as the music sped up, creating a whirlwind of fog that quickly obscured the Piper, the cave, and everything else from view. The music grew louder, filling Jack's head, obliterating his thoughts, taking over his mind, not letting him even think—

Only to stop abruptly, dropping them onto grass much

brighter than it had any right to be, on ground that was both softer and harder than any Jack had ever felt. He groaned, then pushed himself up, noticing a glowing paved stone roadway beginning just a few feet away from the spot where he'd landed. Whereas behind him . . .

Behind him was only mist.

"I think we're here," May said, groaning a little just to Jack's right.

"There does seem to be something . . . different about this place," Phillip said, then gasped.

Jack quickly followed Phillip's gaze, up the paved road to a gate that seemed to be made of silver latticework circles, then past *that* to . . .

"Uh-oh," Jack said.

"No uh-ohs!" May said, glaring at him. "NO! Not after everything we've been through! No more uh-ohs!"

"I do not think we have a choice, Princess," Phillip said.

May started to reply, then finally saw what the other two were staring at. "Uh-oh," she said.

On the other side of the gate, enormous tree-trunk-size vines blocked out all view of what lay beyond as the vines circled and intertwined with one another. Between that and the fist-size thorns growing out of them every foot or so, the overall effect was definitely "Uh-oh."

"Look," Phillip said, his voice choking a bit as he pointed. Just past the gate something lay crumpled over one of the vines. Jack stepped closer, and realized with a start that it wasn't something so much as some*one*.

"NO!" the golden fairy yelled. "My queen!" She leapt into the air and quickly flew at the tangle of vines, reaching out desperately for what appeared to be the body of a fairy queen.

Jack immediately launched himself out to grab her, knowing that it was too late but not being willing to just let the fairy fly headfirst into whatever curse had turned the Fairy Homelands into this overgrown . . . whatever it was.

Unfortunately, Jack was right. He *was* too late.

The golden fairy passed the silver gate and immediately dropped to the ground, landing hard on a vine, her body unmoving.

And a second later, unable to stop, Jack's momentum sent him tumbling past the gate as well, and into oblivion.

BEYONDERS

"Brandon Mull is a wizard with words.
With Beyonders, he has conjured one of the most
original fantasies I've read in years—an irresistible
mix of adventure, humor, and magic."
—RICK RIORDAN, *author of*
the Percy Jackson and the Olympians series

BRANDONMULL·COM

"DO I HAVE FAMILY IN THE IMAGINE NATION?" JACK ASKED. "ARE THEY SUPERHEROES?"

"YOU'RE A MYSTERY, JACK. BUT THAT'S ALL ABOUT TO CHANGE."

DON'T MISS THE THRILLING ADVENTURES of Jack Blank, who could be either the savior of the Imagine Nation and the world beyond, or the biggest threat they've ever faced. And even Jack himself doesn't know which it will be. . . .

EBOOK EDITIONS ALSO AVAILABLE

From Aladdin
KIDS.SimonandSchuster.com

JAMES DASHNER

AUTHOR OF INFINITY RING: *A MUTINY IN TIME*

THE 13TH REALITY

What if every choice you made created a new, alternate reality?

What if those realities were in danger and it was up to you to save them?

Would you have the courage?

FROM ALADDIN
KIDS.Simonandschuster.com